THE
NOSY
DETECTIVES

Louisa Bennet

Clan Destine
PRESS

Published by Clan Destine Press in 2023

Clan Destine Press
PO Box 121, Bittern
Victoria, 3918 Australia

National Library of Australia Cataloguing-In-Publication data:

Bennet, Louisa

The Nosy Detectives
 (Book 3 in the Monty Dog Detective series)

ISBN: 978-1-922904-36-2 (hardback)
ISBN: 978-1-922904-37-9 (paperback)
ISBN: 978-1-922904-38-6 (eBook)

Cover Illustration by Laura Gaitán
Cover background artwork by Judith Rossell
Cover Design by Willsin Rowe
Design & Typesetting by Clan Destine Press

Clan Destine
P R E S S

www.clandestinepress.net

In memory of my beloved Golden Retriever, Pickles.
You will always be in my heart.

1 MONTY

I stand with my front paws in the paint tray. The cool gloopy liquid squelches, a bit like soft mud in a puddle. And do I love puddles? Oh yeah! Some yellow blobs splash onto the grey concrete floor. I look up at the two hoomans in the room but neither of them has noticed. Phew!

This is the first time I've encountered paint, and, naturally, I have to investigate. After all, I am now the furry half of a detective agency: a canine sleuth with a nose for trouble. Rose Sidebottom is the hooman half of the business, formerly a detective. At twenty-one, she was the youngest ever Detective Constable with the Geldeford Police and I'm proud to say that I am her criminal-detecting canine.

It's a Saturday in February and Rose is up an A-frame ladder, wearing baggy dungarees, using a roller to transform the dusty and red brick interior of what used to be a storage shed into a dazzling sunflower-yellow office. Up another ladder is seventeen-year-old Ollie Fernsby, who has somehow managed to get more paint on his hair and clothes than on the ceiling he is trying to paint. He's a good lad from a bad part of town who has apprenticed himself to our newly founded PI agency, despite Rose's protestations that she hasn't the money to pay him and that it might be better for him to focus on his schoolwork. Since Rose resigned from the police force, she has barely had enough cash to put that smelly liquid in the car that makes it go. Her grocery shop gets smaller every week and the content of my food bowl is also shrinking, which has me scratching my ear with worry.

Dogs aren't too good at keeping track of time, but a while ago Rose placed an advertisement in the local paper announcing that our new PI agency was open for business. Rose has had prank calls and one lost dog enquiry. The lost dog found her own way home, which means we have had ZERO cases.

And that's not the only thing bothering me.

Two boxes in Rose's car are bothering *her*. And if they are bothering her, they are bothering me. One is on the passenger seat; the other is in the footwell.

They are covered in an old, woollen blanket that smells of mothballs and beeswax, a pungent mix that makes it hard for me to detect the aroma of the boxes' contents. Every now and again, when the heater is on and blowing towards the back of the car where I sit, I detect the dry, acrid smell of ash. Ash means fire. I have barked warnings, but each time Rose tells me everything is okay. I fear that she is mistaken.

I lift a paw a few inches and watch yellow globules drip into the paint tray. My normally blond furry paws are now vibrant-sunshine-yellow. I ask myself if that matters and come to the conclusion that it's hard to look like a serious dog-tective when you have yellow paws. I decide to go outside and find some grass to roll around in. That should do the trick.

Stepping out of the tray, my paws slip on the smooth concrete. I almost tumble but I right myself just in time and head for the open door. It's early spring and the air is ripe with regrowth – snowdrops poke their little white heads through the frosty grass.

The owner of our shed-cum-office is Malcolm Kerr, part-owner of Geldeford Vet Hospital, who kindly offered us the use of it for free. I like Malcolm, except when he tries to stick a thermometer up my bum, which, to be fair, he has only done once or twice. He's a kind man with big hands and crazy black hair that sticks out like a hedgehog's bristles. Our office is located at the back of the vet building. The vet nurses leave the rear door open during the day so I can wander in and say hi to the visiting patients and, if I time it right, I snaffle a dog treat or two.

Standing in our office doorway, I sniff the air and detect the delicious aromas of cooked chicken, bread, and best of all, a variety of cheeses coming from the vet's kitchen. Ahhh cheese! One of my many weaknesses.

I shake my head and send my ears flapping as I try to clear the distracting food images from my head. What was I about to do? Ah yes, clean my yellow paws.

I turn my head and pick up the sweet scent of grass coming from a garden that backs onto the vet hospital. I set off and accidentally tread on a recently painted sign that is drying on the ground. Ollie has carefully written the name of our new agency on a blackboard in white letters – The Nosy Detectives.

I continue on my way, past Rose's 'poochmobile' as she calls it and then past Malcolm's car, the tyres of which carry the heady aroma of cow poo. I squeeze through a hole in the spiky beech hedge, then lie down on the lawn and move my front paws as if I'm running, hoping to rub off the yellow paint. I stop for a moment to check my progress, but my paws are still yellow. There's a tapping noise and I see an elderly woman frowning at me through a sliding door as she taps her knitting needles against the glass. She slides open the door and flicks a hand at me.

'Shoo! You're turning my lawn yellow! Get out of here!'

I sit up. I'm a super friendly dog but I'm big for my breed. Maybe I scare her? I give her the famous Golden Retriever smile and wag my tail reassuringly. Her frown deepens. The woman shuts the door and picks up her landline phone. Oh-ow! In my experience, whenever a hooman makes a phone call about me, the result is never good. Once, somebody reported me as a stray and I ended up at the dog pound.

I make a hasty retreat from the garden, squeezing through the hedge. When I am out the other side I notice something different about the car park – yellow paw prints form a trail on the black asphalt from the office to where I'm standing. What fun! As hoomans like to say, I have left my mark!

Which gives me an idea. I trot down the side of the vet's building to the main entrance and peer in through the glass door. There are now yellow paw prints from the car park to the vet hospital and when I turn around, there will be more prints from the vet's to the office. This will make it easy for people to find the Nosy Detectives. Ha! Why didn't I think of this before? Rose will be so pleased.

Mavis, the receptionist, glimpses me and gasps. I proudly raise a yellow paw and then trot back around the corner to our office.

'Monty! What have you done?' Rose says from the doorway.

I run up to her and sit, head held high. Yes, I think, I did that. I left my mark! Isn't it wooftastic!

Rose's auburn hair is covered in yellow spots like freckles. She shakes her head and her ponytail flicks from side to side. 'Oh no! You've trodden it everywhere.'

I know from Rose's voice that I've done something bad, although I have no idea what that might be.

'Sit!' she commands, and I obey. 'Stay!'

She heads for her car and takes out an old dog towel which she keeps in there just in case I get more than usually dirty on our walks.

Ollie pokes his head out of the office, sees the yellow paw prints on the black tarmac and bursts into raucous laughter. 'Brilliant! Like it's a path to our door. You know...follow the paw prints. Good on you, Monty!'

'Not sure how Malcolm will feel about it.' Rose shrugs. 'At least it's water-based paint so if we hurry, we can clean it away with some soapy water and a broom.'

'Don't get rid of them,' Ollie says. 'They're so cool.'

Rose spies the sign that I knocked over earlier. Even from where I stand, I see yellow paw prints across one corner of the sign. Rose kneels down and studies it.

'The Nosy Detectives,' she says, reading the sign. Her forget-me-not blue eyes sparkle and she smiles. 'I kind of like the paw prints.' She looks at me. 'Clever dog!'

2 MONTY

It's lunch time and we are all eagerly waiting for Ollie to come back from the fish and chip shop. It's hungry work painting the office and I'm proud to have made a valuable contribution to the sign above the entrance and to the very stylish paw pattern on the floor.

My tail has a life of its own. Right now it's slapping the dog bed where I'm lying, which is a good sign. I don't control it. It conveys my mood without me even trying.

Rose's desk is a trestle table that was stored here before we moved in. As she types on her laptop, the table wobbles but she doesn't seem to mind. On the wall behind her is a photo of Rose at her police graduation, looking smart in her uniform. Ollie suggested she hang it there to assure would-be clients that we know how to solve crimes. Rose was reluctant because she doesn't like to show off how very clever she is, but Ollie talked her into it.

On the wall behind me is a hand-written sign that says *Monty's desk*. I sit at my "desk" busily licking the fur of my front paws, which, even though most of the paint has been washed away, still have a yellowish hue. Rose has assured me that this will fade in time. What hasn't faded is the stink of paint that emanates from the walls and makes me sneeze repeatedly.

Ah-shooo!

I hear footsteps outside and they're coming our way. I'm instantly up, ready to welcome our first client with my Golden Retriever smile.

There is hope in Rose's wide eyes and expectation in her raised eyebrows. When she hears a car engine start, her shoulders slump and she gnaws at her lower lip dejectedly. Yet another visitor to the vet hospital is leaving without so much as popping their head in to enquire about our services. I can't believe it! Surely there must be a crime that needs solving somewhere?

With a sigh, Rose goes back to sending *emails* to friends asking them to spread the word about our new PI business. As I understand it, emails are not that different from a dog's *wee-mails*. Wee-mails are useful for communicating with the local canine community and are by necessity short messages because a dog only has so much pee to leave on a lamppost, hedge, or fencepost. Dogs don't need to sign off their wee-mails because we know who left the message by their unique scent. And through their scent, wee-mails convey the mood of the messenger, without having to use those funny little round faces that Rose calls emojis.

'Just one job,' Rose mutters from behind her laptop, 'that's all we need.'

Rose is softly spoken. So softly spoken that her former boss, DCI Leach, used to nag her to speak up. Rose comes from a Cornish village called Mousehole, which I'd love to visit one day because if there are mice, there is bound to be cheese. Her mum has the same lilting voice as Rose, so I guess it's how hoomans who live in mouseholes speak.

She looks out of the window at the car, and mumbles. Is she thinking about the boxes again? They were in the attic a long time before she moved them, so I can't imagine a client now wants her to look at them.

I am, however, just a dog. What do I know about paying customers? Or boxes for that matter? I'll stick to what I'm good at – following a scent.

I get up from my bed and rest my muzzle in Rose's lap to assure her that everything is all right. Rose strokes my head.

'This will work out, won't it?' Rose says.

I give one confident bark. Yes!

Not that Rose knows how to speak dog, although we have developed a way of communicating which goes beyond the normal *Sit! Stand! Stay!* Rose asks me questions that can be answered with either a yes or a no. I respond with one bark for yes, two barks for no. I'll let you into a little secret. Something Rose doesn't even know, although I think she is starting to suspect: dogs aren't as dumb as we make out.

We understand the hooman language, we just don't let on that we do. It's one of our best kept secrets. The dog nation has a code of conduct called the *Ten Dog Commandments*. This governs our interaction with hoomans and ensures that dogs and people continue to work together in harmony. It's okay for us to be guide dogs, to track criminals, or find hidden drugs because hoomans believe they have *trained* us to do it. It's not okay for us to let on that we are capable of way more. The last thing we want is for our hoomans to feel threatened by our capabilities, because we love our owners very, very much.

In the corner, a printer whirrs as a couple more colourful flyers are churned out. Rose picks them up.

'This can go on the vet's noticeboard. And I'm sure the café up the road will put one in their window.' Rose grabs some Blu Tack. 'Coming?'

While Rose sticks up the poster in the vet's reception area, I leave a wee-mail on a hedge by the entrance. It says:

Monty dog-tective and his hooman are open for business. No case too small. Find us at the back of Geldeford Vet Hospital. Follow the yellow paw marks.

Rose pops a lead on my collar and we drop into the café next door. Diedre, the café owner, has green hair and lots of metal rings through her nose and ears. She must be in a lot of pain, so I always snuggle up to her so that she knows I care. She pins the flyer to a cork board. So far, so good. Heading back to our office, we bump into Malcolm with his Cavalier King Charles Spaniel pup named Lady B, or B for short. B is doing a dainty widdle on a patch of grass beneath a chestnut tree, while Malcolm is on the phone to someone who is speaking very loudly. When B has finished, we sniff each other.

'If you're worried, Mrs Onions,' Malcolm says, 'it's best to bring your Labrador in.'

Rose gives Malcolm a little wave and he waves back.

'Oh dear,' I hear his client say, 'I left the lid off the food container. Could that be why his stomach's bloated?'

'Ah, that would do it.' Malcolm fidgets from foot to foot as he tries to end the conversation. 'Let the receptionist know if you want to bring him in but it sounds like he just needs to process everything he's eaten. I must go now.'

Malcolm ends the call and smiles at Rose. 'I was coming to see you. How's everything going?'

Despite his thick Barbour jacket, I can feel the heat emanating off him and his heartbeat speeding up. Is he ill? I sidle up to him and sniff his hand. Disinfectant, Imperial Leather soap and, naturally, B's unique puppy scent, which smells like oatmeal shampoo and Magic Marker pens. There's nothing to indicate Malcolm is ill.

Rose looks down and swings one boot across the tarmac. 'Nothing yet, but it's early days.' She looks up and smiles, but it doesn't reach her eyes.

'You've only been open two days,' Malcolm says. 'I wouldn't worry. You're famous, remember? You solved The Girl in the Woods murder. People know they can trust you to do a good job.'

Rose's boots continue to swing back and forth, chafing the car park's surface. 'Maybe they think I only do murder cases and I'm not interested in anything else. Right now, I'd take a missing hamster case if somebody offered it.'

I peer up at Rose. Is there a hamster missing? That's an easy one to solve: follow the chewing noises.

Malcolm tugs at the collar of his Barbour. 'I've been meaning to ask, um…' He looks down at his puppy, who wags her tail supportively. Malcolm stutters, 'I…um…it w-would be nice to…we should celebrate your new agency. You know, have…have d-dinner.' The last word comes out like a cough. His heart is beating as fast as a Greyhound running a race. I whimper with concern and lean against his leg. What can I do to help?

'That's a lovely idea,' Rose says. Malcolm stops the collar-tugging and blinks in disbelief. Rose, however, hasn't finished. 'I'd like to wait until we have a paying client. Then I'll have something worth celebrating.'

The corners of Malcolm's eyes and mouth droop. He looks disappointed.

'Oh,' he says, wrapping B's lead round and round one finger. 'I thought we could, you know…pop it in the diary, um, on the 14th.'

'February 14th?' Rose laughs. 'No way! That's Valentine's Day. Pubs and restaurants will be booked solid. And anyway, it's horribly commercial.'

Malcolm is a stocky man with wide, strong shoulders. He's capable of handling heavily pregnant cows, stroppy horses, and Irish Wolfhounds who refuse to get up. He's no weakling. But Malcolm appears to have shrunk inside his coat and his voice is distant. 'I see.'

I think I see, too. Rose most certainly doesn't. In sympathy for Malcolm, I give the back of his hand a lick. B gives a yelp. Her lead is now so short that it's almost choking her. Malcolm notices the lead wound around his finger and loosens it. His cheeks are flaming red.

'Must get back to work.'

Malcolm races into the vet hospital. Rose looks down at me, a frown on her heart-shaped face. 'Was it something I said?'

I have no idea how to respond to that question, so I *hurrumph*, the doggie equivalent of a sigh. When it comes to affairs of the heart, I have no experience. I am only two years old, after all. And I don't understand Valentine's Day or why hoomans get so het up about it. Why is it that hoomans feel that one day a year is the right time to let another hooman know that you love them? Why can't you tell them at any time of the year? On the plus side, this event does usually involve eating, and I'm fond of eating. Especially cheese. Have I mentioned that? And any kind of meat, come to think of it. And I'm partial to dog treats and rawhide chews. Oh and bread, especially with a slice of ham on it. By now I have two long strands of drool dangling from either side of my jowl. It's not a good look. Fortunately, no one sees it as we head back to our office.

'Wait a sec,' Rose says, as we walk past her car. 'I guess I better get to this.'

She drops my lead, knowing that I won't wander too far. One at a time, she carries the lidded boxes into our office and puts them on the floor behind her desk.

She takes a pair of scissors from a little tray full of pens, then cuts the tape that holds the lids on. She sits cross-legged on the floor and removes the lid of the nearest box. I plonk my furry butt next to her and sniff the box. Without a stinky blanket covering it, I now know who packed it. Rose's aunt, Kay, was a Detective Inspector until she died, bequeathing her cottage to Rose. Duckdown Cottage still holds Kay's scent of sunburnt human skin and rust – the smell of Kay's cancer – which only a dog can detect. It's a distressing smell and I jerk my head back.

'Got nothing else to do,' Rose says, eyeing me. 'Does no harm to take a look.'

Our eyes meet. I'm not so sure about that.

I inhale a waft of times long ago. A time of death and suffering. Smoke and ash. Something chemical, not dissimilar to the liquid Rose pumps into her car. The sting of it makes me sneeze. This box is a shrine to a double homicide and a suspect, a boy called Finn Toyne.

Rose has a focus that tells me she means to explore the boxes thoroughly.

This isn't good. Not good at all.

You see, I know something that Rose doesn't.

3 MONTY

'Aunt Kay always believed Finn was innocent,' Rose tells me as she removes a manila envelope from the storage box.

The envelope bulges with photographs. No wait, they're not the actual photos. They're too flimsy. I think they are photocopies. 'The DCI was adamant he was guilty, but he didn't have enough to charge Finn.' She's referring to DCI Craig Leach. He was Kay's boss, just as he used to be Rose's. He's a craggy fellow with a harsh voice. Rose shakes her head. 'I think this case made Kay ill.' She looks at me. Her eyes are watery. 'I think she'd like us to solve it.'

The hair down my spine sticks up, as if I have sensed a predator watching me. I don't think we should touch this case.

I'm not a fan of The Leach, but one thing he and I agree on is that Finnegan Toyne, known as Finn, is a troubled boy. Finn has a temper and can lash out, much like a dog that's been cruelly treated. I once caught Finn staring at a framed photo of Kay with such unblinking, cold-eyed hatred, I backed away from him, afraid. We were alone at the time. Finn was at Duckdown Cottage to keep me company. His reaction to Kay's photo shocked me. Shortly after that, Finn was attacked by an intruder and has been in a coma ever since.

With most hoomans, I either like them or I don't. I don't know what to make of Finn, but I am wary of him.

'Kay photocopied the case files and kept working on it, right up to her passing.' Rose peers into the open box. 'Somewhere in there is her personal notebook where she wrote all her thoughts and hypotheses.'

Rose turns her attention back to the manila envelope. She lays the colour images on the floor in neat rows. The first picture is of the exterior of a house that has been gutted by a fire.

'Hard to imagine it was once a thatched farmhouse,' Rose says.

Only the blackened walls stand. The roof has gone, even the beams, and the windows are jagged holes. The front and back doors are warped and blackened, but still standing. Everything is scorched, including the front lawn and an oak tree to one side of the building. I cringe. Every animal knows that fire is a killer.

'They never stood a chance,' Rose mumbles. She means Finn's parents, Marie and Tony. 'The house doors were locked from the inside. Not that they made it that far. They died in the bedroom.'

The next image is of the kitchen. The floor is covered in ash. Only the sink, the fridge and the cooker survived the flames. In the sitting room, only the metal potbellied stove remains. The furniture is gone.

The next photo is of two blackened hooman forms, curled together, barely visible amongst the ash and debris around them. I whimper and look away.

'What a terrible way to die,' Rose says shakily.

She quickly moves onto the photo of a boy crying. The area around him is dark and smoky, clearly taken at night. The orange glow of the fire is evident on his tear-stained face.

'Ten years old,' Rose mumbles. 'The sole survivor.'

I recognise Finn's black hair and dark eyes. In his arms is a black and white Collie pup which has nestled her snout under his arm, no doubt as terrified as the boy. Everything appears monotone except for his red running shoes. Rose touches the photo with the tip of a finger and traces the contours of Finn's face. Her hand is trembling.

'I'm so sorry, Finn,' she says.

I nudge her arm to get her attention. I want to tell her not to feel guilty. It's not that she blames herself for the fire. Rose didn't know the Toyne family back then and she hadn't even graduated from Police

College. Her guilt is because she blames herself for asking Finn to look after me when she was hunting Patrick Salt's killer. How was Rose to know that the killer would target her house and attack Finn? I sit, stiff-backed, and bark twice.

Rose tilts her head sidewise. 'No? No, what? I don't understand.'

I mean no, it's not your fault so don't feel guilty.

I hear footsteps heading our way: a rhythmic shuffling accompanied by the whistling of a song. I know it's Ollie because he drags his feet when he walks. Ollie arrives clutching two bundles of fish and chips wrapped in paper. My stomach rumbles, my nostrils pulse. What could be better to lift the mood than food?

'Grub's up!' Ollie says, depositing the bundles on the trestle table and taking from his pocket some wooden forks and sachets of tomato sauce.

He removes his olive bomber jacket to reveal a grey sweatshirt spotted in yellow paint, which matches the yellow paint spots on his dark curly hair. They eat at the table. Ollie surreptitiously drops a chip on the ground, and I scoop it up quick smart.

'Ain't that the fire from years ago?' Ollie says, nodding his head at the photos laid out on the floor. He swallows a mouthful of battered cod. 'The one that Finn was blamed for.'

'How do you know that? You would have been twelve at the time.'

Ollie picks up the photo of Finn with his puppy. 'We went to the same school. Half of us thought he was a murdering psycho; the other half thought the cops were bastards for treating him the way they did.'

Rose uses a fork to break off a piece of haddock. 'What did you think?'

'At first I thought no way he done it. He was the cool kid back then, but he wasn't a dick about it. Played electric guitar. Pretty amazing for a kid that age. After the fire, he was different. He wouldn't speak. I mean not a word. Stopped playing guitar. Got into fights at school. He was one angry dude. I guess I'd be angry if my parents died and I was blamed for it.'

Rose swallows her fish. 'I knew he boxed. I didn't know about the scuffles at school.'

'The day Finn got attacked at your place, the headmaster was going to expel him. Finn messed up one boy's face real bad.' Ollie used his fingers to cram a piece of cod into his mouth. 'If you're looking into the case, can I help?'

'Ollie, you know I love your company but you mustn't forget your school work.'

'I know, but if I'm going to be a famous PI, I need experience. And besides, I'm your computer geek and you need me.'

'Okay then. After lunch we'll work through the boxes.'

Ollie shoves a few more chips in his mouth. 'Are you doing it because he's woken up?'

Rose pauses in her chewing. I'm also wondering if I heard him right. We both stare at Ollie.

'Finn's come out of his coma?' Rose asks, eyes wide like an owl's.

Ollie licks tomato ketchup from the side of his mouth. 'Yeah, this morning. I thought you knew. It's all over social media.'

I peer at Rose's face. Her eyes are scrunched up, which tells me she's hatching a plan. She doesn't touch her food. 'Is Finn talking?' she asks.

'Don't know.'

Rose looks me in the eye and strokes one of my floppy ears. 'He liked you, Monty. I think we should pay him a visit.'

It's true that Finn and I once rumbled on the grass and played a game of chase. It was the only time I saw him smile and I felt the tension drain from his body. Maybe he deserves the benefit of the doubt? After all, his mum and dad died when he was young, and he's been in a coma for months.

But my number one priority is always Rose. I am happy to see Finn in hospital but if there is even a hint that he might hurt her, I won't hesitate to protect her. That's my job.

I bark once, a subdued bark. It's a reserved yes.

4 ROSE

Rose felt a nervous flutter beneath her rib cage as she walked up to Geldeford Hospital with Monty trotting at her side. Rose blamed herself for Finnegan Toyne's condition. If Finn hadn't been dog-sitting at her house that day, the intruder wouldn't have hit the boy's head so hard that he fell into a coma. The lad had been through enough in his short life: not only had he lost his parents, but he was also the prime suspect in their murder.

How would Finn receive her now that he was out of the coma? Rose was pretty sure that if Phyllis O'Brien, his grandmother, was with him, she would have some harsh words to say. Rose took a deep breath and stood tall, hoping to quell the anxiety that was causing her to feel a little out of breath.

'I can do this,' she said to herself.

Outside the hospital's main entrance, Rose glanced down at her dog – no, her best friend – and smiled. Monty looked up at her, his big round eyes, the colour of gingerbread, filled with unbridled devotion. With Monty at her side, she thought, everything would be all right.

'Good boy!' she said. 'Stay close and no barking. You're a private investigator now so you need to be on your best behaviour.'

Monty wagged his tail.

Rose brushed a loose hair from the lapel of her jacket. When she'd finished painting the office walls, she had changed into the trouser suit she used to wear as a detective constable, which she kept at the new office for just such situations. She had also tied her paint-speckled hair into a ponytail. If she was going to discuss the cold case with Finn she wanted to look and feel professional. The suit also made her appear a little older than her very-nearly-twenty-two years.

Her birthday was on Valentine's Day, which was a constant source of embarrassment for her. When Malcolm had suggested they have dinner on February 14th, she didn't tell him that it was her birthday or that she intended to have a quiet celebration at home – just her, Monty and a bottle of wine.

They entered the hectic hospital foyer. A busy café was on the left with chairs and tables lining the main thoroughfare. On the right was the receptionists' counter and security guards' desks.

'Morning, detective!' Chris called out, waving at her, a shiny sheen on his chubby face.

Chris was overweight and avoided leaving his chair whenever possible. He relied on Henry, the younger and fitter security guard, to patrol the hospital and its grounds, whilst Chris focused on what he called "more immediate matters", which seemed to involve staring at the CCTV camera feed and talking to Henry on the walkie-talkie. Rose dodged the flow of people coming and going through the main entrance and went up to his desk.

'How are you, Chris?' Rose asked.

'Oh not so bad.' He jerked his jowly face in the direction of the café across the way. 'Fancy a tea? I was just about to go on my break. I've got my eye on a slice of Black Forest Gateaux.'

'Maybe later, Chris. Duty calls. Can you point me in the direction of Finnegan Toyne?'

Chris looked disappointed but he checked his computer and gave Rose the directions to ward twelve. 'Your police dog looks bigger every time I see him. Monty isn't it?'

'Yes, Monty's his name.' She looked at her dog. 'Say hi to Chris,' she commanded, and Monty wagged his tail. Chris seemed pleased. 'Chris, I decided to set up as a PI. I'm here about a cold case.'

He grinned broadly. 'Congratulations! What have you called yourselves?'

'The Nosy Detectives, on account of Monty's super nose.'

'Like it.' Chris chuckled, his several chins wobbling. 'I've always seen myself as PI potential. I'm very observant. If you ever need a partner, you know where to find me.'

'I do.' Rose rummaged in her coat pocket and handed Chris a freshly printed business card. 'If you hear of anyone who needs a PI, can you pass on my details?'

'Certainly can.'

Rose followed Chris' directions to ward twelve. The closer she got to it, the greater her agitation, which was ridiculous, given she had faced crazed killers before. Although it was one particular near-death experience that involved a burning furnace and a killer wielding a shovel that had triggered the onset of Rose's PTSD. It had taken several visits to a psychiatrist and some medication for her anxiety to get her back on track. She no longer suffered from crippling moments of terror and the nightmares were rare these days, but she was still learning to deal with anxiety attacks.

Breathe in, breath out. Nice and slowly.

'Are you all right?' a nurse asked.

Rose hadn't realised that she had stopped walking and had one hand on the wall to steady herself. Or that Monty was whimpering. Rose's face went beetroot with embarrassment.

'I'm fine, thank you.' *Breathe.* 'Been running.' *Breathe.* 'Just a bit out of breath.' The nurse stared at Monty. 'A detective dog,' Rose said, by way of explanation.

It did the trick and the kind nurse walked on.

Just walk in, she told herself. *Say what you want to say, then leave.*

After a few wrong turns, she found the right ward. To her relief, the nurses' station was empty, which meant that she didn't have to explain why she had a dog with her. Rose increased her pace until she found room 1204, the soles of her boots squeaking on the linoleum floor. She knocked, entered, and quietly closed the door behind her.

Finn was the only person in the room. He lay in bed with his eyes closed, his arms resting on a blanket. He was so still she might have thought him dead if it weren't for the machine monitoring his heartrate.

On the bedside table was a vase of daffodils and grape hyacinths which Rose suspected came from Phyllis's garden. On the only chair in the room was the biggest handbag Rose had ever seen. It appeared to be made from a Persian Rug in bright reds, pale blues and cream, with a worn leather handle. It lay open and a crochet hook, a ball of pine-green wool and part of a crocheted blanket was visible, as well as a purse and a Mills & Boon paperback novel. The giant handbag must belong to Phyllis, which meant that she might return at any moment.

Rose vacillated. If Finn was only just out of a coma, would the shock of seeing her be too much for him? She wished she had checked in with a nurse on arrival and asked if it was okay for Finn to have visitors.

She moved closer to the boy's bedside. He looked so peaceful that Rose didn't have the heart to disturb him.

'Come on Monty, let's go home.'

Finn's eyelids opened languidly, his thick black eyelashes parting to reveal eyes so dark it was as if he had no irises at all.

'Oh!' Rose said, frozen to the spot.

Finn stared straight ahead and he didn't appear to see Rose.

Her heart thumped in her chest. She cleared her throat. 'Finn? It's Rose.'

His eyes closed.

'I've brought Monty to see you. He's my dog.'

No response.

'I'll come back another time.'

Rose started to back away, but Monty clearly had another idea. He strained on the lead with such strength that Rose had to let it go. Monty then nudged Finn's arm with his snout. Finn's head wobbled but his eyes stayed shut. Rose bent down to grab the end of Monty's lead. Before she could, he rose up on his hind legs and placed his two large front paws on the bed. The dog's muzzle was a whisker's distance from Finn's face. He then nudged the boy's cheek with his cold, wet nose.

'Monty, get down!' Rose whispered.

She reached out to drag him away by his collar when Finn opened his eyes. Monty nudged his arm a second time. Finn shifted his gaze to the right and came face-to-face with her dog. He blinked rapidly then his dry lips parted in a weak smile. He lifted his pale hand and rested it on Monty's furry head.

Rose had been holding her breath, hoping that Finn wouldn't freak out. He seemed happy to see Monty. She exhaled with relief.

'Finn, it's Rose. Rose Sidebottom. I guess you remember Monty.' Finn didn't turn his eyes away from the dog. His hand slowly stroked Monty's head. She continued, 'I'm so very sorry about what happened to you. I should never have asked you to dog-sit, knowing a killer was after me.'

'Sorry isn't good enough!' The voice was sharp as razor wire.

Rose flinched.

Phyllis stood just inside the room, her take-away coffee cup in one hand. Despite the granny-esque beige fleece, green tweed skirt, and flat, lace-up shoes, she had the build of a professional wrestler and the voice of a town crier.

'You have no right to be here!' Phyllis said.

The seventy-two-year-old stomped over to where Rose stood and slammed the coffee cup onto Finn's bedside table so hard the lid popped off, sending frothy coffee all over the table's surface.

'My poor grandson has only just come to, and you're already hovering around him like the vulture you are. Bloody coppers!'

Phyllis took a packet of tissues from the monster handbag and proceeded to wipe away the coffee-spill.

Monty lowered his front paws from the bed and stood between Rose and Phyllis. The fur along his spine was raised and his tail wag was low and slow. He probably didn't like Phyllis's aggression.

'I've left the police,' Rose said. 'I came here to apologise—'

'Well, you've done it, so off you go! And take that vicious brute with you.'

That was one step too far. Rose felt a flush of fury rise up her neck to her cheeks.

'I'm not your enemy, Phyllis, and my dog loves Finn.' She turned to the boy. 'Finn, I mean what I said. I am so very sorry. If I can do anything to help hasten your recovery, just call me.'

'Stupid girl,' Phyllis chided, 'How's Finn going to do that, hey? He doesn't speak.'

Monty gave Rose's hand a lick, then he looked behind him at Finn.

'What's up, buddy?' Rose said, keeping her eyes on Phyllis who was pointing at the door.

'I want you to leave,' Phyllis said.

'Mmmm…'

Phyllis's head whipped around, and she stared at her grandson.

'Mmmmon-ty?'

Was Rose imagining it? Was Finn trying to speak?

'Finn, my love, was that you?' Phyllis said, taking his hand.

'Mmmonty,' Finn said again.

'Mary, Mother of God!' said Phyllis. 'It's a miracle. You spoke! My beautiful boy spoke!'

Monty trotted back to Finn's bedside and rested his muzzle on the bed clothes. Finn stroked Monty's head again. Phyllis leaned over Finn and hugged him. Somewhere beneath her dangling fleece, Monty kept his head close to Finn.

'My darling boy! Everything's going to be all right. I promise,' Phyllis said, releasing Finn from her embrace.

'Hel…lo gran.'

Finn's eyes came to rest on Rose, who kept her distance, unsure how the boy would react to her now that he was aware of his surroundings.

'Hel…me,' Finn said.

Phyllis glared at Rose. 'You need to go.'

'N…o. S…tay.'

Monty gave Finn an encouraging lick on the arm.

Rose stepped closer. 'You want me to help you?'

'I did…n't…do it.'

The sound of heavy footsteps halting outside the room distracted Rose. The door flew open and Detective Chief Inspector Craig Leach entered the room.

5 ROSE

Rose had always found DCI Leach terrifying and he had always found her a curiosity. Leach had once confided that he couldn't understand how a detective as young as Rose could have solved so many cases. The answer was simple, but he would have laughed at Rose's explanation.

Rose had an uncanny ability of knowing when someone was lying. It went beyond the "tell" that most people have, something they do that unconsciously indicates they had just lied. Most people avoid eye-contact when they fabricate. Some scratch their ear or clear their throat. Rose's ability to sense a lie went beyond that. Her whole body responded in a unique way: pins and needles would tingle in her feet and hands and then travel along her limbs. If the lie was a big one, the sensation became so uncomfortable that she would have to shake her limbs to dissipate the feeling.

As a kid, Rose had tried to tell her primary school friend about her in-built lie detector. Her friend had laughed at her and accused her of lying. Since then, Rose had kept her secret to herself. On a number of occasions, Rose had informed Leach that a suspect was lying, and when she had been proven correct, he had asked her how she knew. She told him it was instinct. But Leach didn't like intuitive coppers and their relationship had been a tense one.

Leach scowled at Rose.

'What, might I ask, are you doing here?'

His Mancunian accent was as pronounced as it had been fifteen years ago when he transferred from Manchester Police to take up his current role as DCI of Geldeford's Murder Squad. His round, shaved head resembled a white snooker ball perched on a squat muscular frame.

Rose could feel her confidence draining away like a leaky water pipe.

'I heard Finn was conscious,' she began, then she spotted her nemesis, DI Dave Pearl, and her words faded away. He stood behind Leach with a nasty grin on his fake-tanned face.

Pearl wore his favourite brown leather jacket and his blond hair was slicked back in an effort to subdue the waves he hated so much. The gossip at the nick was that Pearl took carotene pills which might explain the slightly orange hue to his winter tan.

There was a low rumbling growl and Rose looked down to see Monty staring at Pearl and his muzzle was twitching. Monty had previously made it clear that he wasn't a fan of the copper who had made her life a misery. But the last thing she wanted was for her dog to be accused of aggression. Pearl would use the opportunity to have Monty put down.

'Quiet!' Rose said and Monty stopped growling. 'Sit.' Monty sat.

'Oh for God's sake,' Leach said, 'you brought the bloody dog along!'

'Boss,' Pearl said over Leach's shoulder. 'Dogs aren't allowed in hospitals.'

'I know that, Dave.' Leach directed his next words to Rose. 'It's time you left. I need a private word with Finnegan.'

Rose headed for the doorway, which was currently blocked by Leach and Pearl.

Phyllis strode up to the DCI and stabbed an arthritic finger into his barrel chest. 'Just you listen here, Mister. I know who you are and you're not welcome here. You hounded my poor grandson when he'd just lost his parents. You're a disgrace!'

Now Rose's exit was blocked by three people.

'Nice to see you again, Mrs O'Neil,' said Leach, sarcastically. 'For your information, I have every right to be here. Your daughter's and son-in-law's murders remain unsolved. It's about time Finnegan told us what happened that night.'

Leach tried to walk around Phyllis to get to Finn, but she blocked his path. 'Oh no you don't. Leave the poor boy alone. He's only just come out of a coma.'

'Are you re-opening the case, sir?' Rose asked and then wanted to kick herself for using the word, sir. He wasn't her boss anymore.

'I am. Keep your nose out of it, okay?'

'She thinks she's a PI,' Pearl simpered. 'And how's it going for you, Sidebottom?' Pearl liked to use her surname as a means of humiliating her. She hated the name, but her parents would be devastated if she changed it by deed poll. Pearl continued, 'Let me guess.' He held up his thumb and first finger and created an O. 'From what I hear, zero clients.'

'Shut it, Dave!' Leach snapped, which caused Pearl to blanch. 'Out of the way, everybody. Let Rose pass.'

Rose glanced at Finn, who had been silently observing them. His gaze was firmly set on Leach and his fists were balled. Was Finn afraid or angry?

As she exited the hospital, Rose tried to funnel the sting of Pearl's mockery into action.

Finn had asked for her help. She was happy to give it, and do it as a favour. Finn said that he "didn't do it". He must have meant he didn't light the fire and he therefore wanted her to prove his innocence.

'What do you think, Monty? Do we investigate the fire?' Monty licked his lips which was a sign that he was nervous. 'I know, my friend, Leach won't like it, but I can't be a successful PI if I shy away from difficult situations, now can I?'

6 MONTY

Duckdown Cottage is my doggie heaven. The garden is huge and not properly fenced, which gives me ample opportunity to sneak out and explore the nearby heath when Rose isn't looking. It offers a duck pond that smells enticingly of duck poo and rotting vegetation, and loads of stroppy ducks to annoy. I love to topple the ducks when they are sleeping on one leg. It's a bit like Ten Pin Bowling. I never harm them, of course, just ruffle their feathers a little. And they get to chase me around the duck pond and occasionally nip my tail, so it's fun for everyone.

The cottage is unusual. It leans slightly to one side and the front door is jammed shut. The roof leaks and the paint peels but it's perfect in my eyes. I have a cosy dog bed in the kitchen where my ratty friend, Betty Blabble, lives behind a hole in the skirting board. My mother, Summer, a senior dog, spends much of her time curled up in her bed next to the warm radiator. Best of all, Duckdown Cottage is Rose's home.

It's early evening and Rose is cooking her dinner while I oversee the process. I lie near enough to Rose so that if any foodie bits fall to the floor, I can immediately snaffle them. If it's on the ground, it goes to the hound, as the saying goes. Rose is making spaghetti bolognaise –

one of my favourites – which she does in a wide pan she calls a wok. If she can't finish her meal, I dispose of the leftovers in my tummy. This clean-up service is a role I now share with Summer, who, unlike me, eats in a dainty way and is pickier about what she will and won't eat. Me? I'll try anything. So far snail and lettuce are the only two things I've spat out.

Rose's phone rings and she answers, the phone in one hand and the wooden spoon in the other.

'It's Phyllis.' The old lady's voice booms.

Rose stops stirring her bolognaise, the wooden spoon poised above the wok.

'Phyllis O'Brien?' Rose is as surprised as I am that Phyllis has contacted her, considering how much she appears to dislike her.

'Of course! Who else is it going to be? Now listen to me, Finn wants you to prove his innocence. That blasted man is determined to find my grandson guilty and Finn wants you to make sure Leach can't frame him. I think he's a fool, but there you go. It's his wish and I have to honour it. So, will you do it?'

Rose's eyes light up. 'I'm happy to look into the case but I can't guarantee the outcome.'

'I suppose you'll want payment,' Phyllis grumbles. 'I don't have much money. I'm a pensioner, see? I want a flat rate.'

'Phyllis, I won't charge you. I'd be glad to help. But you should know there is a possibility that I can't prove him innocent.'

'Whyever not?'

'Because I might find evidence of his guilt.'

'Tish and nonsense! I knew this was a waste of time. Once a cop, always a cop. You lot all think the same.'

'That's not true. I have an open mind about this. I want to know the truth.'

I swear I can hear Phyllis grinding her teeth down the other end of the phone.

'Come to my place at seven-thirty,' the old lady says. 'I have something to show you.'

Rose looks at the wall clock. 'Okay, you're at number twelve, Beehive Lane in Nether Wallop, correct?'

'You coppers!' Phyllis tuts. 'Spies, the lot of you.' She ends the call.

Rose stares at the phone. 'I wonder what she wants to show me. And how did she get my mobile number?'

I've never been to Nether Wallop and I'm always up for exploring new places, so I wag my tail excitedly until I notice the smell of burning bolognaise. I bark a warning and point my nose at the cooktop.

'Oh no.' Rose uses the wooden spoon to scrape the burnt bottom layer of meaty yumminess from the pan, then she switches off the gas burner. 'You don't mind a bit of burnt food, do you?' she says to me.

It would be my honour to get rid of those bits for her, and Summer can help me too. I trot over to where my mother is snoozing, a front paw twitching and her muzzle quivering. She is dreaming, probably of chasing rabbits or squirrels. It's my favourite dream too. I decide not to wake her. Rose always divvies up the leftovers between us so that Summer doesn't miss out.

Rose serves herself a bowl of bolognaise. 'No pasta for me tonight. I'm trying to lose weight. I can barely fit into my jeans.'

Rose sits at the oak table that's dinged and scratched but as sturdy as a rock, and she eats her dinner. I stare longingly at the burnt food still in the wok.

'Oy! Monty!' says a squeaky voice from the hole in the skirting board. I turn my head and see a pointy, whiskery nose and two bulbous eyes like black ball-bearings. 'Save some for me, will ya?' Betty says.

I can't bark a response because that would annoy Rose. I point my nose at the back door, which is code for "meet you outside."

There is an air vent in the exterior wall with a sizeable hole in it and this is Betty's back door. I head outside through the stable-style kitchen door that leads directly to the back garden. Rose leaves this door ajar most of the time so I can come and go as I please. It's a cold February night but Rose doesn't seem to mind. I guess the kitchen is toasty warm from her cooking.

Our meeting place is the old tools shed that's overgrown with ivy. Out here, I can talk to Betty: Rose thinks I'm barking at a neighbour's dog. Rose is aware that a rat is living under her roof but, unlike most hoomans, she doesn't object. In fact, Betty has almost become a pet, although I would never say as much to Betty, who defends her freedom fiercely.

You see, Betty is no ordinary rat. Born and raised a Eurotunnel rat, she settled in our village after a particularly bitter breakup with her ex-partner. She's super smart and, thanks to Ollie's patient training, she has learned to carry on her back a "rat cam", one of Ollie's many inventions. Rose now feeds Betty once a day, leaving tiny pieces of food outside her hole in the skirting board. Ironically, this has resulted in my rat friend losing weight because Rose keeps Betty's diet healthy.

It's pitch-black outside and the sky is cloud-free and full of twinkling stars. My breath forms little warm clouds that surround my nose for a second or two and then are gone. I smell hedgehog and fox on the other side of the hedge. I pass a huge willow tree, its branches like an open umbrella, beneath which the ducks, two Canadian geese and a pigeon called Cyril are sleeping. I resist the temptation to charge through the willow's dangling branches to knock over the sleeping ducks because I want Betty's advice. The tumble-down shed is full of rusting garden tools and plenty of spiders that have set up home there. I lie down and wait for Betty to join me. The grass rustles and Betty appears, closely followed by Summer, who walks arthritically, her back legs a little wobbly.

'We can't have your mum missing all the fun, now can we?' Betty says, wandering over to a rake and scratching her back on its teeth.

'You were asleep, Mum,' I say. 'I didn't want to disturb you.'

'That's all right, son,' Summer says, sitting awkwardly. She slumps her back end to one side and then lowers her front legs slowly. 'Betty says you have a case to solve. I want to do what I can. I'm so proud of you, Monty. Who would have thought that one of my pups would become a dog-tective?' She rests her jaw on a paw and sighs contentedly.

Betty comes over and rests her upper back against my paw as if I'm an armchair. 'I have to point out that this isn't really our first case, is it, Mr Monty? You and me, we've solved crimes before.'

'That's true,' I say, 'although this is our first case as The Nosy Detectives.'

Betty uses a long claw to pick a miniscule piece of food from her sharp teeth, which she then swallows. 'You're right about that, Mr Monty.' Betty wriggles and when she's comfortable she says, 'So, tell us about the case.'

I glance at Summer, whose eyes are already drooping with sleepiness. I worry that the cold floor isn't good for her arthritis. I must keep the briefing quick so we can return to the warm house.

'This is the story of a ten-year-old boy who lost both parents in a farmhouse fire,' I begin. Summer's eyes open at the sound of my voice. 'That boy is Finnegan Toyne, known as Finn, and he's fifteen now.'

Summer interjects, 'I know about that fire. Every dog for miles around knew about it. The smoke carried on the wind far and wide. Just the boy and his pup survived. Am I right?'

'Yes. He was in a coma for a while. Not because of the house fire.' I lower my head and whimper. Terrible memories swarm around my head. 'He was dog-sitting me, here at Duckdown Cottage. An intruder smashed the back of Finn's head with a bottle and cracked his skull. Rose blames herself, but I should have done more to stop him.'

'Now, now, Mr Monty, it wasn't your fault,' Betty says. 'I was there, remember? Not only did he try to kill Finn, he went and flushed me down the toilet, the evil toerag!' Betty leaps up and shadow boxes, her front paws clenched into tiny fists. 'Take that, you scum!'

'He's serving a life sentence, Betty,' I say. 'He won't hurt you again.'

Betty pauses, mid-right-hook. 'I'm not afraid of the likes of 'im. I'm just saying you did everything you could, given you were shut outside, and the intruder was in the sitting room. Anyway, I've made my point.' Betty reclines against my paw again. 'Please continue with the story, Mr Monty.'

It's time to give Summer a bit of background information. Summer came to live with us just before Christmas. Before that, she lived a terrible life on Wiggins Farm: Rose and I rescued her from a puppy farm.

I begin.

'Rose's aunt Kay was a detective and she's the reason why Rose became a police officer. Kay worked the Toyne double murder case and The Leach was her boss. Kay came to the conclusion that Finn didn't light the fire that killed his parents, but The Leach was convinced of his guilt.'

'Oooh,' says Betty, 'I really don't like that Leach fella. Although I dislike that prancing pony, Pearl, even more.'

'They really thought a child did it?' Summer asked, twitching her ears in incredulity.

I continue, 'They still do. I don't know the details, but Rose says there are strange aspects to the case that make him look guilty. Anyway,

Finn came out of his coma today. The Leach has reopened the case and is determined to get a confession out of the boy. Finn asked The Nosy Detectives to find the real killer.'

Betty is up again. 'So let me get this clear. Rose, you, me and Summer are going to find the hooman who lit the fire at Toyne Farm. Correct?'

'Correct.'

'The Leach and that cocky idiot, Pearl, want to collar Finn, is that correct?'

'Correct.'

'And what does Rose think about all this? Does she think Finn did it?'

'She wants to find him innocent.'

'And you? What do you think?' Betty asks me.

'I don't know what to think. I used to like Finn. I guess I still do. But part of me is afraid of him. There's a darkness in him. I saw it only once and I never want to see it again. I think Finn is capable of doing bad things.'

Summer cocked her head. 'What did you see him do?'

'He looked at a photo of Kay as if he wanted to kill her. His body thrummed with hatred. It scared me.'

'Perhaps he thought Kay was attempting to frame him for arson?'

'It's possible,' I say.

'Right then, we need to get cracking,' Betty says, whipping her stunted tail around and slapping it on the floor, 'because I for one am not going to be outwitted by The Leach and that Prancing Pony! So what do we do first?'

'This is what I know,' I say. 'The fire happened the night of Finn's tenth birthday. There was a party. The fire started when the guests had gone home and Finn's parents were asleep in bed. Finn and his puppy survived.'

Summer says, 'How did the boy and pup escape?' She attempts to scratch behind her ear with a back paw but her hips aren't as flexible as they used to be. She gives up.

'All I know is that the boy was found outside the house, clutching his puppy. Nobody knows how he came to be there.'

'He walked out the door, of course, or climbed through a window,' Betty chides. 'He was young and quick, unlike his mum and dad.'

'That's what I thought,' I say, 'but Rose says the doors were locked from the *inside.*'

'Most peculiar,' says Summer. 'Is that why this detective you call The Leach thinks Finn started the fire?'

'I think so.'

Betty pipes up, 'What is Rose's plan of attack?'

'I don't think she has a plan yet. We're going to see Finn's grandmother later tonight. Phyllis says she has something to show us.'

Betty squats on all fours, arches her back and hisses in the general direction of the open shed door. I leap up, ready to head off the danger. I can't see or smell anything untoward.

'That witch!' Betty booms. 'Stay away from her, Monty. She's EVIL.'

I search the starry sky for a pointed hat and broomstick, but I don't see one. 'You think Phyllis is a witch? I thought they didn't exist.'

Betty remains squatting on all fours but she has stopped hissing. 'No, silly, I mean Tiffany is the witch.'

None the wiser, I'm relieved when Summer asks who Tiffany is.

'The cat. Tiffany-the-ginormous-cat. She's the size of a grown pig, I swear. And she casts spells. She has Phyllis in her thrall. You watch yourself, Mr Monty. She could turn you into a tree or something worse. She could turn you into a cat! Yikes! Then you might try to eat me!'

'Betty is right, Monty,' Summer says. 'Some cats have magical powers. They can control their hooman.'

'I thought that was a fairy tale,' I say.

'To be honest, I've never met a witch-cat,' Summer says. 'I'm just telling you what my mother told me when I was a pup. She talked about famous hoomans who were bewitched by their cats. There was a wise hooman who lived many years ago by the name of Nostradamus. I remember his name because it reminded me of nostrils. This wise man had no idea that his cat, Grimalkin, had bewitched him and was channelling his own visions through his master. And take the Bronte sisters' cats. These felines fiercely guarded Charlotte, Emily and Anne, doing their utmost to ensure that they never married because the cats wanted to keep them at home. When Charlotte finally married the curate of Haworth, her cat was so furious he cast a spell that led to her death not a year later. But I think I should be clear that cats can do *good* magic too.'

Betty folds her arms. 'Never known a cat to do good.'

Summer continues, 'Take Sir Winston Churchill. He stopped a very bad hooman called Hitler from invading England. His ginger cat, Jock, stayed at Churchill's side when London was being bombed, slept with him at night and even slipped into the cabinet war room meetings. The story goes that at night he would whisper into Churchill's ear the military strategies that won the war.'

I stare at Summer, awed at her knowledge of hooman history.

'Sorry, Summer,' Betty says. 'No offence, but I don't believe it. Cats is cats!'

Most of the cats living in our village keep to themselves so my experience of cats is limited. 'I imagine Tiffany wants the same thing as Phyllis. So there's no reason for her to get in our way.'

Betty shakes her head. 'I won't let you go there alone. Far too dangerous.'

'I won't be alone. I'll be with Rose.'

'I'm coming with you.'

I know there's no point arguing with Betty, so I thank her and move on. 'We can help Rose solve the case. We just have to work out how.'

Betty and Summer nod.

'That's the hard bit.' Betty says.

I scratch my ear as I think. 'What we need is a fly on the wall. Someone who can secretly listen in to the police questioning Finn. Someone small enough that hoomans won't notice.' I look at Betty. She's small and can move fast. She also can carry a rat cam.

Betty's whiskers twitch fast. 'You want me to hang out at the hospital?'

'I think that would be helpful.'

Betty leaps into the air and claps her front paws together. 'Yippee! I looooove hospitals. I don't know what it is about ill people, but they leave so much food on the floor. And have you seen the size of a hospital kitchen – eeenorrrrmous!'

'When Rose next goes there, you can hitch a ride in the car.'

Betty rubs her tummy. Once she is at the hospital, I may find it difficult to get her to leave.

'The pup is also a witness to the fire,' Summer says wisely.

'That's true,' I say. 'But I don't know the pup's name or where he lives now.'

'Don't you worry about that,' Summer says. 'A few well-placed wee-mails and a bit of patience and we'll find that puppy.'

'I now see where you get your brains from,' Betty says to me, nodding at Summer.

Summer lowers her head shyly and I give Mum a loving boop on the nose.

'I'll try to sniff Finn's bedroom for clues. And who knows? Maybe Tiffany can help us.'

'Not a chance in hell,' Betty mutters.

7 MONTY

Rose pulls up outside an end-of-terrace house in the village of Nether Wallop.

The red brick houses are small, with one window downstairs and one upstairs at the front. The only streetlight in the village is outside number two, which leaves Phyllis's house, at number twelve, in deep shadow. The front garden is a tangled mess of weeds and creepers which obscure the square paving stones that lead to the doorstep. Rose's shoe snags in some ivy. She trips but manages to pull her foot free. The fur down my spine rises, my ears pricked on full alert. Is Summer right? Does a witch-cat live here? The windchime dangling from the porch roof clinks in a tinny way and sets my teeth on edge. The corn chip smell of cat is very strong. The lights are on in the front room and through the lace curtains I can just make out the shape of a hooman sitting in an armchair. The TV is very loud.

Rose rings the doorbell and it sounds like a hornet buzzing. The TV is suddenly muted. 'Who the blazes is that at this time of night?' Phyllis says from the sitting room.

'It's Rose Sidebottom,' she calls out. 'You asked me to drop by.'

Phyllis mutters, 'Did I?'

Finn's grandmother takes a while to get to the door. The security chain clanks as she fiddles with it, then the door squeaks open. I think Phyllis has forgotten that we were coming because she's wearing a red fleece dressing-gown with a cord tie and slippers on her feet. Then I notice what is draped around Phyllis's shoulders like a shawl. It is the largest grey cat I've ever seen. Her round, yellow eyes shrink to slits, and she hisses at me.

'Your kind are not welcome here,' Tiffany says.

I step back and my furry bottom collides with a tubular umbrella-stand that wobbles but doesn't fall. Rose looks at me, probably wondering why I'm pulling backwards on my lead.

The cat grins with satisfaction and meows the word, 'Coward.'

Right! That's it. Time to show this cat that she can't mess with Monty-the-dog-tective.

Rose places her soothing palm on my head. She must sense that I'm on edge. I decide to give the cat another chance. I bark, 'I'm here to help find out who killed Finn's parents.'

Tiffany laughs. Have you heard a cat laugh? Hoomans call it purring.

'You stop your nasty dog scaring my poor Tiffany,' Phyllis says, stroking the cat's fur.

The cat whispers in Phyllis's ear. 'Don't let the dog in.'

Phyllis glares at me. 'That dog can't come—'

Rose interrupts. 'We're a team. If you want me to find who killed your daughter, Monty comes with me.'

I wag my tail. *Yeah! Take that!*

'Get over yourself, you smug git,' purrs the cat.

My jowl wobbles with frustration. I want to respond but if I bark again, Phyllis is likely to banish me and I must stay with Rose. If I don't, the cat might bewitch her.

'Oh all right,' Phyllis says, 'but mind he doesn't hurt my poor kitty.'

Fat chance! I eye Tiffany's claws as they appear and then retract from her paws. They are very long and very sharp.

The hallway is narrow and musty. Phyllis leads us into the sitting room that smells of ages long past and is stuffed full of furniture: a wooden writing desk with lots of little drawers and a delicate handle; dining chairs of all shapes and sizes in polished wood and faded fabric, none of them matching; a leather armchair with a sagging seat; a walnut display cabinet with figurines inside. The walls are covered in old paintings and decorated plates. Why would anyone want to put a plate on the wall? What a waste!

Phyllis sits in an armchair of faded burgundy corduroy that has stains on the armrest and where the back of her head goes. Tiffany hasn't moved from Phyllis's shoulders. The cat must weigh quite a bit and I marvel that an old lady can carry her around with apparent ease. There is a two-seater sofa opposite with blue and cream stripes on it. One of the sofa cushions is covered in grey cat fur. I suspect this is where Tiffany sits of an evening.

Rose avoids the fur-covered spot. When she's seated, I sit at her feet where I can best keep an eye on things.

'You said you had something to show me?' Rose says.

'Oh that's right. I do. I'll get it in a minute.' Phyllis clears her throat. 'Tell me what you know.'

Rose does just that. Most of it I know. Then she asks Phyllis about petrol and my ears prick up.

'I understand that when Finn was found outside the burning cottage, he had petrol residue on his hands and shoes. How do you think that happened?'

The old lady straightens her back and raises her chin. 'It's obvious, isn't it? The arsonist used petrol. Finn must have touched some of it when he escaped the house.'

Rose realises that this is a touchy subject because she moves on. 'I want to ask you about the people who attended the party on the night of the fire. I can't see an obvious suspect.'

'You're wasting your time on the guests. I know who killed Marie and Tony and she isn't on the guest list.'

Rose opens a small, hard-covered notebook and pulls a pen from the spiral binding. 'Who do you think did it?'

'Sasha Bassinger, of course.' Phyllis stares at Rose as if the name is proof enough of the woman's guilt.

'Who is she?' Rose asks.

I glance at Tiffany. Her shoulders bob and her purring is deafening. She's laughing at Rose. How dare she?! I feel a growl rising up my throat and it takes all my willpower to stop it.

'Don't you know anything, girl?' Phyllis says. 'That evil woman hounded my daughter and son-in-law to sell Toyne Farm. Haven't you heard of Bassinger Homes? Property developers. Tony refused, and damned right too. That farm had been in his family for six generations. There's motive for you!'

Tiffany skips off the old woman's shoulders, lands on the chair's arm, then jumps down to the carpet. I watch the cat slink off behind a leather chair. Now that Tiffany's overpowering corn-chip smell has gone, I detect Phyllis's unique scent of lavender soap and moth balls.

'What makes you think Bassinger is capable of murder?'

'Because without Toyne Farm, there was a bloody big hole in her planned development. One hundred and twenty houses and flats. Do you know the Meadowbank gated community?'

'Yes. I have a friend who bought a terraced house there.'

Rose must mean Big Man Joe, my favourite police officer. Some of the houses there are huge. Joe's is one of the smallest.

'Well, imagine Meadowbank with a section cut out of it.'

'When did Bassinger Homes acquire Toyne Farm?'

'About a year after the fire. You see, Finn was traumatised. He wouldn't go back to the farm. His psychiatrist said that he might never be able to. Once the insurance company had paid up, the decision was made to sell the land.'

'Who made that decision?'

'The two executors. Me and an accountant called Frank Featherman.'

'You were willing to sell to the person you believed lit the fire? Why?' Rose asked.

'Had to. Nobody else wanted it. I mean, who wants to live where two people were murdered?'

'I'd have thought you'd have done anything to avoid Bassinger getting her hands on the land.'

'Don't you dare judge me! I had a traumatised grandson. I had the coppers sniffing about. Psychiatrist bills to pay. His future to provide for. What else was I going to do?'

'I didn't mean to offend you,' says Rose placatingly. She moves quickly on. 'Tell me about Marie's and Tony's wills.'

'They wrote what's called mirror wills, leaving the farm to Finn. I was appointed his guardian. Finn was to live with me at the farm until he reached the age of eighteen, at which time he could sell the farm if he wished. The manner of his parents' passing changed everything. He said he never wanted to go back there. As executors we made the decision to sell the farm and set up a trust fund with the proceeds, which Finn inherits when he reaches eighteen.'

'I didn't know you could do that.'

'His parents left identical letters with their wills. I think they're called letters of wishes, or something like that. In them they stipulated that in certain circumstances they would wish the farm to be sold and a trust fund set up for Finn.'

Rose nods sagely and writes notes.

I am lost. Insurance? Wills? Trust funds? I have no idea what Phyllis is talking about. I scratch my ear to make me feel better.

'Mirror wills?' Rose asks.

'Basically, the wills are identical. They reflect each other, see?'

'Oh, I see. Back to Bassinger. I've seen her police statement.' A copy of it must be in one of the boxes that Rose keeps in her office. 'She has an alibi,' says Rose.

'It's a lie! She's the only one who had something to gain.'

'I'll talk to her, of course,' says Rose. 'Is there anyone else who might have wanted either Marie or Tony dead?'

'Everybody loved my darling girl,' Phyllis's voice has softened and her eyes wander to a silver-framed photo of a young girl in school uniform with long fair hair in pigtails. 'My beautiful Marie.' She sighs. 'She made such gorgeous clothes, you know. Designed them herself. And she was such a wonderful mother.'

'No enemies?'

'As I said, everyone loved her,' Phyllis snaps.

'And Tony?'

'I already told you, Sasha Bassinger. She hounded him.'

'How do you mean "hounded"?'

'It started with emails. Then she sent her lawyers after him. When that didn't work, she showed up at the farm. She offered more money and when he said no, she threatened to spread a rumour that his strawberries had pins in them.'

'I remember that scare. It made the national news. Somebody stuck pins inside the strawberries they picked. I thought they arrested that person?'

'They did. But when Bassinger was threatening Tony, the police hadn't found the culprit yet. That bitch knew if she spread a rumour like that, nobody would buy his strawberries and it would ruin them.'

Rose nodded. 'Do you have proof of her threats? A recording perhaps?'

'Not that I know of.'

'Do you have Tony and Marie's mobile phones?'

'I do as a matter of fact. I insisted the coppers return them.'

'Can I borrow them? I want to check the contact lists and messages.'

'I want them back.'

'Of course. I have some more questions but first I'd like to see Finn's bedroom.'

My tail thumps the carpet with excitement. Perhaps some smells from Finn's past still linger.

'I suppose,' Phyllis grumbles.

I catch sight of a grey tail as Tiffany rushes from the room. I can guess where she's going: Finn's bedroom. Rose and I follow Phyllis up the stairs and, sure enough, the cat is curled up on the single bed. Her yellow eyes challenge me. I find it hard to look away. Focus! I tell myself and raise my nose, inhaling the many scents.

Even though Finn hasn't used the room for a while, the dominant smell is teenage sweat with the tang of a sandalwood deodorant. I detect cheesy socks under the bed, and leather. I approach a guitar on a stand and sniff the strings, then I turn and find boxing gloves hanging on a hook at the back of the door. The room is small. There are posters on the walls of muscular hoomans posing in boxing gloves, and rock bands with angry expressions, all dressed in black.

'He likes heavy metal, I see,' Rose says, nodding at the posters.

'He wants to play in a band one day,' Phyllis says, opening a top drawer. She takes out two mobile phones and some cables. 'I want them back, remember.'

Rose puts them in her handbag and continues to look around. 'No photos of his mum and dad.'

'Don't you go drawing the wrong conclusions,' says Phyllis. 'I had to put every photo of Marie and Tony away. They made him cry. His psychiatrist said he was suffering from PTSD as well as grief. It's no wonder he couldn't speak.'

There's that "pee-tee-ess-dee" word again. I swivel my head and watch Rose's face. Rose nods but doesn't tell Phyllis that she understands what Finn was going through. Rose's pee-tee-ess-dee made her so ill that she couldn't work.

'Was the psychiatrist helpful?' Rose asks.

'Not really. She seemed nice enough, but Finn just got angrier and angrier as he got older. After eighteen months, I stopped the sessions and tried guitar lessons instead. He found music soothing and he played like a pro.'

'How did he communicate with his psychiatrist if he didn't speak?'

'He used a pen.'

'Did he keep a notebook or a diary?'

'Yes, a notebook, but I can't find it.'

I flick a look at Tiffany and I am pretty sure her grin is smug. Does she know where the notebook is? Did she hide it?

'Shame, that could have been useful. Who was his psychiatrist?'

'Lady by the unfortunate name of Dr Doom.' Rose blanches. Dr Doom is her psychiatrist, or she was while the police service was paying. Once Rose left the force, they stopped paying and Rose stopped going because she can't afford it.

'I know of her. Can you arrange for me to speak to her?' Rose asks.

'If you must.'

Phyllis opens the second drawer down and pulls out a silk scarf that reeks of a floral perfume with a hint of musk. 'I found this. It's Bassinger's scarf.'

'Why would Finn have her scarf?' Rose asks.

'Exactly.' Tiffany jumps off the bed and skedaddles out of the door. I hesitate. Do I stay in the room or follow Tiffany?

Phyllis continues. 'She toyed with Finn's affections. He was an only child and his parents worked hard. He craved attention and that Bassinger bitch gave it to him. Invited Finn to her son's party, a few months before Finn's. She must have coerced Finn into giving her the house key so she could light the fire and then lock everyone in.' Phyllis looked down. 'I think the poor boy blames himself, see? That's why he didn't speak for so long.'

'Did the investigating officers know about the scarf?'

She nodded. 'Weren't interested. Take it and ask that cow why she gave a scarf to a ten-year-old boy.'

Rose pulled on latex gloves and folded the scarf inside a zip-lock bag. 'Is this what you wanted to show me?'

'And this,' Phyllis said. From the same drawer she took out a USB flash drive and handed it to Rose. 'That has all the photos taken on the night of the party. Perhaps you'll see something the cops didn't.'

While the hoomans are talking, I slip out of the bedroom and find Tiffany licking a paw on the landing. She raises her head and her eyes glint. 'I won't let you frame Finn,' she hisses. 'He didn't do it.'

'Just give us a chance.' Tiffany resumes her licking. Cats are very good at pretending you don't exist. I continue, 'If you know where the notebook is,' I bark as quietly as possible, 'please show me.'

'You'll never find it,' Tiffany says.

'It might help prove his innocence.'

'Quiet, Monty!' Rose calls out.

I'm going to have to be succinct. 'What happened to Finn's puppy? Where is it now?'

'How should I know? An ugly brute. She had peculiar eyes. One was blue, the other brown.'

'Name?'

'Something stupid like Panda.'

With a name like Panda and different coloured eyes, the dog should be easy to find.

8 ROSE

Rose, back in the sitting room with Phyllis, was relieved that the huge cat had hopped through the extra-large cat-flap. She had the strange sensation that the cat didn't approve of her and there was no doubt that she disliked Monty.

Monty sat between Rose and the coffee table and had unfortunately planted one of his paws on top of her right foot, causing it to go numb. She bent down and lifted the paw away. As the blood supply returned, there was a sharp stab of pins and needles. This was different from the tingle she felt when somebody was lying to her. That was more like a prickly wave that travelled up her limbs. So far, she hadn't experienced any such prickling sensation, which meant that Phyllis had, so far, told Rose the truth. Phyllis genuinely believed that Bassinger was guilty and Rose had to admit the property developer had motive. But that didn't mean Phyllis was right: according to Bassinger's boyfriend's police statement, Bassinger had been with him all evening.

'I really need to talk about the party guests,' Phyllis opened her mouth. Rose didn't give her time to object. 'I have to explore all avenues.'

Phyllis rolled her eyes but didn't protest further.

'Can I ask why there were only five kids at the party?' Three boys and two girls.

'Food poisoning. It was such a shame for Finn. Earlier that day another kid had her birthday party and the meat in the sausages was off. Finn and his three best friends weren't invited, and Sadie and Matilda didn't like pork, so they were spared the poisoning.'

'Okay. Let's start with the vicar, Reverend Mabey.' She pronounced it "Mar-be".

'You don't seriously think the vicar did it?' Phyllis said.

'Everyone's a suspect. How did Marie and Tony know the vicar? Were they religious?'

'Marie and the vicar's wife, Lorraine, were great friends. Marie taught Sunday School. Tony donated fruit for the Harvest Festival. He wasn't into religion, but he'd turn up at the occasional church event.'

'Was Lorraine at the birthday party?' Rose had noticed that Mrs Mabey's name was absent from the list.

'At the start, yes. She helped Marie with the cake then she left after the first hour. She's a bell-ringer, you see. They had practice that night.'

Rose thought it strange that Lorraine would choose bell-ringing over her friend's party.

'Did either Marie or Tony have a falling out with the vicar or his wife?'

'Not that I know of. They are both lovely people, if a little annoying.'

'How do you mean annoying?'

Phyllis leaned forward with a cheeky smile. 'Well, he's such a ditherer. Keeps changing his mind. Maybe this, maybe that.' She grinned. 'We call him Reverend May-be.'

'Oh I see.' Rose moved her pen to the second name. 'Tell me about Frances Buttermere.'

Phyllis scowled. 'That woman is a wretched busybody. You be careful what you say to her. In fact, I'd rather you didn't talk to her.'

'I'm sorry, Phyllis, I have to talk to everyone who was anywhere near Toyne Farm that night. If Buttermere was so unpopular, why was she invited to the party?'

'Because if she wasn't, she'd spread nasty gossip. She really is spiteful. Is it any wonder she's a spinster?'

'Did she bear a grudge against Marie or Tony?'

'She dislikes the whole village, so I'm sure she'll have something nasty to say about them. Although, at the party, she was on her best behaviour. She even brought a present.' She looked down. 'It was destroyed along with everything else.' She pulled out a scrunched-up tissue from her right sleeve and dabbed her hooded eyes.

Monty shifted his haunches and whimpered. Rose guessed he sensed Phyllis's distress.

Rose glanced at the list. 'What about Mervyn Mumford?'

'Merv? He used to own the farm next door. His wife died a long time ago. He brought up his son, Alfie, all on his own. A lovely boy. Was best mates with Finn. I should ring him in the morning and tell him the good news.'

'Who owns Mumford's farm now?' Rose asked.

'Oh Lord, you're behind the times, my girl. Merv sold it to Bassinger Homes. He told me that once Tony was gone, he lost the will to keep his farm going. I think it was the best thing for Merv and his boy to move on, start afresh.'

'Where do they live now?' Rose asked, scribbling notes.

'Little Wallop. Merv spends most of his time at the tennis club. I hardly see him these days.'

'And who is Wendy Macintyre?' Rose asked, her pen pointing at the name.

'Marie's best friend. She died poor thing. Breast cancer. Must be three years ago.'

'Did she have motive to kill Marie?'

'Lord! No!'

Thanks to Kay's notebook, Rose knew that Macintyre's boyfriend had confirmed she was home with him from 9.45pm.

So far, not one of the partygoers seemed to have a motive. However, there were more names on the invitation list: all juveniles.

'Sadie and Matilda Jones. Did they have any reason to dislike Finn or his family?' The sisters now lived in Australia.

'Are you serious? They were ten years old!'

'I know, but it would help me understand the big picture if I had a handle on everyone at the party.'

'The answer is no. And their parents collected them, so they can't have done it. They were tucked up in bed.'

'Okay. Alfie Mumford, Jimmy Fox and Sam Chang, also ten-year-olds. Did they argue or fight with Finn, or get up to any mischief that night?'

'I was too busy heating up party pies and quiches, and keeping everyone fed and watered. The boys did what they liked.'

'What time did the party end?'

'Around nine. Jimmy's mum collected Jimmy and Sam and took them home around that time. So did the girls' parents. Alfie stayed on a bit longer with his dad. They left around ten, from memory. The vicar left early, maybe eight o'clock. He would!' Phyllis muttered. 'That bloody Buttermere woman hung around until ten-ish. She wouldn't take a hint and Marie was too polite to tell her to leave. So I reminded Buttermere that this was a farm and they would be up at dawn, so everyone was off to bed. I was the last to leave, at about eleven o'clock. It took ages to clear up the mess.'

Rose felt a tingle travel up her legs and arms and this time it wasn't her dog's fault. Somewhere in Phyllis's answer was a lie. 'Why did you say "he would" about the vicar?'

'Oh it's nothing. He likes to go to bed early when he has a service the next day.'

Another tingle ran through her body. Another lie. It made sense that the Rev Mabey would want an early night to prepare for the Sunday service, but Rose suspected there was more to it than that.

'So after you went home, was there anybody else in the house except Marie, Tony and Finn?'

'I didn't see anyone. But there had to be someone, didn't there?'

Phyllis desperately wanted the arsonist to be someone other than Finn but Rose had to admit that it wasn't looking good for him, with Sasha Bassinger as the only other possible suspect. Rose referred to her notebook, checking the timeline of events she'd put together from the photocopied case files. 'And the fire was reported at one thirty-eight by Mumford. Could he see the fire from his house?'

'Oh yes, he was further up the hill. Just a bridleway and fields between the two properties.' Phyllis crouched forward as if she had indigestion.

'Phyllis, are you all right?'

'I feel sick every time I think about it. I didn't know about the fire until Merv called me around two in the morning. By the time I got there, the house was an inferno.' The old woman's voice trembled. 'Dear God! It was a terrible sight.'

Rose wanted to hug Phyllis but she didn't think the old lady would appreciate her doing so. *Stay on course*, she thought. *You're here to solve the case*. 'How do you think Finn ended up outside the house with his puppy?'

Phyllis's eyes narrowed. 'He didn't start the fire, I'm telling you. He was a good boy.'

'Okay, but how did he get outside if the exterior doors were locked?'

'Through the toilet window, downstairs. He was slight enough back then to crawl through the tiny window.'

'Why not a bigger window?'

'There'd been a burglary a few months earlier, so Tony put bars on the downstairs windows. Except the one in the toilet.'

'Why didn't Finn keep his puppy?'

Phyllis glanced out of the window. 'Tiffany wouldn't have a dog in the house.'

9 MONTY

Rose is asleep upstairs. I am curled up on my bed in the kitchen with my jaw resting on my matted toy duck. I can't sleep. My thoughts charge around my head like tumbling puppies in a pen. I listen enviously to Summer's snoring. The fridge clanks every now and again as if it has a screw loose, and the wall clock ticks rhythmically. Outside these four walls, everything is quiet.

While Rose and I were with Phyllis, Summer howled a message to the dog universe, asking for information on a Border Collie named Panda who once belonged to Finn Toyne. When time is of the essence and the message must travel a big distance, dogs use a howl-a-thon. Think of it as a canine cellular network. It's simple really: each dog repeats the cry of the dog before it. We throw back our heads and howl like our wolf forefathers.

Once the message is put out there, all we can then do is wait for an answer to come back, which may take days or weeks. It means that the source of the message, someone close to them, must stay alert and listen for the response.

A fox screams, as they do at night. Then I hear the distant howl of a dog, far far away, that trills in the still air. My guess is that the canine is as far away as Geldeford. I can't decipher the message, but I lift my head expectantly. Is it a one-off cry or is it a howl-a-thon? I wait and, sure enough, another dog takes up the cry. Ha! It's definitely a howl-a-thon. The same length and pitch of howl, a touch clearer, but still I can't work out the message. Then another dog, a smaller one yip yip yips the same message.

I take myself outside, the better to hear. As usual, Rose has left the back door ajar so I can squeeze through the gap. I step onto the lawn, which is crunchy with white frost. I recognise the breathy bark of Mr Squishy, the pug who lives in the next-door village of Milford. His cry is taken up by my good friend Jake, the three-legged Staffie who lives in a caravan in Winterfold Heath with his hooman, Ed. The howls continue until they reach our village of Farley Green. Bear, the German Shepherd, booms out the message in his bass voice, as clear as the water in my water bowl:

For Monty at Duckdown Cottage. The dog you seek is at the Peasemarsh Pound. She's called Panda. Hurry! She is due for destruction tomorrow.

My tail droops. Flashes of my cage at the Peasemarsh Pound burst into my brain: I remember hard surfaces and bars and the smell of wee-mails that reek of terror. I hear my fellow prisoners baying to be rescued. The hoomans who worked there meant well, but they had more dogs than they had cages and if a dog wasn't adopted, or was pronounced aggressive, then he or she was for the chop. No wonder the dog pound is known by the canine fraternity as Dogmo: the canine equivalent of Gitmo. I had managed to escape death row and had helped twelve other dogs escape with me, one of whom is my good friend Jake, the three-legged Staffie.

I never want to see that wretched prison again.

But if Panda is due for destruction tomorrow, then we must act tonight!

I take up a wide stance and prepare for a howl. I lift my head and look at the stars. I take a few large breaths and then exhale from deep in my chest:

Thank you, my fellow dogs. Message received.

As soon as my howl is over, there is not a yip or a growl or a woof to be heard. Their job is done and the dogs return to their sleep. It is the hoomans who are making "a racket" now. Complaining they have been woken. Cursing those bloody dogs. I feel warm breath on the back of my neck and snap my head around to find Summer standing close, her eyes glistening in the moonlight.

'Howl-a-thons are so special. They bind us together,' Summer says. 'I'm sorry the news isn't better.'

'We have to get to Dogmo tonight. I need to wake Betty.'

'But how will you get there? It's a long way.'

'I don't know. Come inside. It'll chill your bones out here.'

Back in the kitchen, I poke my nose into the hole in the skirting board and whine, hoping it won't disturb Rose upstairs.

'Bleedin' Nora!' squeaks Betty. I pull my snout from the hole. A few seconds later, she stumbles out of her nest as if she were drunk. Betty is a deep sleeper. 'What's up?' she asks, yawning.

I explain about Panda's situation.

'Well, what are you waiting for? We have to rescue her.' Betty is now wide awake.

'Yes, but how do we get there?' I keep my bark as hushed as possible so as not to wake Rose. 'And then we have to break in. I once managed to break out. Breaking in might be a lot harder.'

'Then we need to eat,' says Betty. 'Fuels the brain.'

Before I can stop her she ducks into the hole and returns with a slice of bread that's almost as big as she is. 'A piece each.' Betty tears the bread into three pieces; two are small, one is large. She hands Summer and I the small pieces and starts to gnaw at the large one. Summer and I swallow our bit, but Betty likes to fill her cheeks with as much of the bread as possible and then she swallows one crumb at a time.

'We tayth the train,' says Betty. Trying to speak with her mouth full of bread causes her to lisp. 'To Geldeford. Change trains. Then tayth the latht train to Peathmarsh.'

Betty knows the train service timetable by heart. She's a Eurotunnel rat from way back and trains are in her blood.

'When is the last train, Betty?' I ask.

'The last one leaves Milford at seventeen patht eleven. That one goes to Geldeford. The Peasmarth train leaves Geldeford at eleven forty-five.' Crumbs go flying from her mouth and she races to suck them up. 'Whath the time now?'

The village church clock chimes eleven times as if to answer Betty's question. 'We have to go now.' I gaze at Summer. 'Do you want to come?'

'I'm too old for that,' she says, 'I'll just slow you down. But take care.'

Summer gives my neck a fond nudge and then settles on her bed.

'When does the first train from Peasemarsh run in the morning?' I ask Betty, who is busy tugging the remaining piece of bread back through the hole in the skirting board.

'Ten past five in the morning.'

It looks like we are going to be out all night, which isn't a problem as long as Rose doesn't wake early and discover I'm missing.

'Right then,' I say. 'Up you get.'

Betty knows what to do now. She climbs up my front leg at surprising speed, given the weight of crumbs she holds in the pockets of her cheeks. She positions herself in the middle of my shoulder blades and hangs onto my collar like a jockey. 'I'm ready. And remember, Mr Monty, don't touch the live rail. I'll point it out as soon as we're through the hedge.'

The tall yew hedge that separates our garden from the railway line has no foliage in winter and there are numerous gaps for me to squeeze through. Thankfully the half-moon sheds some light.

'It's that one. The farthest rail,' Betty says.

I can't see where she points but I know which rail she means. I hop into the middle of the track where there are wooden slats and start to run. I gather speed.

'Woohoo!' Betty yells. She loves to ride on my back. 'Yee-hah!'

The frost has made the slats slippery but I keep going. Ahead is the dark tunnel. On the other side is Milford station: it's the last stop before the train terminates at Geldeford. I have to be through the tunnel before the train comes. I speed up, my tongue lolling from my mouth. In the distance, far behind me, is a rattling sound. I sniff the air: the faintest smell of engine oil, burning rubber and the tang of metal. It's the train. Soon I feel the slats beneath my paws vibrate – the train is approaching fast. The tunnel is pitch black inside but at the other end, bright lights illuminate the tiny station. I keep up my pace. The rattling grows louder, becoming a roar. The air in the tunnel suddenly gets shunted forward and it's as if I'm being shoved from behind. I almost lose my footing. The train has entered the tunnel and created the pressure behind me.

'Hurry!' squeaks Betty.

The dank arched walls are lit up by the train's headlights. The noise is deafening. My ears twitch in discomfort. I feel more air pressure behind me. I leap off the track and dive into tall grass, then I scurry up the steep slope leading to the platform. The electric light lends an orange glow to the damp bench and the shiny ticket machine. A young couple is on the platform, at the other end. Nobody else. The train whooshes past us, buffeting my fur. Betty slips towards one of my shoulder blades as she is sucked towards the monstrous beast. She soon rights herself. The train screeches to a halt and the doors open automatically with a beep, beep.

'The last carriage,' directs Betty. 'Now!'

I jump through the open door of the carriage, hoping there is no hooman inside who will notice me and sound the alarm. I'm running so fast that I almost collide with the doors on the other side of the train. Just in time, I manage to stop. The doors behind us close. I am panting hard and desperate to drink water, but that will have to wait.

It's only then I notice two boys are in the same carriage. I poke my nose around the edge of the seat. They must be about the same age as Finn. They lounge back with their trainers on the opposite seat and talk loudly. One of the boys laughs.

'Don't. I'll piss myself laughing!'

The train sets off with a sudden jolt. I don't know what will happen if the boys get up and discover us. If they grab my collar, I am trapped. But they only appear interested in their conversation. There is a yeasty smell of beer in the compartment and the greasy, salty smell of hot chips. The laughing boy snorts like a pig.

'I'd give anything to see that loser's face! Priceless!'

They continue their chatter and I hunker down and wait for us to arrive at Geldeford. Even from inside the sealed train, I smell the city. Car exhaust fumes, all the food smells that emanate from the cafes and restaurants and takeaways, and all the many smells of hoomans. Geldeford is an old city. A cobbled street runs all the way down the hill. Rose told me it was originally built in Roman times. Many of the buildings that line the high street have black beams and lead-light windows. I'm not a city dog. I love the countryside too much. But the food smells are very enticing and my stomach gurgles. The train begins to slow.

As we enter the enormous city station, the train is bathed in white light. There's a judder and the train jerks to a halt. The doors beep and start to open. I stand, ready to leap out the moment the gap is wide enough. The boys' shoes scuff the floor. I only just jump out in time.

'Was that a dog?' one boy says.

I don't look back. I've ridden the train to the city before. I know that I have to run as fast as I can along the platform, then take a left. The station is busy with late night revellers. I slalom around people. A group of women wobble on their high heels and share a joke with a guard. I use the opportunity to charge past the guard and sprint down platform three where a train is waiting, the doors open.

'Look at the dog!' someone shouts, and people stare.

I duck into a narrow gap between a shop selling coffee, and the guards' hut. There's only just enough space for me to squeeze through. I stop, panting heavily.

'We'll wait here till the last minute,' says Betty. 'I'll tell you when.'

Seconds tick by and my heart still races. A guard blows a whistle and waves a baton.

'Now!' Betty says and I charge out of our hiding place and leap onto the train as the doors close. There is a solitary rail worker on board, in a yellow jacket with reflector stripes, who closes his eyes to sleep.

We made it. We're on our way to Peasemarsh.

10 MONTY

Crumbly Lane has steeply sloping banks on either side so I have to walk in the road. Trees form an arch over us, blocking out the moonlight, which means I have to tread carefully. Only one car has passed us by and when I heard it coming I scampered up the bank to avoid being seen. We're not far from the Peasemarsh Pound and with every step I'm growing more nervous. Just thinking about the hideous place makes my stomach churn. What if our plan goes wrong and I get caught breaking and entering? And what's more, the pound is set up like a prison. How on earth am I going to free Panda?

I hear an owl tewit-tawooing in the distance. I hope that he isn't going to lecture me. What is it about owls and their sense of superiority? Granted, they are the only birds I know that can recite Shakespeare, but do they have to do it to belittle the animals they happen to fly past?

I hear the flap of wings and an owl swoops under the tree canopy and flies over me. I brace myself for the verbal onslaught. The owl screeches at me:

'Life...is a tale
Told by an idiot, full of sound and fury,
Signifying nothing.

You ter-wit!'

The owl disappears on its hunting mission. I breathe a sigh of relief. I've had worse Shakespearean quotes hurled at me.

'Rude bird!' says Betty.

My thoughts return to Panda's escape. When I was held at the dog pound, I managed to escape because I know how to flick latches and turn doorhandles. I flicked the latch on my cage, freed the other prisoners, and then discovered an open window. I doubt the hoomans running the pound will make that same mistake twice. Then my thoughts move onto Panda. She must have been traumatised by the farm fire when she was a pup, and then she was wrenched from her special hooman – her boy, Finn. I still can't understand how Phyllis could be so cruel as to make Finn give up his beloved pup. Wherever Panda has been since then, it can't have worked out because here she is, at the pound, an unwanted dog and destined to be put to sleep. In my heart I know that whatever the risk, I must at least try to free her. She deserves a second chance.

'Are we there yet?' Betty moans from her position between my shoulders. 'Me bum is getting sore.'

'Almost.'

The road bends to the right and there's a T-junction ahead. Straight ahead is a five-bar, wooden field gate that has been padlocked. It is the entrance to the Peasemarsh Pound, which is surrounded by wire-mesh fencing. I don't have to tell Betty that we have arrived. The air reeks with fearful dogs. Two are barking, another is whimpering, calling out for their owners to save them.

I zip across the road and peer through the five-bar gate. Two cars are parked out front. Oh dear. This late at night there shouldn't be anyone there, just the dogs locked in their cells for the night. Lights are on in the reception area and several other rooms. Why would the staff work so late? There are four other buildings, all connected by a covered walkway. Us dogs refer to them as cell blocks A–D. At least I can be sure that Panda is not in cell block C – that one is reserved for cats.

Betty has climbed off my back and stands on her hind legs, the better to see the place. 'You want me to take a look? Find a back way in or something?'

I nod. Betty scampers across the gravel car park. A security light bursts into life and Betty is bathed in light. She scurries as fast as her legs can carry her to the reception exterior wall, then disappears around a corner. I observe the windows and entrance for a sign that a hooman has noticed the security light switch on, but no-one appears. My attention moves to one of the cars. I sniff the air. It smells familiar. I need to be closer. I can't get through the mesh fencing, but I should be able to jump the wooden gate. I move back so I can get a good run-up. Then I set off, gathering pace with every step. Just before I reach the gate, I leap high into the sky. The dazzling security lights blind me temporarily. My back paw catches on the top bar, but there is enough momentum for my body to keep moving forward and I land on the gravel with a crunch of little stones.

I race over to the car I recognise. Just one inhalation of the wheel and I know whose car it is. It belongs to the nice vet, Malcom Kerr. There can be only one reason why Malcolm would come here at night: an emergency medical situation.

If the hoomans are busy attending to the sick animal, they are less likely to notice us. But if Malcolm does see me, he will take me home to Rose, who will be upset.

I hear Betty squeaking my name. 'Oy! Over 'ere.'

I follow Betty's voice to the back of the main building. From inside, there's the rumble of voices. I recognise Malcolm's. From what I can overhear, one of the dogs escaped and was hit by a car. H e w a s t o o b a d l y i n j u r e d t o m o v e .

'I'm sorry,' Malcolm says to his companion. 'I did what I could.'

Oh no! A dog has died. Betty and I look at each other and our heads droop.

'Brave soldier,' Betty mumbles.

It can't be Panda, I think. I know it's a selfish thought, but Panda is who we have come all this way to rescue.

'Poor little thing,' says a woman. 'Someone left her cage open by mistake.'

Would a hooman refer to a fully grown Border Collie as little? I don't think so. Betty and I lift our heads.

'There's no easy way in,' Betty says. 'And no way to work out where Panda is being kept. Only one thing for it,' Betty says, 'you gotta call her name. Them hoomans will think you're just one of the pound's dogs.'

I have been avoiding barking, fearful that I will be discovered. But Betty is right. With any luck my barking will be ignored by the hoomans.

I begin. 'Panda! This is Monty, the dog-tective. I'm here to rescue you. Speak up so I can find you!'

A cacophony of canine cries erupts from everywhere, everything from deep bark to high-pitched yaps. They're all begging me to free them. Help me, they woof. This is not the response I'd been hoping for. It's so loud there is no way I can separate Panda's voice from the other dogs.

'Quiet!' I command. 'I need Panda to speak up!'

'Take me!'

'Help me!'

'I can't stand it anymore!'

The wails are distressing. And they're drawing the attention of the hoomans.

'What the blazes is going on?' I hear the woman say from inside the building we're hiding behind. 'Maybe they heard a fox?'

I try again. 'Listen up, I can't help you all. I wish I could. Panda, this is your last chance. Please tell me where you are?'

'I'm Panda. Block A. Help me. I'm destined to die tomorrow.' Panda has a jerky, nervous voice.

'Okay, I'm coming to get you.'

Betty and I head for Block A. The door has no handle, just a slot for a key, which means I can't open it my usual way. We need the key. In my experience, hoomans like to keep keys in one of two places: they hang them on a key rack or they leave them in a tray or bowl by the door. Given this place needs many keys, I hazard a guess that the key to Block A hangs on a rack in the main building.

'Betty, we'll sneak into the main building and find the key. We're looking for this sign.' I find some sticks and create the letter A.

'Okay, boss. How do we get in?'

'Through the front door. It's how the hoomans got in tonight and I can't imagine they've locked it.'

Betty follows me to the front of the building. I give the door a shove with my shoulder and it swings inwards. I peek through the gap. Malcolm and the woman are just visible in another room. On a table is a miniature poodle who isn't moving. My heart saddens. I hope the little dog has gone to the great dog park in the sky.

'Look!' says Betty, her nose pointing at the reception desk.

Bingo! Behind the desk is a row of storage cupboards as high as my head, and on the wall above is a key rack with multiple keys dangling from hooks. I run in, heading for the cupboards, then I hoist my front paws onto the top of them so I am much taller and can just reach the keys.

'Which one?' Betty asks.

Good question. Behind the books are little labels with writing on them. My eye is dawn to a row of keys labelled A–D. I point my nose at the key labelled A.

'Got it,' says Betty.

She climbs up my rear leg and runs along my spine until she is balancing on top of my head. She huffs and puffs as she strains for key A. I stretch my body and neck to make me as tall as possible. There's a clink, then Betty climbs off my head and sits between my shoulders. I can't see her but I'm guessing she now has the key between her jaws, so I nip outside, quick smart.

Once I'm at Block A, I aim my snout as close as possible to the lock in the door. Betty then balances once again on my head. I hear tapping sounds as she attempts to slide the key into the lock, using her front paws to grip the key.

'It won't go in,' she says.

I daren't answer. If I did, my head would jerk up as I barked and Betty would fall off. A prisoner inside Block A must hear the tapping because she sounds the alarm. My shoulder muscles tighten: the noise will draw unwanted attention. Betty persists and finally she slides the key into the lock. She doesn't have the strength to turn it.

'Phew!' Betty says. 'Over to you.'

Betty scampers down to the ground and I bite the key between my left back teeth and turn my head. With a click, the door opens a fraction. The dogs inside Block A launch into a tirade of barking, which is sure to bring the woman who works at the pound. I have to move fast.

I charge in, with Betty close behind me, then come to a halt. It's very dark inside Block A, but my sense of smell indicates where the dogs are located.

Now is the right time for me to bark.

'I'm Monty, the dog detective. I'm here to free you. Barking will bring your jailers. Stop barking!'

Some dogs cease, but three keep going: a Beagle, a Miniature Schnauzer and a mixed breed dog. The Beagle is baying so loudly it's enough to scare foxes for miles around.

'Quiet!' I woof sternly.

The beagle is the last to give up on his baying, but it tapers off into a whimper. I can only hope that the instant silence is enough to stop the pound lady from inspecting the block.

'Panda! Are you here?' I bark.

From the furthest cage, a black and white dog with a thick coat presses her nose to the cage bars. 'I'm Panda.'

I approach her cage. Her eyes are different but in the darkness I can't work out their colour.

'I'm here to free you. Don't run, okay? Stay with me.'

'What do you want with me?' Panda asks, her bark fearful.

'I need your help.'

I prod the latch with a paw. I'm relieved to see Dogmo hasn't upgraded the simple latches they use to hold the cage doors in place – a metal hook that slots into a loop. I use the bridge of my nose to pop the latch up and out of the loop. Panda creeps out, then she crouches submissively.

'Don't send me back to the farmer.'

'Stick with me and Betty and you'll be fine.'

Betty says, 'Monty's a good dog. I vouch for him.'

Panda doesn't run. Instead, she sticks close to me as I move along the row of cages, popping latches.

In the next cage is a cross-breed with German Shepherd in him.

'Get me out of here,' the cross-breed whines. 'Nobody will adopt me. They say I'm too big and scary.'

'Hang on, my friend,' I say as quietly as I can.

I pop the latch. The German-Shepherd-cross bolts from her cage and charges out of the door.

Next is an elderly boxer with a very large lump on her ribcage.

'I want to run free one more time before I die. I know I don't have long in this world.'

I free her and she thanks me before she, too, disappears into the night. The next cage holds a medium-sized Staffie who reminds me of a younger version of my mate, Jake, who I helped free from this very dog pound some time ago. The Staffie flees from the cage without a moment's hesitation. The Husky in the next cage has her paws up on the cage door and her eyes are wide with terror. I free her and move on until every cage is empty. Then I slip through the exit, followed by Panda and Betty. The security light is on and the lady from the pound peers out through the main entrance. Betty clambers onto my back, then we run for it.

The woman shouts, 'They're escaping!'

Panda and I are almost at the cross-bar gate when Malcolm's voice booms across the car park.

'Monty? Is that you?'

11 MONTY

Panda cowers behind me. I am a friendly dog but in this instance I make it clear to Malcolm and the Dogmo lady that I won't let them take Panda back. I adopt a defensive stance and stand between them and the Border Collie.

'I don't like the look of that brute,' Dogmo lady says. 'Can you hang onto his collar while I leash Panda? Then I'll call the police. Has to be kids who broke in and thought it a laugh to free the dogs. Bloody kids!'

Malcolm doesn't move. He glances at me with a wry smile on his face. 'Panda must be very special for him to have come all this way.'

'Him?'

Malcolm points at me. 'I think you'll find Monty flipped the latches.'

'That's ridiculous. No way could a dog do that. It's only ever happened once before and it was probably kids who freed the dogs back then too.'

'I've seen Monty do incredible things. Anyway, tell me about Panda.'

'Look, it's late and I need to call the police.'

'Please, humour me.'

'Panda was left here by a farmer. We think she's been cruelly treated.

She snarls and tries to bite everyone who goes near her. Not her fault, but we can't adopt her out when she's aggressive. She's being euthanised tomorrow.'

I whine, 'Save her, please!'

Malcolm rubs his chin. 'Can I take her and see if I can find a suitable home? Let me take her off your hands.'

I lick his hand to say thank you.

Dogmo lady agrees, clearly delighted to have the responsibility for Panda off her hands. Soon we are in the back of Malcolm's car and heading towards Geldeford. Malcolm doesn't know that Betty is curled up, fast sleep, with us. Panda stares out of the rear window, mewling at the night sky. She's not sorry to be leaving Dogmo. She's afraid of where Malcolm will take us.

'Why did you do it?' Malcolm asks, throwing the words over his shoulder in my direction.

I don't know how to tell him that this is Finn's dog and that Panda may know the identity of the arsonist who murdered Finn's parents. So, I *hurrumph*.

Soon we enter Geldeford.

I sniff the cold night air that blows into the car through an open window. The city smells are familiar and so is the noise of traffic, and people yelling as they leave the pub. I hope Malcolm is taking us to Duckdown Cottage, although I'm not looking forward to the disappointment on Rose's face when she learns where I was tonight. Rose knows that I go into the garden at night and once or twice I haven't been home when she wakes up. She tells me off for going to Winterfold Heath but she's not unduly concerned because we live a hop and a skip from the heath. However, Rose has no idea of how far I travel sometimes.

I feel like a very bad dog.

Maybe I am. But Betty and I have saved Panda from death row. Well, to be truthful, Malcolm unwittingly assisted. When he shouted my name in the car park I had two choices – run or turn back and face the consequences. I couldn't ignore his call: Malcolm has been so good to us. And besides, he'd seen me and would have told Rose anyway. I thought it best to throw myself on his mercy.

I see Malcolm watching me in the rear-view mirror, his face lit up momentarily by a streetlight. 'Why did you open the cages?' he asks, then mutters, 'He can't answer, stupid!'

Malcolm is far from stupid. In fact, he's one of the cleverest hoomans I know.

He turns the steering wheel and we head up the ramp to the dual carriageway. Rose's cottage in Farley Green is four miles down that carriageway.

Panda sits up. 'As soon as he opens the boot, I'm going to run for it,' she says in a breathy, terrified voice.

'Give it a chance,' I say. 'Malcolm is a vet and a very nice hooman. He knows lots of dog lovers. He'll find you a nice home.'

'I don't trust hoomans. My first owner gave me up when I was terrified and needed his love. Then the farmer who took me starved me if I failed to herd his sheep the way he wanted me to. He was going to shoot me for being a lousy sheep dog when I ran away. I was a stray for a while, then a woman offered me some food which I stupidly took. She handed me in to Dogmo.'

Betty, who a few seconds ago had been asleep, scurries over to Panda and strokes her paw. 'There, there, petal,' Betty says soothingly. 'You have our word, we'll find you a good home.'

'Keep it down in the back,' Malcolm calls out. 'You'll wake the neighbourhood.'

The car headlights illuminate the junction where he's turning off the carriageway and from the smell of the sandy heath and the wood smoke, I know we are almost home. Before we arrive, I have to ask Panda a question.

'Would you like to live with Finn Toyne?'

'And live with his nasty grandmother and her ginormous cat? I'd rather be a stray.'

'Finn was only a child back then, and children don't get to do whatever they want. He wanted to keep you, I'm sure of it.'

'I loved him,' Panda says. 'But the night of the party he was cruel to me. I wanted to greet everyone at the party and play with his young friends. He put me in a cardboard box, stabbed some holes in it and sealed the top and left me there all alone in the machinery barn. I heard the party. The laughter. I smelled the food. I didn't understand why he wanted to punish me like that. I whimpered and cried but he didn't come. Not until there was fire. Then he took me in his arms and said he was sorry.'

'What happened after that?' I ask.

'The house was full of fire. Finn was crying. A fire engine arrived. I remember the wailing sound. The air was thick with black smoke and oh, that smell. It was burning flesh. I will never forget it.'

'Who lit the fire?' If I could cross my toes, I would. This is the big, BIG question.

'Don't know. I was in a box in the barn. All I do know is that afterwards Finn was broken. He didn't speak. And he hid from everyone, even me.'

Malcolm closes the window. 'Guys! Keep it down, will you? You're making enough of a racket to wake the dead!'

As the car hums along the narrow road, I slump to the floor, my hope of discovering the identity of the killer dashed. My thoughts turn to Rose and how she will react when she discovers I broke into the Peasemarsh Pound.

Malcolm and Rose are drinking hot chocolate in the kitchen. Rose is wrapped in her pink fleece dressing gown. Panda lies next to Summer, her different coloured eyes darting from Rose to Malcolm fearfully. Summer licks Panda's ear, trying to comfort her. At the first opportunity, Betty scurried into her hole in the skirting board. I don't blame her. I'm tired too but I must make sure that Panda is okay. I lie on the floor next to Rose and rest my head on her sheepskin Ugg slippers. She looks down at me and her hair falls across part of her face.

'How on earth did you get to Peasemarsh, Monty?'

I stare blankly at her. Would Rose believe me if I said I took the train?

'I can't fathom it, either,' Malcolm says. 'I know Monty escaped from there once, but that doesn't explain how he managed to find the place again. And this is the bit I haven't yet told you. He freed ten dogs from their cages, not just Panda. Lord only knows how he did that.' It's Malcolm's turn to peer down at me. I'm feeling scrutinised and look away. 'Did you train him to open latches?'

'No. Perhaps his previous owner did. What I can't understand is how he knew where Panda was. I mean, how could he possibly know she was there and in that particular cage? It's like he went all that way to rescue her.'

'Can she stay with you for a few days?' Malcolm asks. 'I want to see if I can find her a new home.'

'Of course.' Rose chews her lower lip. This means she's thinking. 'I wonder...' Her voice trails away.

'Wonder what?' Malcolm prompts.

'Dogs have an amazing sense of smell. Would Panda know the scent of the arsonist? Is that why Monty went to fetch her?'

Her hand rests on my head. *Yes*, I think. That's why I went there, but Panda doesn't remember.

'From what you've told me,' says Malcolm, 'the night of the fire would have been traumatic for the boy and his dog. Panda isn't likely to forget, although she may be so traumatised that she doesn't want to remember.' They both turn their heads to look at Panda who leans closer to Summer and hides her face.

'How might she react if she met the arsonist again?'

'She'd probably show signs of fear. Low stance, tail low, teeth bared perhaps, or she might try to flee.'

Panda lifts her head. Her tail wags. 'I remember,' she barks. Everyone in the room looks at her but only Summer and I understand what she's saying.

'Go on,' I say.

'The night of the fire. Two hoomans spoke angrily. I could hear them from my box. They must have been in the barn. One was a woman, the other a man. I was too young to understand but I know who the female was.' She pauses and licks her lips in fear.

'Who was it? I ask.

Rose tells me to be quiet. She goes over to Panda to stroke her. 'You're frightening Panda,' Rose says. 'It's all right, you're safe now.'

Panda looks at me and I nod.

'The woman was Finn's mum,' Panda says.

'And the man?' I ask. I know I'm disobeying Rose and I feel bad about it, but Panda is the only witness we have right now.

Rose once again tells me to stop barking.

'I don't know his name,' Panda says, 'He had a whining voice. I peeked through the holes in the box. He wore a white dog collar around his neck. I remember thinking it was strange that a hooman would wear a dog collar.'

I know who she means. The argument was between Marie and Reverend Mabey.

I race over to Panda and give her a congratulatory lick on the ear. This is important information.

At the back of my mind is a burning question: how do I tell Rose?

12 MONTY

It's Sunday morning and the church bell rings eight times as I pant in Malcolm's face, my wet nose a hair's breadth from his cheek. He's asleep on Rose's sofa with his legs resting on the arm and a blanket tucked under his chin. It's light outside so why isn't he up and about? Panda, Summer and I have already patrolled the garden, chased a few ducks and checked the dog bowls at least twice, wondering when we will be fed.

Malcolm wriggles his nose, then his hand comes up to his face and encounters my furry muzzle. His eyes spring open, he stares at my nose for a moment, then yawns. For a hooman, he has a wide jaw and a very good set of teeth.

'Monty,' he says.

Yup! That's me. I pant even more enthusiastically, my wagging tail creating quite a breeze. I give his cheek a boop with my nose. Hi there!

He looks at his wristwatch, then moans. He closes his eyes again.

Is he really going back to sleep when we have a crime to solve and a home to find for Panda? It's time for me to venture upstairs and try my winning good morning smile on Rose. Strictly speaking, I'm not permitted upstairs. But I have ventured up there when Rose is unwell and when there is an emergency, and there's an emergency right now!

I climb the stairs. There are two bedrooms and a bathroom. One bedroom belonged to Aunt Kay and I find the dolls on her bed creepy. Their glass eyes stare at me in a way I don't understand. In contrast, Rose's room is cosy and welcoming. She has an especially thick duvet on her wooden bed and she disappears under it, as if she's hiding. However, I know she's there – I hear her shallow breathing and know her scent. The tips of two fingers and her nose poke out from under the covers. I put my nose as close as possible to her nose and pant enthusiastically, my tail wagging so fast it would be a blur if I could see it. Her nose crinkles and the two fingers turn into a hand which blindly and gently pushes my muzzle away from her.

'Go away, Monty. It's Sunday.'

And how does that make any difference? Sunday's as good a day as any to solve crimes and find a dog a new home. Her hand withdraws beneath the duvet and Rose turns her back on me. All I can see of her is the top of her head. Oh dear, that's not the reaction I was looking for. I blame the duvet; it's too thick and too cosy. I carefully take a corner of the duvet between my front teeth and slowly walk backwards. Gradually Rose is revealed in her pyjamas with penguins all over them. Rose tries to grab the duvet but it slides off the bed.

She turns around, rubs both eyes. 'There's no peace for the wicked, or at least for a dog owner like me.' She sits up and checks the alarm clock on the bedside table, then frowns at me. 'We didn't get to bed till two.'

There's plenty of time for a nap later. I place my head on the sheet and stare lovingly at her. She strokes my head, then pushes me aside so she can get up. Once she has her slippers and dressing gown on, I lead her down stairs and into the kitchen. She puts the kettle on with a big yawn, readies two mugs with tea bags, then scoops out dry dog food into three bowls and puts some water into each water bowl. She then tells me, Panda and Summer to sit. We plonk our butts on the lino floor in unison, two of us drooling – that would be the golden retrievers.

'Eat,' she says, and we do.

Malcolm appears in the kitchen in the same clothes he wore last night, his black hair sticking out at crazy angles. Rose hands him a cup of tea and he sips it.

'Monty woke you, didn't he? I'm so sorry,' Rose says.

'It's okay. I probably should get going. B will be wondering where I am.'

'I'm sorry for the disturbed night,' Rose says.

'Please don't apologise.' He takes a chair at the kitchen table and Rose follows suit.

'Is it too early to ask a question?' Rose asks.

'Fire away.'

'Do you know why Finn gave up his puppy?'

'He wasn't allowed to keep her. Phyllis doesn't like dogs much.'

'So there's no chance Finn would take her back? I hope he'll be cleared of the murder of his parents soon and he can get on with his life.'

'You think he's innocent, don't you?' Malcolm asks.

'I do. I just can't imagine a ten-year-old doing something so wicked. I mean, is someone so young really capable of such ruthless planning? He would have had to sneak out, pour petrol in the house, lock the doors, and set fire to the place without setting fire to himself.' Rose shakes her head.

Malcolm puts his mug on the table. 'This means a lot to you, doesn't it?'

'Yes, it does.'

'Let me help you, Rose. I might know some of the suspects.'

Yes, I think. Say yes. We need all the help we can get!

'You've been such a kind friend already, I can't ask any more of you.'

He shifts in his seat. 'Friend? Oh, well, I suppose I am.' Malcolm sighs heavily and his shoulders slump. 'I'd like to help. I like…your, err…company.'

'But how can you spare the time?'

Oh Rose, just say yes!

'I'll make the time.'

Before I know it, I've barked, one loud, single bark, which is a YES. Rose jumps in her seat.

'What do you mean, yes?' she says, looking me in the eye.

Malcolm is quick to step in. 'I think Monty wants my help. And he's right. This is a big task and if any of your suspects are clients of mine, I can do my best to help you contact them, at the very least. Perhaps I can provide an introduction?'

'I don't want to impose on you. And Ollie helps me with online research.'

True, but Ollie has school to attend and after our last adventure, when Ollie got badly hurt, his mum made it clear that she doesn't want Ollie involved in anything dangerous in future, and what could be more dangerous than hunting a killer? I decide I have to make my views clearer and I trot over to where Malcolm sits, then I lift a paw and place it on Malcolm's thigh. He strokes my head.

'I think Monty has cast his vote,' Malcolm says.

Rose laughs. 'I think you're right about that. All right, then, I'd love your help. When's a good time to take you through the list?'

'Now's a good a time as any.'

'How about I make breakfast first? It's the least I can do.'

Rose makes scrambled eggs on toast and they eat it hungrily. I sit under the table hoping for a crust or a bit of egg to flop to the floor, but I have no such luck. When the empty plates are in the sink, Rose finds her notebook and pulls a chair close to him. Malcolm's cheeks bloom with pink blotches and his body temperature has escalated. Rose talks through her suspects, starting with Sasha Bassinger, whom Phyllis adamantly believes is the killer.

'Hmmm. Sure, Sasha had motive,' Malcolm says, 'but murdering two people is a bit extreme just to procure some land, don't you think? I don't know her personally but my business partner does. His son works for her. Are you happy for me to ask Fred about her?'

He means Dr Fred Rochester, the older vet with thick white hair.

'Yes, but it would be good if Bassinger doesn't know that I'm looking into the case. I don't want her prepared for my visit.'

'No problem. Fred is totally trustworthy. I'll explain what you're doing and ask him to be subtle. The police investigation is all over the news, so it will be easy for him to drop it into conversation.'

Rose continues down her list of suspects.

'Mervyn is a client,' says Malcolm. 'Has two cats. Their enteritis boosters are due about now. I'll encourage him to bring them in. He's a charming fellow. I can't imagine he'd do anything sinister.'

When Rose has been through her suspects, Malcolm scratches his head. 'Isn't there somebody missing? I don't mean to criticise of course.'

'Who's that?'

'Phyllis.'

My ears are pricked. Did he say Phyllis? I'm paying close attention now.

Rose stifles a laugh. 'But she's employed me to prove Finn is innocent.'

'Do you know about his parents' wills?'

'A little.'

'My mother is a wills and probate solicitor. Now that the case has been reopened, she mentioned that she hoped the police would ask Phyllis about the will.'

'Why?'

'Is Phyllis a beneficiary?'

Rose paused. 'I can't reveal what I know, but I can talk hypothetically. If Phyllis has hypothetically set up a trust fund from the sale of Toyne Farm, I suppose she might be able to use some of the capital for the purposes of helping Finn with his education.'

'I know there are strict rules about that sort of thing, but is it possible that she's squirreling away some of that capital for herself?' Malcolm said.

'Are you saying that Phyllis might have killed her daughter, son-in-law and potentially her grandson to get hold of some cash?'

'People have done worse things. And don't detectives always look at the closest relative as the suspect?'

'Fair point. But my gut tells me she just wants the best for Finn and I really can't imagine her stealing from Finn's inheritance.'

I come out from under the table and wander into the garden where it is quiet, and my doggie brain can hopefully focus on what I've just heard.

Would Phyllis steal? I wonder. She reminds me of a she-wolf defending her pack. Her pack was Marie, Tony, and Finn. I can't see her turning on her pack and killing them. Nor can I see her stealing from the sole survivor of her pack – Finn. I think she is more likely to do whatever it takes to defend them.

13 ROSE

'Shall I take Panda, or leave her here?' Rose asked herself as she toyed with the clip on the leash Malcolm had given her.

In sync, Panda and Summer looked up. Perhaps it was the clinking of the clip. Rose watched Monty trot over to Panda and nuzzle her. Panda then rose and followed Monty to where Rose stood. It was as if Monty was telling Rose to take Panda with them.

'You're right,' Rose said, giving Monty a pat. 'Panda must know the killer's scent. However young she was at the time, I can't believe she would forget something like that.' Rose clipped the spare leash to Panda's collar and noticed that the address on the collar was for the Peasemarsh Pound. 'When we find you a good home, we'll get you a new tag.' Panda looked up at Rose nervously, her tail between her legs. 'It'll be okay,' Rose said, stroking the dog's head. Then she looked at Summer.

'Want to come too?'

Summer sighed and lowered her head on her dog bed.

'I don't blame you,' Rose said. 'I'd much rather be cosy in bed.'

Rose said goodbye to Summer and left the back door ajar so that she could visit the garden if she wished. Then she, Monty and Panda set off for 15 Meadowbank Close: Sasha Bassinger's home address.

Malcolm had headed home a while ago. His hypothesis that Phyllis might be creaming off money from Finn's trust fund and therefore benefitting from Finn's parents' death seemed ludicrous. Certainly, money was a motive for murder but Phyllis lived a frugal life. If she were mishandling the fund for her own benefit, it wasn't obvious.

The tree-lined roads were icy, and the windscreen kept steaming up with too much doggy breath, which meant she had to drive with the windows down. As she navigated an S-bend on the single-track lane leading to Nether Wallop, the church bell struck ten times.

Nether Wallop was a larger village than Farley Green, boasting a post-office-cum-grocers, a pub, a small cricket pavilion, a flint Norman church with a magnificent arched entrance, and a community hall where the Scouts and Girl Guides met, as did a weekly art class and the amateur dramatics society. Rose drove past Phyllis's house but she didn't catch sight of Phyllis or Tiffany. A little further on was the vicarage, a plain house painted cream with a grey tiled roof. In the summer, the climbing roses made the house look quaint but today, on a dreary winter's day, it appeared rather barren. Next door, the stained-glass windows of the Norman church glowed, lit up from within, and the arched wooden door was wide open.

Monty had his head out of the rear window. He started barking frantically. Panda did the same, squeezing her muzzle out of the same window.

'What's the matter, guys?' Rose glanced at her dog in the rear-view mirror and saw a rat on Monty's head. Her eyes met with the rat's ball-bearing-shaped eyes.

'Hello, Hoover,' Rose said. 'It's quite a party in the back there, isn't it? Coming along for the ride?'

The rat squeaked loudly, then scampered out of sight.

Hoover, as Ollie had christened the rat because of how she sucked up crumbs like a vacuum cleaner, was like a pet and yet she didn't live in a cage. Rose knew that Hoover lived in a hole in the kitchen skirting board and that she and Monty were pals. Ollie had trained Hoover to wear a "rat-cam" camera on her back. Rather than concern herself with why Hoover was tagging along, Rose focused on her task: how was she going to get into a gated community when she didn't have an appointment?

Rose kept driving and Monty pawed at the door. Why were he and

Panda so frantic? Something was wrong. She pulled over to the side of the road and turned in her seat.

'Do you need the toilet?'

Monty shoved his head further through the open window, so far, in fact, she was convinced her was trying to clamber out. His nose was pointing directly at the church entrance. Why was St Bartholomew's making Monty so agitated? It was true that Reggie Mabey, the vicar, was on her list to interview, but nothing indicated that he had motive to kill two of his parishioners. And there was no point trying to talk to Mabey until after the service: he'd be distracted by his preparations.

Rose set off again and gradually Monty's barking subsided. Within minutes she came upon Meadowbank, the tips of the red tiled rooves poking above the high brick walls that surrounded the private community. At the entrance was a boom gate with a hut to one side, and a black-uniformed security guard within.

Rose halted at the boom gate. The guard stepped out of the hut clutching a clip board. *Oh no*, she thought, *he's one of those do-it-by-the-book types.* How could she persuade this man to let her in when it was his job to keep her out? Rose hadn't made an appointment with Sasha Bassinger. Without a warrant card, Rose had doubted that the high-powered businesswoman, who owned the largest house in the gated community, would see her. As it was a Sunday, Rose hoped to catch her on the fly.

The guard made a note of her number plate and then came up to her window. 'Good morning, miss. I don't have your registration number on my list. Who are you here to see?'

His cheeks were plump and riddled with burst blood vessels, as was his bulbous nose. Despite the coffee on his breath, Rose was sure she detected the sour smell of red-wine-breath.

'I'm here to see Sasha Bassinger about a cold case.'

'Are you police? I got a phone call from Geldeford nick. A detective. I have their car reg. Doesn't match yours.'

It was clear that one of her former colleagues in the Murder Squad, perhaps even DCI Leach himself, had made an appointment to interview Sasha. What if he was on his way? Rose had two choices – talk her way in or leave. She decided to do what guilty suspects frequently did in police interviews – avoid directly answering the question.

'You should have been given my details. Apologies for that. I'm here to interview Mrs Bassinger and I'm running late, so would you mind letting me through?'

He glanced around him, then back to Rose. 'I'm a big reader of crime fiction. Love a good mystery, I do. Maybe I can help, you know, solve the case. I know everything that goes on in this community and believe you me, I've seen some things in my time.'

'That might prove helpful. What is your name?' She jotted down Aaron Brown's mobile number.

'You mind telling me which cold case?' Aaron asked.

'I really shouldn't, but since you asked so nicely, it's the Toyne family murder.'

'Oh yes, I remember that one. A fire, wasn't it?'

'That's right. Now if you wouldn't mind, I need to get on. I'm already late.'

'Of course, of course.' He clicked the remote and the boom gate lifted. 'Call me any time.'

Rose drove in as quickly as was polite and headed for the far end of the development. The further she went, the bigger the houses became, until she came across a mansion with so many windows you could house a school inside. But this was no school. The lawn was so perfect, Rose wondered if it might be fake grass. The garage was wide enough to take at least four cars. A fountain and a dolphin sculpture sat in the middle of the u-shaped drive.

'Somebody's doing well for themselves,' said Rose to herself, staring at a sleek, red Jaguar XF parked outside the garage.

Rose parked in the road and turned to Monty. 'Are you going to behave yourself?' Monty dropped his head and looked at her sheepishly, but he wagged his tail. 'I need you to behave like a police dog. Obedient and quiet. Can you do that for me?'

He snuffled her shoulder. She took that as a yes.

'Panda, I'm going to leave you here for this one. Be a good girl.'

Panda lay down. With Monty on a leash, Rose walked up to the double front door and rang the doorbell. At first there was no response, then Rose heard a woman's voice.

'Who the blazes is that! Go and see who it is, darling. And if it's that dreadful woman from number eighteen, tell her I couldn't give a toss about raising money for the church roof.'

'I'm busy!' a man replied. 'On the phone.'

Heels clomped on a solid floor and one of the double doors flew open. Sasha Bassinger looked Rose and her dog up-and-down. 'You're not Frances. Who are you?'

Bassinger was a petite, dark-haired woman in a tight skirt and heels so high it was incredible that she didn't topple over. Despite Bassinger's five-inch heels, she stood just a tad taller than Rose. Clearly, what she lacked in height, she made up for with bullishness.

'My name is Rose Sidebottom and this is Monty, my detective dog. I'm investigating a cold case and I'd like to ask you a few questions. Can I come in?'

Sasha's big green eyes, highlighted by dark eyeliner and mascara-laden lashes, flicked from Rose to Monty again. 'Show me your warrant card.'

'I'm a private investigator looking into the murder of Marie and Tony Toyne five years ago. You knew them, I understand?'

'A PI?' Her gash of red lipstick twisted into a snarl. 'Go away.' She began closing the door. 'That useless security guard!' she muttered.

'Sasha, please, I just need a few minutes—'

'Bugger off!' The door slammed shut.

Rose's cheeks burned. So far, Rose had learned nothing useful about Bassinger except that she was unhelpful and rude. Rose headed for her car just as a vehicle entered the sweeping drive and came to a sharp halt. Two men got out, one wide and bald, the other blond and tall in a leather jacket: DCI Leach and DI Pearl.

'What are *you* doing here?' Leach said.

Rose stood stock still; Leach had that effect on her. As he lumbered towards her with a scowl on his face, Rose tried to come up with an answer that was the least likely to enrage her former boss. Monty, who was looking directly at Pearl, pulled on his leash, his fur bristling.

'If that dog so much as sheds on my jeans, I'll have him destroyed,' Pearl said.

'Stay calm,' she told her dog.

Pearl had made her life hell from the day she joined the Murder Squad. He fancied himself a heartthrob and had set his cap at her. When she had declined his offer of a drink at the pub, Pearl took the rejection badly. And then there was his deep-seated resentment about Rose's promotion to detective constable in just three years when Pearl had waited ten years for the honour. Pearl put her meteoric promotion down to nepotism because her Aunt Kay had been a DI in the same squad.

'Hello Craig. Hello Dave.' Both men scowled. Now that she was no longer a police officer she didn't have to say sir or boss anymore. This clearly irked them. Inside her puffy jacket that made her look like a blueberry, she was sweating. She continued, 'I've been employed to investigate the Toyne murders. I won't tread on your toes. Anything I come across that's critical to the investigation, I will of course share with you.'

Leach's eyes narrowed. 'Who asked you to do this?'

'That's confidential.'

Pearl said, 'It's obvious, boss. Has to be the grandmother.'

'Phyllis O'Brien?' asked Leach.

Rose nodded.

Leach flicked a look at the house. Bassinger was watching them from a downstairs window. He steered Rose away and continued the conversation with their back to the house.

'You have every right to work in parallel to us. But be very careful of Finn. He's not the lovely kid you think he is, and Phyllis is a crafty old coot. She'll have you believing all sorts of rubbish.'

'Thanks for the tip. Can I ask you something?' Rose said.

'Make it snappy.'

'Do you really think a ten-year-old murdered his parents?'

'Look Rose, I find the idea of kids who kill horrifying. But kids do kill. Take the Jamie Bulger case and the two ten-year-olds who murdered him.'

'Isn't it more likely the killer is an adult? Locking the doors from the inside and the use of petrol is beyond a kid's capability, surely?' Rose said.

'Rose, he had means, motive and opportunity.'

'What motive?'

Leach tapped his nose. 'Mind your own business.' He walked away.

Why was Leach so adamant that Finn was the arsonist? What did he know that she didn't?

14 MONTY

I push my head between the car's two front seats and rest my muzzle on Rose's shoulder. *I'm here for you, Rose*, I want to say. *I'm your buddy and protector.*

'Good boy, Monty,' Rose says, giving my furry ear a kiss. 'That was a bit scary, wasn't it? I feel like a schoolgirl caught stealing from the tuck box cashbox.'

Earlier, when we stood in Bassinger's driveway, I nearly cocked my leg on DI Pearl's jeans. I've been longing to do it for a while now, and his snide comments were almost the last straw. Fortunately, Rose calmed me down. I wish I knew how to help Rose relax. Her heart is still racing. I try licking her ear, which is very small and bereft of any fur.

'Yuck!' she says, but she giggles too. This is a good sign. 'You know what I think?' If I could answer, I'd say that Rose needs comfort food. Food always cheers me up. 'I fancy a hot chocolate. The pub will make one for me.'

Panda stares out of the back window, seemingly oblivious to what's going on, but I imagine there's a lot of thinking inside her head.

I pant enthusiastically at the idea of a pub, then my eyes are drawn down to the pocket at the back of Rose's seat. Betty is nestled inside it, her upper half poking out, and she's doing a wiggly dance. She's excited about going to a pub.

The last time my rat friend was let loose at a pub, she caused total chaos when she tried to steal a diner's lunch. The pub was shut down while a pest control program was actioned. I can't have Betty shut down another pub.

I lie down so that Rose can't see me in the mirror anymore and I shake my head at Betty. Betty squeaks with fury, her front paws on her hips.

I give a half-bark, which is me trying to keep my voice down. 'You can't go in there, Betty. Rats are a no-no in pubs. Please don't get Rose in trouble. I promise I'll bring you a treat.'

Betty glowers, but she takes her paws off her hips, which I interpret as acceptance. 'I want a nice big piece of bacon,' she squeaks, barely audible over the rumble of the tyres and the rev of the engine.

'I'll do my best.'

The pub, The Drunken Duck, offers all-day breakfast and coffee, as well as lunch and dinner. Their Sunday roasts are very popular. Rose can't afford to eat out often, but she pops into The Drunken Duck for takeaway cappuccinos every now and again. It's her treat, just as mine is a rawhide bone. As Rose pulls into the pub car park I wonder, as I do every time we come here, why there is not a duck anywhere. I have asked the ducks at home about this peculiar situation, and this makes them laugh so hard they fall over, and I never receive an answer. I have a soft spot for this pub because the landlord, Jethro, doesn't object to dogs entering his establishment. I suspect that his two Dachshunds, Shiraz and Chardonnay, usually shortened to Shardie, insist that dogs are always welcome. They might have very short legs, but they have Jethro wrapped around their tiny paws.

The pub's side entrance leads us into a conservatory with a peaked glass ceiling. A family of four are eating breakfast and I inhale the intoxicating smell of fried bread, eggs, sausage, bacon and baked beans. I'm not so keen on the baked beans because they cause me to fart a lot and Rose complains about the smell. I mindlessly veer towards their table and Rose has to tug the lead to keep me going in the right direction. Panda, as usual, is in a world of her own and doesn't appear to even notice the food on the table. The main part of The Drunken Duck has wooden beams, a burning log fire and walls covered in framed duck photos and paintings, as well as some lifelike ducks in display boxes, which I find unsettling because they look so real. Rose orders her hot chocolate and sits at the bar on a tall stool while Panda and I sit at her feet. I find a crisp that someone dropped last night and swallow it whole.

'Two dogs now, I see. And what would they like to order?' Jethro asks, wearing his cloth cap which he is never seen without. Rumour has it that he sleeps in the cap. Shiraz and Shardie will neither confirm nor deny on this matter. 'How about a pig's ear each?'

I am salivating.

'Thank you, Jethro. Add them to my bill.'

'On the house.' Jethro takes two pigs ears from a jar and comes around the counter. 'Shake!' he commands.

Too easy. I lift a paw and he shakes it, then hands me the deliciously oily treat. He asks Panda to shake too. She cowers and hides behind Rose's boots.

'She's a rescued dog,' Rose says.

'Poor love.' Jethro leaves the pig's ear for Panda on the stone floor. As soon as the publican goes to make Rose's hot chocolate, Panda quickly eats the pig's ear.

While Rose sips on her hot chocolate with a marshmallow floating on the top, I focus on snapping and chewing my treat. From around the corner of the bar, two black and tan, short-haired Dachshunds appear.

'Monty, good fellow, how terribly nice to see you!' says Shardie, in a yellow collar.

'Hello, there! It's been too long, my friend,' yaps Shiraz, in a red collar.

Why they have such cultured accents, I don't know. Perhaps their mother was with a well-to-do breeder? Jethro has a different accent; he speaks through his nose a lot and I've overheard Rose ask him why he left Birmingham to run a village pub. Jethro said he had wanted a quieter life. With Shiraz and Shardie in charge, I'm not sure he's ever going to have a quiet life – they like to get their way.

'How can you eat that!' exclaims Shardie, pointing her nose at the remnants of my pig's ear. 'I prefer something more, shall we say, refined, like venison jerky. Keeps me slim too.'

'You can't beat peanut butter chews if you ask me,' says Shiraz.

They plonk their butts on the stone floor and watch me devour the last piece of my treat. I then lick the floor, just to make sure that I haven't missed a morsel. 'I don't want to sound greedy–' I begin.

They burst into yippy laughter. 'Oh you are hysterically funny!' Shardie says, when she finally calms down. 'Aren't Golden Retrievers *always* greedy?'

She has a point. 'I have a friend waiting in the car.' I mean Betty. 'Can I take her some bacon rind?'

'Jethro likes to give it to the birds. But I can sneak some out of the kitchen for you.'

'She'd love that, thanks.'

Shiraz tilts his long-snouted head to one side. 'The word on the wee-vine is that you're now a fully-fledged dog-tective?'

'Yes, and we have our first murder case.'

'Congratulations, young hound!' Shiraz says.

Rose tells me to be quiet. This is the problem with a pub; my barking disturbs customers. Rose resumes her conversation with Jethro. I get up and wander through the conservatory, doing my level best to ignore the breakfast smells, but by the time I walk past the kitchen, I'm drooling.

'May I suggest,' says Shardie, following me, 'that I retrieve the bacon rind now? Perhaps you can partake, as well as your friend.'

Shardie waddles into the kitchen and returns seconds later with five strands of bacon rind dangling from her jaw like shoelaces. She drops them at my feet and screws up her black nose. 'Yuck, not my thing at all.'

I sniff approvingly. I remind myself not to wolf them down. I made a promise to Betty. I scoop them up with my jaw and push open the side door with my head. The Dachshunds follow. We veer to the right and into the beer garden, which, given it is freezing cold, is empty of hoomans. Shiraz and Shardie jump onto a wicker two-seater and lie down. Their faces are now level with mine, as long as I remain standing.

'Tell us all about the case,' Shiraz says, his bulbous eyes like dark brown marbles.

I tell them all about the Toyne fire five years ago and how the case has been reopened because Finn is able to speak again. I explain that Finn's grandmother has appointed The Nosy Detectives to find the killer. Our problem is that The Leach is set on finding Finn guilty.

They nod sagely.

'And what do *you* think, young Monty? Is the boy guilty or not guilty?' asks Shardie.

'I don't know,' I say. 'He has a temper, that's for sure, and he hates Rose's Aunt Kay for some reason, but I find it hard to believe that a ten-year-old hooman could do something so terrible.'

'I see,' nods Shiraz, his name tag jangling. 'Do you have any suspects?'

'Yes.' I relay the names I can remember, which isn't many. The church clock chimes eleven times. The Sunday church service is finishing. 'Ah, yes, the Rev Reggie Mabey is a suspect. He was at the party that night. His wife left early.'

Shiraz and Shardie glance at each other. They are almost mirror images, except Shiraz is slightly more black than tan. They come from the same litter.

'Shall I tell him, or will you?' Shardie says.

'Be my guest,' says Shiraz.

In sync, they turn to look at me.

'Our vicar,' says Shardie, 'isn't the saint he appears to be. He's been having an affair for as long as I can remember. We've lived seven dog years, and the affair has been going on all that time.'

'What is an affair?' I ask.

Again, the Dachshunds look at each other. 'Shall I explain, or will you?' Shiraz asks.

Now I remember why conversations with these two dogs can take a while: they defer to each other all the time. This time Shiraz answers my query.

'So, young pup, when a male dog and female dog come together to produce pups, they have a special bond. With me so far?'

I nod.

'Two hoomans who love each other like to make a commitment for life. They call this marriage or a de facto relationship. The vicar is married, but he is secretly humping another female. Her name is Karen Price. I still can't believe that his wife hasn't noticed him skulking off to visit her'

'Okay, but how does this make the vicar a murderer?' I ask.

'Well,' Shiraz continues, 'what if Marie or Tony was about the expose the vicar as an adulterer? It would have ruined his life. He would lose everything: his vicarage, his wife, his kids.'

I think this through. 'A witness saw Marie and the vicar arguing the night of the fire,' I say, not wishing to bring up Panda's name.

'There you are, then,' says Shardie. 'Sounds like you need to do some sniffing around the vicarage. Perhaps we can help? Hoomans tend not to notice us. We could be your eyes and ears in Nether Wallop, and report back via wee-mails.'

'That would be great,' I say. 'I think Rose plans to interview the vicar now that the morning service is over.' Just then, Rose pokes her head out of the pub door and calls my name. 'I better go. Before I do, did any other name ring a bell?'

Shiraz and Shardie look at each other. 'Will you tell him or shall I?' Shiraz says.

'Monty!' Rose calls again, 'Come!'

I don't have time for them to make up their minds about who is going to tell me. I say goodbye to them.

'Not so fast, Monty, you should make sure that Rose talks to Frances Buttermere,' Shardie yips.

'Why her?' I ask, already walking away from them.

'She's the village gossip, that's why,' Shardie yips louder.

'Monty!' shouts Rose. I run over to her, ashamed at keeping her waiting. She leashes me and, with Panda at my side, we head up the path to the church where the vicar is bidding farewell to the last of his congregation. I repeat the name Frances Buttermere over and over again, hoping I can keep her name in my head.

15 ROSE

Rose couldn't work out how Monty had managed to snaffle some bacon rind, but he had it dangling from his mouth as they left the pub. Even curiouser was his insistence that he return to the car. She assumed he wanted to stay there while she spoke to the vicar. When she opened her car's rear door so that he could jump in, he simply dropped the rind, then turned to face the church as if to say, let's get a move on!

'Is that for Hoover?'

The appearance of the rat from the rear-seat pocket answered her question. It struck her that she had quite a large group of animals living with her. But it didn't bother her. In fact, she preferred the company of animals to that of people.

Rose locked the car and walked the two dogs up the churchyard path. Only a few stragglers from the service remained behind. Rose was surprised at how young Reverend Mabey looked. She knew from her research that he was forty-one and married with four kids, but he didn't look a day over thirty. She had heard that the Anglican Church was finding it difficult to recruit new vicars. She guessed Mabey was much sought after, given that the other vicars in and around Geldeford were all reaching retirement age. Mabey was fresh-faced, with fine dark hair and a genial smile and was clearly popular with several ladies in the village who crowded around him at the church entrance, competing for his attention.

Rose decided to wait until his fan club had left the churchyard before she broached the subject of the Toyne murders. Mabey glanced at her and smiled, before his focus was reclaimed by a stiff-backed woman in her sixties, who was dressed up as if she were having tea with the Queen. She wore a hat with a peacock feather sticking out of the dark blue band. Her elegantly cut wool coat in a matching blue was unbuttoned. She waved a hand about and a ring glinted in the sunlight. The diamond was huge. Eventually the women left the churchyard – peacock lady was the last to leave. As she passed Rose and her dog, she stared at them with suspicion.

'Hello and welcome to St Bartholomew's,' Mabey said. 'Did you wish to speak with me?'

'Yes!' Rose made her way to him, Monty and Panda staying close at heel.

Peacock lady snorted in what appeared to be annoyance, then departed.

'Lovely dogs,' Mabey said.

Monty sniffed his cassock.

'Thank you,' said Rose. 'Is there somewhere we can talk privately?'

'Of course. Come through to the vestry. I think everyone has left. We can chat in there.'

'Can I bring the dogs with me?'

Mabey hesitated. 'Well, it's not normally allowed, but I suppose it won't matter if nobody knows.' He smiled conspiratorially and Rose smiled back. He really was charming.

Rose followed Mabey into the church through an arch with zig-zag mouldings around the doorway. The interior was simple, with wooden pews and another stone archway separating the altar from the body of the church. To the right was a short passageway that led to the vestry, where the choir robes hung on wall pegs. Mabey halted suddenly at the entrance and Rose almost collided with his back. A young woman with a retroussé nose and 50's-style winged glasses sat on a low, backless bench beneath a row of white choir robes. Everything about her was neat, from her perfectly centred parting to the little velvet bows on her peach-pink cardigan. She gasped when she saw Monty and Panda, then stood so fast, her handbag fell off her lap and landed on the stone floor.

'Oh, how clumsy of me.' She picked up her bag.

'Ah, Karen, I didn't realise anyone was here. This is…' Mabey turned to face Rose. 'I'm sorry, I forgot to ask your name.'

'Rose Sidebottom. And they are Monty and Panda. They're friendly.'

Karen gave Rose a little wave. 'Hello.' There was an awkward silence. 'Right, I'll leave you to it.' She then scurried out of the vestry.

'Mezzo-soprano,' said Mabey, by way of explanation. 'Beautiful voice. Please sit.'

They sat side-by-side on the bench. Monty lay down on the floor but Panda stayed standing and faced the door. 'Are you new to the parish?' he asked, no doubt hoping to recruit her to his Sunday service.

'Not really. I'd like to talk to you about the fire that killed two of your parishioners five years ago.'

All the colour drained from his face.

'Terrible business.' He shook his head. 'Are you a detective?'

'Yes. I run The Nosy Detectives with my dog, Monty.'

If Mabey thought it strange that she had a dog as a business partner, his expression didn't give him away.

'So you're a…what do they call it…a PI?' He appeared pleased with himself for remembering the acronym.

'I am. I've been asked to look into the unsolved murders of Marie and Tony Toyne.'

'But why now?'

'Because Finn, their son, has come out of his coma and can speak.'

Mabey stared at Rose, speechless, as if she had just told him that the Titanic never sank. A bead of sweat had formed in the cleft of his upper lip and he used the back of his hand to wipe it away.

'Is something wrong, vicar?'

'No, not at all. That poor boy. He's been through hell.'

'Yes he has, and from your reaction, would I be right to guess that you think Finn is innocent?'

'I don't know, I mean, I'm not a detective. But I like to see the good in everyone.'

'Tell me what you recall about the night of the fire.'

'It's so long ago, I don't think I can.' He stood. The bench wobbled. He wanted this discussion over. But Rose had just got started.

'Please, tell me what you can remember about the party. You were there all evening, I believe?' She pulled out of her pocket a small notebook and pen.

Mabey sat heavily. 'Yes. Lorraine and Marie were great friends, you know.' He sighed, remembering. 'They had decorated the farmhouse in birthday banners and balloons. Marie made an amazing cake, shaped like a dog, just like the pup they bought Finn as a present.' He frowned at Panda. 'Hold on a sec. Is that…?'

'Yes this is Finn's pup, all grown up.'

'I often wondered what happened to the dog. Finn adored him.' He dragged his gaze away from Panda. 'Anyway, back to the birthday party. Um, let me see. Oh yes, Lorraine baked sausage rolls and pizza. It was such a joyous night. Until the tragedy.'

'Your wife, Lorraine, left early, I understand?'

'Yes, she wanted to stay but she had bell ringing practice. They were rehearsing for a competition, you see. They had a good chance of winning the county finals. Of course, they didn't win. How could they? They were all so devastated about what happened at the farm.'

A light tingle in Rose's feet and hands – a sign that the vicar wasn't being totally truthful – took her by surprise. Rose dug deeper. 'Was everyone devastated at their deaths?'

Mabey's eyes widened. 'How can you ask that? How could anyone *not* be devastated?'

A nice deflection, Rose thought, but also a fair point.

'Did Marie fall out with anyone that night?'

'What do you mean? I can't believe you think someone bore Marie a grudge.'

'Would you mind answering the question please?'

'As far as I can recall, no she did not.' A sharp zing of pain shot up Rose's arms and legs. She had to open and close her palms and wriggle her toes to get rid of the sensation. Mabey was lying.

'I hear there was an argument that night. You must have heard it.' Rose was winging it, but she was now pretty sure that Marie had fallen out with someone. Was this why she and Tony were murdered?

'I don't know what you're talking about,' he said sharply. 'You might be better off talking to the other party guests.'

Monty stood up and barked twice at the vicar. Did he mean that no, the vicar *did* know about an argument? Rose stroked his head.

The vicar leaned away from the dog.

'And what about Tony? Did he have any enemies?' Rose asked.

'He was a lovely man. The only person he might have fallen out with is that woman from Bassinger Homes. She and her lawyer were brutal. They harangued poor Tony. They wanted his land, no matter what.'

'Did Sasha Bassinger join the birthday party?'

He laughed. 'No. If she had tried, Tony would have shown her the door.'

'What time did you leave?'

He looked down. 'Don't know. It was so long ago. Perhaps nine o'clock.'

Sharp pins and needles flared in her legs and arms. Ouch! Rose jotted the time down in her notebook, knowing that Phyllis had said that he left the party at eight.

'And when did you reach home?'

'Soon after that. It's only a five-minute drive.' More stinging in her limbs. What was Mabey hiding?

'What time did your wife get home?'

'Shortly after me.' The stinging subsided. At least that was true.

Mabey's face was sweaty. 'What is it you're not telling me, vicar?'

He shook his head. 'I don't know what you mean.'

There was an ear-splitting scream, then a crash.

Monty was the first to react. He charged into the main part of the church, closely followed by Rose and Panda, then the vicar. In the aisle was a shattered porcelain vase. Water spread out from beneath red and white flowers, ferns and holly.

Rose recognised the woman who was screaming. It was the peacock lady, although she no longer wore the hat or her coat. Instead, she had an apron tied around her waist, presumably to keep the messy business of flower-arranging off her clean blouse. She was standing on a pew and pointing at the ledge of a stone pillar. Standing on that ledge, were two rats, one grey, one brown. Monty peered up at them and let rip with an almighty bark.

'Rats!' screeched the terrified lady.

One of the rats looked remarkably like Hoover: a grey well-fed rat with a stunted tail.

'Oh no,' Rose mumbled.

16 MONTY

I watch Betty and her new buddy squeeze through a hole in the flint and grit church wall, although Betty struggles to wriggle her large tummy through the tight space.

While the peacock lady shrieks and the vicar vacillates about what to do, and Rose does her best to calm them, I bolt from the church, turn down the side pathway and careen to a halt where the hole in the wall leads. It's too high up for them to jump to the ground so they jump onto a branch of a yew tree that's covered in red berries. Betty's unique scent of burned rubber, engine oil and pizza makes it easy for me to follow her path. A lower branch shakes and the brown rat, followed by a panting Betty, jumps to the ground.

'Dog!' the brown rat shrieks, spying me. 'Run for it!'

The brown rat scoots across the paved path and heads for a gravestone.

'Sid!' Betty shouts. 'He's my mate.' She gasps for breath. 'Blimey! Can't run as fast as I used to.'

'They're coming,' I warn her. 'Hide!' I fear that either Mabey or peacock lady will try to stamp on her.

'I'm knackered,' she wheezes. 'Can't run anymore.'

'Then climb on my back.'

'Thanks, mate!'

Betty climbs up my leg and grips my collar. Mabey dashes out of the church porch, his white cassock flying behind him. The soles of his shoes slide on the frosty pavers. He steadies himself and then spots me.

'There's the dog!' yells Mabey, waving a broom in the air. 'He's found the rats!'

Betty yells as me to get moving. I set off in the direction that Sid took, dodging gravestones.

'Monty!' Rose calls. 'Stop!'

This is what hoomans call a moral dilemma. I have to choose between obeying my owner or saving my friend. I want to do both.

Obeying my master, or in this case mistress, is one of our Ten Dog Commandments. As young pups, our mothers teach us these commandments and make us promise to abide by them. Those that don't are ostracised from their kind. They are ignored at the dog park. Their wee-mails are unread. If they join a howl-a-thon, other dogs ignore their cry. It's a terrible punishment and one I never wish to endure. I love my hooman dearly and am proud to be in her pack, but dogs also need to feel part of the greater dog universe too. The Ten Dog Commandments tell us to:

1. Love your owner.
2. Obey your owner, who is pack leader.
3. Defend your owner.
4. Never embarrass your owner.
5. Never appear smarter than your owner.
6. Never show you understand hooman language.
7. Never be seen using hooman technology.
8. Cooperate with other creatures for peaceful purposes.
9. You may abandon your owner if ordered to kill another animal for entertainment or profit, or a hooman, unless your hooman's life is at risk.
10. If in doubt, play dumb and wag your tail.

If I keep running I will break commandments two and four. That's very bad. On a positive note, I am obeying commandment eight as I attempt to save Betty from a battering with a broom. As my mind grapples with this dilemma, my rhythm is broken, and I stumble. Betty squeaks with fright and almost slides off my shoulders but she clings to my collar.

'Over there!' screams peacock lady, waddling around the corner as fast as her swollen ankles allow her. 'Kill them!'

My decision is made. I speed up. Once Betty is safe, I will return to Rose and try to be the best dog I can be to make up for my disobedience.

'Pssst! Over 'ere,' squeaks Sid. He's in front of a hole in the trunk of an old oak. I swerve past a stone angel and stop just in time. Betty scampers down my leg and both rats dive through the hole in the tree.

'Betty, I'll collect you later,' I bark. 'I'll throw them off the scent.'

I charge for the churchyard entrance, zig-zagging through gravestones like a skier doing the slalom.

'Monty! Stop! Not the road!' Rose cries.

I am not going on the road. I'm heading for the wheelie bin around the corner, its pungent smell of rotting food easy to trace. I skid to a halt next to the bin and bark at it. Rose is the first to catch up with me. The broom-wielding vicar hasn't left the churchyard yet, and peacock lady has stopped chasing me altogether. She is gasping, mouth wide, like a baby bird begging their mother for food.

Rose clips on my lead, then whispers in my ear. 'Was that Hoover?'

I sit and give her one clear bark. Yes. I wish I could find a way to tell Rose that Betty's name is Betty and not Hoover.

'Is she in there?' Rose looks at the red, plastic lid of the big bin.

Two barks from me.

'That's a no, then. Good, I don't like killing animals.' She glances behind her, then at me again. 'You understand me. I know you do. But it's impossible. A dog doesn't understand human language.'

I'm silent because I don't know how to respond. I yearn to answer with a yes, I do understand her. But, as commandment ten says, if in doubt, play dumb.

Mabey bursts on the scene, throws open the bin lid and waves the broom at the tied, plastic rubbish bags inside as if he's wielding a sword at his enemy. I bark at the bin.

Mabey uses the stick end of the broom to poke at some of the rubbish bags. I sit and watch, happy in the knowledge that Betty is far away. Finally, peacock lady waddles over. 'That won't do,' she directs Mabey, 'you'll have to take all the rubbish out. If you don't find them, the whole village will be infested with filthy vermin.'

'I'm sorry, Frances, I don't have time to rummage in bins searching for rats.' He looks at his watch. 'I have Sunday School is ten minutes.'

'But Lorraine runs Sunday School.'

'I know that, Frances, but my wife needs my help today.'

Is Rose's lie detector telling her that Mabey is lying? He smells slightly of vinegar and that's a sign he's panicking.

'Of course, vicar,' peacock lady says. 'I'll find a pest exterminator on Monday. Just you leave it with me.'

'Excuse me,' says Rose, stepping closer to the lady, 'Are you by any chance Frances Buttermere?'

'I am, and who might you be?' Buttermere replies, lifting her chin and giving Rose a haughty look.

Mabey bids Rose goodbye and rushes away. I suspect he's relieved to have escaped the clutches of the peacock.

'I'm Rose Sidebottom. I was a detective with Geldeford Police and now I'm a PI. I'd really appreciate your time to answer some questions relating to the fire five years ago at–'

Buttermere interrupts, 'Toyne Fruits Farm, yes, how could I forget? Dreadful. To think I was there only a few hours before the fire started!'

'Which is why I'd like to talk to you. Have you got time now?'

Buttermere puffs out her chest. 'I'd be delighted. Always happy to help our wonderful police officers, and, of course, our private investigators. Let me clear up the broken vase, then we'll chat over a nice cup of tea. Oh and I have some Bakewell Tarts I made yesterday. You'll have to try one. They've won prizes at the village fete, you know.' She loops her arm through Rose's and steers her along the pavement and into the churchyard. I trot along next to Rose. 'Thank the Lord we bumped into each other. I know everyone in this village, and there are a few dark horses I can tell you.' She winks at Rose. Then her face darkens when she notices me close at heel. 'I'm very sorry but the dogs can't come inside. You understand, I'm sure.'

I don't know what Rose understands, but I am certain that I don't understand at all. It's my duty to be with Rose at all times, especially when she's about to enter a stranger's home. The last time I was stopped from joining Rose on a case, she almost died. I won't ever let that happen again.

Rose pulls her arm away from Buttermere. 'In that case, Monty and

Panda can wait outside your house, but I won't tie him up. I've made that mistake before, and I was almost murdered because of it.'

Exactly!

Buttermere gawps. 'Oh my! You poor dear! How terrible. Well, as long as your dog doesn't trample my plants, I suppose that's all right.'

Relieved, I wait on the church porch until Buttermere and Rose exit. Buttermere's voice has reverberated off the church's solid surfaces and made it easy for me to eavesdrop. The woman hasn't stopped talking the whole time she used the dustpan and brush to clear up the broken vase. We then head for Buttermere's thatched cottage, two doors down from the rectory. Rose tells me to sit outside Buttermere's front door and to stay there.

I obey, although when the wooden front door with cast iron hinges shuts on me, I begin to panic. If Rose is in trouble, how will I get inside to help her? I hear their voices coming from the back of the house and the clank of cups and plates and the bubble of the kettle boiling. I just need to take a quick look and once I know Rose is okay, I'll return to the exact spot where Rose left me.

I duck down a side passage and creep along the back of the cottage, where wrought iron chairs and a table are covered in dead leaves. Rose is seated near the lounge room's French doors, which allow me to see her clearly. How that woman can talk! For every question Rose asks, Buttermere replies with an epic story about each of the party guests on the night of the fire.

'Did anyone have reason to kill Tony and Marie Toyne?' Rose asks when Buttermere stops her chatter to take a bite out of a Bakewell Tart.

Buttermere chews. I hear her teeth grinding. 'I'm sure you've already thought of Sasha Bassinger. She had everything to gain from their deaths.' A plate clanks on a hard surface. 'But she's a little too obvious, don't you think?'

'Who do you think killed them, Mrs Buttermere?'

'Ms Buttermere. I never married. Well, there is another person who stood to gain financially from their death.' She goes silent. I think this is termed "milking it".

'Who do you mean?' Rose asks.

'Mervyn Mumford,' Buttermere said, dabbing each side of her mouth with a cotton serviette.

'The farmer?'

'Not just any farmer. He owned the adjoining farm. Bassinger Homes wanted to buy his farm *and* Toyne Fruits. One wasn't much use without the other, because Tony and Marie's farm was like the inside of a horseshoe and Mervyn's was the U that wrapped around it. The farms around here are peculiar shapes. I'm told it's got to do with warring factions stealing land in King Henry VIII's time. Anyway, Sasha didn't want to have to build her gated community with the Toyne's farm in the middle. It was a blight on her plan.'

'Are you saying that Mervyn killed Tony and Marie?'

'It's possible, don't you think?'

Does this mean we now have three suspects? Sasha Bassinger, the Rev Mabey, and Mervyn Mumford? Oh boy, we have our work cut out for us. I wish Betty were here. She's really good at homing in on the important details. I'm already confused.

Betty! I had forgotten about her. Was she still in the tree trunk with Sid? How will she get back to Duckdown Cottage if she can't get into Rose's car?

From where I am seated, I can see the churchyard and the very tree where I last saw Betty. Rose continues to ask Buttermere questions and Buttermere seems overjoyed about casting aspersions on her "friends" and neighbours.

I head for Buttermere's front door, where Panda waits patiently. I tell her I must find Betty and I'll be back soon. Panda sits up.

'Don't leave me alone. I'm coming with you.'

If I hurry, Rose won't even know that I left my post. We run into the churchyard, dodge the gravestones and stop at the oak tree. From inside the tree trunk I hear Betty squeaking in a giggly way.

'Oh Sid, you are a naughty boy!' coos Betty

'Betty! It's Monty,' I bark. 'We have to get you in the car.'

'Tell 'im to wait,' Sid says.

'Can't do that,' Betty says, 'we look out for each other.'

Betty pokes her nose out of the hole. 'Where's our Rose?'

'Talking to someone. Come with me to Rose's car. When she opens the door to let me in, you can hop in too.'

'Look, Monty, you're my best mate but I only just met Sid, you see, and we're getting on very well, if you get my drift.' She winks.

I'm not sure I do see. 'Can't you see Sid another day? Rose has another major suspect. That makes three, too many for me to cope with. I need you to help me draw up a plan.'

'Oooh, I love making plans. Hold on, I'll just say goodbye to Sid.'

I look down the street to Buttermere's cottage. The front door opens and Rose steps outside. Yikes!

'Betty, we have to go now. Rose is leaving.'

'Okay, coming. See you again, Sid.'

Betty leaves the hole in the tree with her fur dishevelled. She scurries up onto my back and then I run to where Rose has parked the car in the street. Across the road is Buttermere's cottage.

'Where did Monty go?' I hear Rose ask.

I bark. She sees me. 'There you are!'

Rose says goodbye to Buttermere, then jogs over the road and opens the rear car door. Panda and I hop in and so does Betty, still clinging to my collar. Rose steps back when she notices Betty on my shoulders.

'So it was you in the church!' Rose says, chuckling. 'I know I'm wicked for saying this, but it was very funny when you scared Mrs Buttermere.'

17 ROSE

Rose was five minutes' drive from the office. It was a Sunday but what else did Rose have to do? Rake the leaves? Go supermarket shopping? Mop the kitchen floor? Anyway, Rose would rather solve the case. Ollie had offered to help out for a few hours and in return she promised to buy him Sunday roast lunch. She admired the teenager's dedication – most boys his age would be chilling at home, playing football, seeing mates or doing a paid job.

Her thoughts turned to Malcolm and she wondered what he was doing today. Maybe he was spending the day with family or friends? She often saw him walking his dog, B, on the common. He was always alone. The vet hospital was closed on Sunday so he might be free to join them for a bite to eat. But what if Malcolm took her suggestion the wrong way? Their friendship was really good, and she didn't want to blow it.

Her phone rang.

'Rose, get over 'ere quick,' said Ollie. 'Coppers turned up. They're taking your boxes. I tried to stop 'em.' In the background, Rose heard a male voice barking orders.

He had to mean the photocopies Kay had made of the original case files. There was nothing in those boxes that the detectives didn't already have – except one item. She hadn't yet had the chance to go through Kay's personal notebook. Rose couldn't allow others to read it. A lump formed in her throat which no amount of swallowing could shift.

'Who are they?' Rose asked.

'One's called Pearl. Don't know about the other.'

Rose felt like a ghostly hand had run its fingers up her back. She shuddered. 'I'm almost there. Don't get in their way Ollie. I'll deal with it.'

She wanted to sound in control, but she felt the opposite. Pearl had a way of undermining her self-belief. He would probably made a big deal out of the fact she had copies of the case files, which, to be fair, was unusual, but Kay had been the lead detective on the case and it had been her choice to bring them home.

Monty popped his head between the front seats and nuzzled her neck.

'It'll be all right,' she said, speeding up.

Soon, Rose turned into the vet hospital's front car park then slowed before taking the blind corner that led to the rear carpark and her office. As she did, an unmarked grey Vauxhall Insignia almost collided head-on with her car. The wheels screeched as the unmarked police car halted. Pearl glowered at her from the passenger seat. To her relief, DS Varma was driving. Varma was known as "the gentleman detective". He was polite and courteous, even to the vilest suspects. And he had always been kind to Rose, especially in her early days at the Murder Squad. Pearl, however, was the first to get out. Rose was still fiddling with her seat belt when Pearl tapped on her car window. Rose wound down the window.

'Been holding out on us, Sidebottom?' said Pearl.

'I'd like to get out of the car.' Rose tried to open the door, but Pearl stood in the way.

By now Varma had joined Pearl. 'Sir, why don't we talk in Rose's office? No need to make a public scene.'

Pearl stepped back and made a mock bow. 'Be my guest.'

Rose got out. *Don't back down*, she told herself. *Kay would want me to have her notebook*. But she nervously shuffled from one foot to the other.

'I hear you've removed items from my office. Do you have a warrant?' Rose asked.

'Why do we need one? You're a former detective. Why would you object to helping us with our enquiries?' Pearl said.

'Dave, I'm more than happy to collaborate, but you can't just take things from my office without my permission.'

'We've reason to believe that you have taken evidence. In particular, DI Lloyd's notebook.'

'That's rubbish and you know it,' Rose said, her cheeks red with fury. 'Anything I have relating to the Toyne murders are photocopies made by DI Lloyd when she was working the case. I did not make the copies or tamper with original evidence. Why don't you check the signature list at the evidence storage facility?' Cold case documents were stored there and required an officer's signature to remove them. 'The only item not in the cold case evidence boxes is Kay's personal notebook, and it's *personal*. I want that back *and* I want all the photocopies too!'

Rose had done well to sound strong, at least until the last sentence when she had become shrill, which always happened when she was agitated. Monty, who had been watching the proceedings, barked, his eyes fixed on Pearl.

'No can do,' said Pearl. 'We had a tip-off that you were withholding evidence.'

Rose caught Varma grimacing but the pins and needles in her hands and feet already warned her that Pearl was lying. By now Panda had joined in the barking, their heads poking out of the side window.

'How do you know about the notebook?' Rose asked.

'Anonymous tip-off, as I said.'

More pins and needles. It was so uncomfortable that she had to flex her fingers.

'Rose,' Varma said, clearly hoping to calm the situation his superior had created, 'would you mind if we looked through Kay's notebook? We'd be most grateful.'

Pearl gave Varma a filthy look.

'If you had simply asked me, I would have gladly said yes. But you took my files and the notebook without my permission, so the answer is no, you cannot. Now give me back my boxes. I'm not going to move my car out of the way until you do.'

Pearl stared at their two vehicles, nose to nose, and there was no way Pearl could drive around Rose's Jazz.

'You help us, we help you,' said Pearl. 'Come on Sidebottom, we were colleagues not so long ago.'

And you made my life a misery, Rose thought. She pulled her phone from her pocket and dialled her lawyer, Sylvia Blight. She made sure Pearl could see who she was calling.

'All right, you can have the boxes back,' Pearl said. 'But if you want our help one day, don't waste your time asking, because we won't be listening.'

Pearl went for a smoke while Varma carried the boxes back into her office.

'Sorry about that, Rose. Look, if you learn something useful to the investigation, call me. Whatever the DI says, I'm happy to cooperate where I can. And you know that if you're ever in trouble, you can call me, any time.'

She thanked Varma and watched them drive away.

Ten minutes later, Rose was sipping a cup of sweet tea and Kay's notebook was on her desk. Adrenaline was racing through her veins even now, and her hand trembled as she lifted the mug to her lips. Monty had taken up a guard dog stance at the door and Panda lay on the dog bed, her eyes nervously watching Ollie and Rose.

'You were amazing!' Ollie said. 'That Pearl bloke is a right dickhead. Can't believe you got them to give everything back.'

'Neither can I,' Rose replied. 'I think knowing Kay would want me to keep her notebook gave me the courage to stand up to him.'

Rose sipped her tea. She didn't usually have sugar, but she needed that burst of energy because she was feeling suddenly drained. Ollie sat on his wheelie chair next to her.

'Before those nobs turned up, I was busy,' he said. 'I scanned in the party and crime scene photos. They were a bit washed out, so I've enhanced the colours and the contrast. Want to see?'

Rose shifted out of the way and Ollie sat in front of her laptop. He opened the photos file.

'I started with the party pics. They're time-stamped. See?' He pointed at the rows and rows of images.

Rose nodded. Ollie scrolled down, then enlarged one photo, date stamped 8.02pm. It was a photo of the party guests and family: Finn held his puppy in his arms, next to a birthday cake with lit candles.

Beside him were his mum and dad, and then three boys and two girls of similar age to Finn. In the back row were three adults. Rose pointed at the screen.

'There's the Reverend Mabey. And I recognise Frances Buttermere: she does like to dress up for an occasion.' Buttermere was wearing a navy blue, silky dress, a long string of pearls and a matching blue hat with a feather in it. 'And that must be Mervyn Mumford.' Mumford had a weathered face and a sour expression: his lips were a tight slit. Everyone else was smiling, so why was he so grumpy? 'And the boys must be Alfie Mumford, Jimmy Fox and Sam Chang.'

'Yup. That one is Alfie,' Ollie said, pointing. The tallest of the boys had fair hair and a confident air about him. It was hard for Rose to believe that when that photo was taken, Alfie was ten years old, because he looked more like fifteen. Ollie pointed to the next boy. 'That's Jimmy.' His hair was cut short and he had a stocky build and deep-set eyes. 'Sam is the shy one. Never said much. Used to follow Finn about like a puppy dog,' Ollie said, then looked at Monty. 'No offence, Monty.'

From his position facing the entrance, Monty wagged his tail but he didn't take his eyes off the door, clearly determined to ward off Pearl should he return.

'How well do you know the three boys?' Rose asked. 'Did you go to the same school?'

'Yeah. They were younger than me, but I remember them. They were a close-knit gang of four and Finn was the leader. Back then he was the most popular kid in school. Might have something to do with his really cool electric guitar. He could really play it, too. We all said he'd form a band and tour the world.'

Rose raised her brows. 'The Finn I know isn't like that. He's withdrawn and definitely not popular.'

'The murder of his mum and dad changed him.'

'Did you keep in touch with any of them?'

'Not really. I wasn't in their hemisphere. They were clever and I…I hated school.'

'What else do you know about them?'

'I remember when Finn came back to school after the funeral. He didn't speak. I mean nothing. It freaked everyone out. They said it was because he was guilty. Jimmy and Sam got sick of the jibes. They kept their distance. The only one who stayed loyal was Alfie. He stuck by Finn until Finn eventually pushed him away.'

'Interesting.'

'I haven't shown you the best bit,' Ollie said. 'Take a look at this.'

On screen was an amateur video clip of the same group of revellers crowded around Finn on his birthday. The time stamp placed the recording at seven minutes past eight. Finn was blowing out the candles on his cake and everyone sang *Happy Birthday*. Ollie played it, then looked askance at Rose. 'Notice anyone missing?'

'Yes,' Rose said, 'the vicar.'

'Yeah and I checked his police statement. Mabey said he left the party around nine. I reckon he left between 8.02pm and 8.07pm because he was in the photo but not in the video.'

'I guess he could have been in the loo or something.'

'Yeah but I flicked through all the photos after that time and the vicar isn't in any of them.'

Rose gave Ollie a huge smile. 'Great work, Ollie! I think our vicar has some explaining to do.'

Monty walked over and gave Ollie's hand a congratulatory lick.

18 MONTY

There's a knock on our office door. I know it isn't Pearl because the knock is hesitant and then from beneath the door I detect Malcolm's and Lady B's scents. I wag my tail happily and Rose opens the door. B, his Cavalier pup, follows Malcolm into the room and as soon as she spots Panda she races over to have a good sniff.

'Not disturbing you, I hope?' he asks.

'Not at all,' Rose says.

'All right, mate?' Ollie says, pausing in his reading of the case files. He's seated cross-legged on a cushion on the floor, his back to the wall. Resting against his knee is Betty and every now and again, Ollie scratches her tummy, which she loves. On the floor is his spiral-bound notebook. Rose gave Ollie the notebook and pen and told him that if he wanted to be a PI, he must have them with him at all times.

Rose has been reading Kay's notebook. She leaves it open on her desk and goes to B who does little circles and yips happily as Rose strokes her.

'I'm glad you dropped by,' Rose says. 'We're going to the pub for lunch later. Want to join us?'

Oooh! Love pubs. So many delicious smells. So many food bits dropped to the floor.

'Yes, um, that would be very nice. I'd like that. I just need to make a quick phone call.'

Malcolm backs out of the office.

'If you're busy, that's okay.'

'No, I mean yes, I mean, I just need to call someone,' Malcolm says. 'It's nothing. I can ask Fred to do it.'

'You're working? Why didn't you say? Another time,' Rose says.

I stare at Malcolm, who is perspiring heavily. It's clear, even to me, that he wants to come to lunch but for some reason he's doing a great job of putting obstacles in the way. Sometimes hoomans make their lives so complicated. I don't understand it.

'Oh, I didn't mean to…right, yes, another time, of course.'

Rose's eyes and mouth have drooped. I think she is disappointed.

I *hurrumph*.

'I wanted to update you on Panda,' Malcolm says. 'I've put out feelers.' Panda and B stop their game of chase and watch Malcolm. 'Dogs that have been abused can be aggressive because they're afraid. This means that finding her a new home is tricky. It takes a very special person who is prepared to take on a nervous dog like her and gain her trust.'

'She hasn't shown any aggression to me,' Rose says.

'Well, you're one of those special people. Panda senses you are relaxed with her and she knows you love dogs.'

'I wish I could adopt Panda but it's a tricky time for me. And I already have two dogs and a rat to take care of.'

'How is Hoover doing?' Malcolm asks.

He knows that Betty is part of Rose's family. He also knows Betty is a genius with a rat-cam. Betty squeaks and Malcolm spies her, reclining against Ollie's knee.

Ollie says. 'She's very chilled out today.'

I wonder if that has something to do with Sid, the rat she seems fond of.

'Hello, Hoover,' Malcolm says.

In a trice, Betty is on all fours and hissing at Malcolm.

'Woah, there! Did I say something wrong?' he says.

Betty hates being called Hoover. The trouble is that none of the hoomans in the room know her real name. This situation needs resolving. But how? Then I have an idea. For it to work, I need access to the vet hospital. I take hold of the end of Malcolm's oil-skin coat and tug at it.

'What does he want?' Malcolm asks.

'Let's see,' Rose says. 'Let's follow him.'

Perfect! I release the edge of his coat, walk out of the door, cross the car park and stand outside the hospital's back entrance. The door is ajar. Malcolm and B live above the vet surgery and use the back exit to come and go.

'I think he wants to go inside,' Rose says.

'Is this about food?'

'Could be. But I think it's more than that,' Rose says.

While they are talking, I take the opportunity to relieve myself and leave a message for the dogs coming and going to the vet hospital:

Live in Nether Wallop? Watch the vicar. He has a secret and I need to know what it is. Monty, Duckdown Cottage.

Malcolm pushes open the back door and I rush down the corridor, and past the communal kitchen and the consulting rooms. Before me is the reception desk. Before anyone can stop me, I charge around the desk to the drawer where the nurses and vets keep their name tags. Everyone here goes by their first name.

The handle is a circular knob. I clamp my teeth down on the knob and pull. It opens easily.

'Did you see that? He opened the drawer!' Malcolm says.

All the name badges are neatly laid out in alphabetical order. And before you ask: I know the hooman alphabet. Only one person in the vet hospital has a name starting with B and her name is Betty.

I plunge my snout in the drawer and wrap my tongue around the name badge beginning with B.

'Monty! Stop that,' says Rose, clutching my collar.

I have Betty's name badge in my mouth. By now my ratty friend has joined us. I drop the name badge in a large globule of saliva onto Betty's back.

'Thanks a bunch, Mr Monty,' Betty complains. 'That's all I bleedin' well need.'

'It's your name, Betty. On a badge,' I say.

Betty stares at the badge. 'I can't read. What good is it to me?'

'Show it to Rose. Show her that's your name!'

Betty picks up the badge and drops it at Rose's feet.

Rose picks it up, then wipes it with a tissue. 'Betty.'

Betty then points her claw at her chest and squeaks, 'I'm Betty.'

'I don't get it,' Ollie says. 'What's Hoover doing?'

Betty arches her back and hisses.

'I think I get it,' Rose says. She gives the name badge to the rat. 'Is your name Betty?'

Betty does a little jig, dancing on her hind legs.

I give a single bark. Yes!

'Blimey,' says Ollie, 'we've been calling her the wrong name all this time. Hello Betty!'

Betty does a pirouette. She sways and falls over. 'The world is spinning,' she says. 'Thank goodness Ollie finally cottoned on. I can't keep twirling like that.'

'I hate to ask the obvious, but how does a dog know which name badge spells Betty?' Ollie asks.

All eyes are on me. I give them my innocent-eyes look. Rule ten of the Dog Commandments – if in doubt, play dumb.

'I have no idea,' Rose says.

'Oh, I forgot the reason I came by,' Malcolm says. 'There is someone who might take Panda, but he's a little unusual. I wanted to know what you think.'

'Who were you thinking of?'

'Ed Penrose. He lives in a caravan on Winterfold Heath.'

'I know Ed. He does handyman work. Old guy.'

'That's him.'

'I thought he didn't like dogs.'

'So did I but he's taken on this stray Staffie called Jake and they're inseparable now. The guy hasn't got a penny to rub together, but what he lacks financially he makes up for in kindness and compassion.'

I know Jake, the three-legged Staffie. I know Ed. I go to Malcolm and bark a single yes – that's a great idea!

19 ROSE

After lunch, Rose dropped her dogs home. She loved their company, but it would be easier to interview suspects without having to worry about them. Ollie waited patiently in the car while she took Monty and Panda into the back garden and then they drove to Mervyn Mumford's bungalow in Little Wallop. However, when Rose knocked, there was no answer.

'We could snoop around the back,' Ollie suggested.

Ollie had begged to come. He wanted to learn how to be a private investigator and he couldn't do it, he said, from the office. He had a point, but Rose made him promise to let her do the talking.

'I may know where he is,' Rose said. 'He's a tennis player and quite a good one, I hear.'

Rose googled him and found a local news article about Mervyn and his tennis partner winning a mixed doubles competition at a tournament last summer. He was a member of Geldeford's prestigious Aces Tennis Club.

She started the car. 'Good thing we left the menagerie at home. I can't imagine such a posh tennis club welcoming dogs and rats.'

'Me neither.' Ollie snickered, indicating his low-slung, baggy jeans and black hoodie. 'Not sure if they'll welcome me, come to think of it.'

'Let's see how we go.'

The Aces Tennis Club was on the outskirts of Geldeford, backed by rolling green hills. The ivy-clad Tudor club house was impressive. So many parking spots were allocated to committee members, such as the club captain and treasurer, that the car park was well-nigh full. Rose eventually found a spot near the groundskeepers' shed. On entering the club house, she went up to a counter where a smart woman with her hair in a French twist was asking another woman to complete a membership form. While the new member scribbled away, Rose asked the receptionist where she might find Mervyn Mumford.

'Visitors are most welcome, but we have a dress code here. No trainers.' She stared down at Ollie's trainers.

'I'm investigating a murder. I'm Rose Sidebottom and Ollie is my trainee. I apologise for his footwear, but I promise you we won't be long.'

'Oh it's you! I thought I knew your face. You solved that missing girl case not so long ago.'

'That's right,' Rose said. 'Could you tell me if Mervyn is here?'

'I can, but your trainee can't enter the bar. I'm sorry. He's welcome to wait here.'

'That's stupid,' Ollie began.

'That's quite all right. Ollie, why don't you wait here? I will be quick.'

Ollie sat in a leather chair and folded his arms across his chest.

'Mr Mumford's in the bar,' the receptionist said. 'Go ahead.'

Comfortable armchairs surrounded circular glass-topped coffee tables and, at the elegant, polished walnut bar, the manager was busy serving club members their drinks. Beyond the bar was a dining area where people were eating lunch. The smell of roast beef made Rose's empty stomach gurgle. Rose recognised Mumford from the photo of him at Finn's party, taken five years ago. Same weathered face, a little greyer and definitely smarter in his tennis whites. He was seated on a bar stool, laughing at something the bar manager had said.

Conscious that she looked scruffy in her puffy coat, she removed it, tucked it over one arm, and approached Mumford.

'Excuse me,' Rose began, 'Mervyn Mumford?'

He put his pint glass down on the countertop. 'That's me,' he said cheerily.

She took the vacant bar stool next to him, although it wasn't easy, given that it was tall and she was short. 'Rose Sidebottom. Can I get you another?' She nodded at his half-drunk pint.

'Thank you very much,' he said. 'Guinness.'

Rose ordered a Guinness, and a lime and soda for herself.

Mumford continued, 'I haven't seen you here before. New to the club?'

'I'm not a member, but it looks like a lovely place to play tennis.'

'It is. I'm retired. Spend most of my time here. It's a very sociable place.'

Rose vacillated between telling, or not telling, Mumford the real reason why she was there. 'Have you been a member long?'

'Almost five years. My wife died some time ago and my son has his own life. When I sold my farm, I needed a way to connect with people. You know, make new friends.'

The barman served the drinks and Rose paid for them.

'Thank you, kindly.' Mumford sipped the fresh pint. He licked the white froth from his lips.

Rose drank her lime and soda.

'You look way too young to retire,' Rose said. 'What made you decide to sell your farm?'

He leaned closer so their shoulders almost touched. 'Had an offer I couldn't refuse.' Then he sat straight again. 'What about you, Rose? Thinking of joining the club?'

'I couldn't afford the fees, I'm afraid, although I was quite good at tennis at school.'

'You could always play here as my guest. Or my son's guest. He's more your age. His name's Alfie.'

Mumford was such a friendly fellow that Rose felt guilty about misleading him. 'I'd like to come clean. I'm here because I wanted to talk to you about the deaths of Tony and Marie Toyne.'

'Are you a journalist? I don't think the club likes journalists prowling the corridors, but I don't mind chatting, providing it's off the record. You look like an honest person.'

Oh boy! By being so nice, Mumford was making it very hard for her to ask questions.

'I'm a private investigator. Are you aware the police have reopened the case?'

'No. Glad they have, though. I think it's a crying shame they never caught the killer.'

'Can I ask you about Finn's tenth birthday party? You and your son were there?'

'Yes.' Mumford smiled. 'Such a happy occasion. It breaks my heart every time I think about what happened that night.'

Rose sipped her drink. She wanted to keep the pace relaxed. 'Tell me about the party.'

'It was wonderful. Finn was ecstatic about his puppy.'

'Did anyone disappear during the course of the evening?'

He gave her a questioning frown. 'I don't know.' Her limbs tingled. For the first time since she'd sat down with him, Mumford was lying. 'Why do you ask?'

'Just wondering. Did any guests clash with Tony or Marie that night?'

'Ah, I see where this is going. Has that wretched woman been gossiping again?'

'What woman?' Rose feigned ignorance.

'I shouldn't speak ill of her. She's a lonely old woman.'

'Who do you mean?'

'Frances, of course. Will that woman ever give up?' He sighed.

'You mean Frances Buttermere?'

He nodded.

'Give up what?'

'Ever since Evelyn died – that's my wife – Frances has set her cap at me. She's been single her whole life. I think she was in love with me once, a long *long* time ago, and when I became a widower, she did all she could to ensnare me. But I was having none of it. Evelyn was the love of my life and I'll never marry again,' he said sadly. Rose experienced no tingling. He was telling the truth about Evelyn and Frances.

'Tell me about the row you had with Tony on the night of the party.'

He raised his eyebrows. 'Did Frances say that? Well, it's not true. We went to Tony's study at one point to talk business. We didn't row.' He shook his head. 'Frances is a bitter woman and she wants to make me pay because I wouldn't marry her.' A surge of pins and needles shot up Rose's legs and arms.

'What did you and Tony talk about in his study?'

Mumford put down his pint glass. 'This is starting to feel like an interrogation. Where are you going with this?'

'If Tony and Marie refused to sell their farm, then the offer from

Bassinger Homes to buy your farm would have been withdrawn, am I right?'

'No, you're wrong. The offer may not have been as good, but Sasha still wanted my land, either way.' Pins and needles seared though her feet and arms. Rose opened and closed her fingers, trying to ease the stinging sensation. She also wriggled her toes. *Ouch!* 'If you must know, I went to Tony's study that night to talk about Finn, not Bassinger Holdings. Finn had always been a nice lad but he'd started acting up at school and he was getting my son into trouble. So I asked Tony to have a word with Finn about it. Now, if you'll excuse me, I've got to pick up my son.' He got off the bar stool. 'Good day to you, Rose, and I hope you find the killer. I can promise you, it isn't me.'

He left the bar. Rose's pins and needles were still there. What did that all mean? Mumford wasn't telling the whole truth, but had Finn really been leading Alfie astray?

When she returned to the clubhouse entrance, Ollie wasn't there. She texted him and a few seconds later he replied with:

Outside the pro's shop.

'Excuse me,' Rose said to the receptionist, 'which way is the pro's shop?'

'Out this door, turn left. You'll see it a bit further up the hill.'

Rose found Ollie sitting on a low wall outside the shop.

'Hey, Ollie, everything all right?'

'Thought I'd do some sniffing around. I bumped into Alfie. We chatted.'

'Interesting.' Rose sat next to him. 'What did he say?'

'I asked him if he knew Finn was conscious. He said he didn't, and he'd drop by the hospital. Then he said something weird.'

'Like what?' Rose asked.

'He said that Jimmy wouldn't be happy about it.'

'Jimmy Fox?'

'Yeah. Then Alfie legged it, like he realised he shouldn't have said it. Said he had to meet his dad or something. I mean why would one of Finn's mates be unhappy he was out of a coma?'

'Good question,' Rose said smiling. 'We'll make a detective of you yet.'

20 MONTY

While I wait for Rose to come home, Betty uses my front paw as a headrest as she tells me for the umpteenth time how wonderful Sid is. I had hoped to catch a nap, but Betty will not stop talking.

'This could be the one, Mr Monty,' Betty says, wriggling her stunted tail. 'What do you think?'

'I only caught a glimpse of him, Betty. What do you know about him?'

She fiddles with one of her whiskers. 'You mean apart from the fact he's devilishly handsome? He's a church rat, so that has to be a good sign, don't you think?'

'Does that automatically mean he's a good rat?'

'Of course it does. Otherwise why else would he live in a church?!'

'Perhaps he likes the bread and wine they keep there, and the food they have at the harvest festival, and the tea and cakes they serve at the mothers and babies meeting, and–'

'So what? If he lived in a house he'd have way more food to pick at, but he chose to be in a church. I see it as a sign of good character.'

I'm not convinced. Betty's been through a series of relationships with selfish rats who abandon her. I just hope Sid isn't one of *those* rats. I try another tack.

'What do you like about him?'

Our roles have swapped: Betty usually offers me motherly advice, but I guess now that Summer is with us, Betty feels a little on the outer.

'He was so brave,' Betty coos. 'Did you see how he rescued me from that broom-wielding vicar?'

'I saw him run away.'

'Did not!'

Now I've offended her. Oh dear. 'Does he have a girlfriend?'

Betty paces up and down the length of my dog bed. 'We haven't discussed that sort of thing. I've only just met him, after all. He wouldn't flirt with me if he was married, now would he?' I'm too young to know the answer to that. Betty continues, 'He's a bit younger than me. I hope that's not a problem.'

'I just don't want you to get hurt,' I say. 'Perhaps you should get to know him better before you give your heart to him.'

'And what would you know, Mr Monty? You've never had a girlfriend,' she says peevishly.

This is true. I am only two years old – which is fourteen in hooman years. 'Fair point.'

'I want to see him again. And Valentine's Day is coming soon.' Betty flops down on her furry butt, looking dejected.

'Why is Valentine's Day important?' I ask. 'It's a hooman celebration, isn't it?'

Betty stares up at the *Dogs' Trust* calendar on the wall. The February dog is a scruffy little fellow with a cheeky grin named Sooty. 'What is the date today?' Betty asks.

I wander closer to the calendar. 'I haven't mastered dates yet. Why do you ask?'

'Valentine's Day, of course. The day when lovers declare their feelings. When is it exactly?'

I *hurrumph*. The question is beyond me. 'Rose knows all about dates. She's always checking to see what day it is, although I get the feeling that she doesn't have time for romance.'

'You're telling me,' Betty says, rolling her eyes. 'That poor vet. He tries so hard but she just can't see what's staring her in the face.'

'You think Malcolm wants Rose to go on a date?'

'Does he ever! He just can't seem to ask her. Now wouldn't it be lovely if they went out together on Valentine's Day?'

'Ah. I think Malcolm's already tried that.'

Betty shrugs her tiny shoulders. 'Well I plan to be on a date with Sid that night.'

'I can get you there,' I say. 'I'll cut across Winterfold Heath.'

'You are such a good friend,' Betty squeaks, 'but somehow I have to work out when Valentine's Day is exactly.'

'We'll find a way.' I glance through the window. The sky is clear. 'I'd like to drop by Ed's caravan and say hi to Jake. We could take Panda with us, then she can make up her own mind if she likes Ed or not.'

We both look at Panda, who lifts her head from the lino. 'I'd like to meet him, but I'm scared of Jake. If he attacks me, I'm dead.'

'Jake won't attack you. He's got a heart of gold. It was his previous hooman who forced him to fight other dogs.' Panda lowers her head to the floor. She doesn't look convinced. 'I'll be with you. And maybe Summer would like to come. Betty too.'

'Okay,' Panda says.

Betty jumps up. 'Let's go!'

Summer wanders in from the garden and I explain our plan. 'I'll come. It'll be nice to walk on the heath.'

We all set off. Betty rides on my shoulders. Panda darts ahead and then runs back, then runs off again, while Summer ambles and sniffs every tree trunk and log. It's a cold day and the shady puddles are iced over. The bracken and heather ripple in the wind but the sun shines. To the east, tall fir trees, straight as pencils, form a dense forest and this is where we are headed.

'What if he doesn't like me?' Panda asks.

'We'll think of a Plan B,' I say.

'Mr Monty always has a Plan B,' Betty says, warm and snug in the fur of my back.

I don't have a Plan B. But Malcolm is searching for people to adopt her and I know that Rose won't let Panda be put to sleep.

'Tell me more about Ed,' Panda says.

'Ed is an old man who does odd jobs for Rose around the house. He used to be Phyllis's neighbour in Nether Wallop, but the bank took Ed's home and he now lives in a caravan. I don't know why the bank took

Ed's home but I can't think of anything much worse than losing your safe place. These days, Ed's only companion is Jake, who I met at the dog pound when I was imprisoned there. Jake once told me that Ed lost his job and his house and then he fell through the cracks, although I'm not sure what cracks. Anyway, Ed must have survived his fall because Rose and I sometimes catch glimpses of him picking wild mushrooms in the forest.'

I stop and sniff the air.

'Can you smell that?' I ask Panda and Summer.

'Wood smoke, sausage fat and coffee,' says Summer.

'Then we're almost there,' I say.

Ed's caravan is well camouflaged by huge ferns that have sprouted around it and also a collapsed tree that lies near the door. Wood mice, a hedgehog, foxes and voles live inside the partly hollow trunk. I give a quick bark to alert Jake of our arrival. There's a creak as a door opens, then a thud. Twigs and bracken snap like pencils beneath Jake's sturdy form.

'Pssst!' Jake's voice is like sandpaper dragged down a rough fence. 'Is that you, Monty?'

I trot over to where Jake's scarred face pokes out of the bracken.

'Yes, my friend. I need your help,' I say.

Jake glances at Betty on my back. "Ello Betty, long time no see.'

'Hello gorgeous,' Betty says, giving Jake a wink.

I continue with the introductions. 'This is my mother, Summer.'

'Honoured, ma'am,' Jake says, lowering his head.

'And this is Panda. I helped her escape from the pound.'

'You went back there?' Jake has a whole body shake. 'That place gives me the 'eeeby-jeeebeys.'

Jake head-butts his way out of the bracken, then grimaces. 'It's me fourth leg, see? It still gives me gyp even though the thing isn't even there. Would you believe it?'

'Sorry to hear that, Jake.'

Jake sniffs the air. Panda senses he is sizing her up. Hoomans size people up visually. We use scent. Intimidated, Panda hides behind my furry butt.

'Shy thing, ain't she,' Jake says.

Just then I hear Ed's croaky voice from inside the caravan. 'Jake! Where are you, boy?'

'Come and meet the boss,' Jake says.

We follow Jake. The caravan's tyres are flat and one of the windows is boarded up. A bent man as gangly as a scarecrow stands in the doorway, wearing an old, olive-green trench coat and army boots. He peers at us through smudged glasses.

'Well, well! We have visitors!' Ed says, grinning to reveal a toothless mouth.

Ed has false teeth that he only uses to eat. He once told me the dentures don't fit him properly and make his gums bleed, so most of the time he leaves them in a jar of water. Ed leaves the van and he pats each one of us. All that is, except Betty, who he hasn't noticed. He smells of rich earth, body odour, and tobacco and when he reaches out to touch me, I notice his missing little finger, which was bitten off by a horse, or so the story goes.

'It's Monty, isn't it?' He strokes my head. Then he notices Betty on my back. 'Would you look at that!' He cranes his neck forward. 'Ain't you a nice plump rat!'

Oh-ow! Betty won't like that.

She gets on all fours and hisses, her back arched.

'Ooh! And feisty,' says Ed, chuckling. 'Don't you worry, little friend, I ain't gonna eat ya.' Then he notices Panda behind us. 'And ain't you a beautiful dog. A mere pup. And look at them amazing eyes.' He then turns his attention to Summer. 'Ah, the matron of the pack. I bet you have your work cut out for you, keeping this rabble under control, hey?'

Summer snuffles his hand and then lies near the wood fire. Ed continues, 'Well ain't this a cause for celebration? I'm guessing you're all hungry? Hmmm?'

I bark once. That's a yes from me. Panda and Summer wag their tails. Betty stops hissing at the mention of food.

Ed chuckles. 'I might just happen to have some sausages that my mate at the butcher's gave me. A bit past the sell-by date but who cares, hey?'

Before we know it, Ed has a heavy frying pan perched over the flames and a pot of black coffee bubbling. In the pan are three fat sausages. This troubles me: one hooman, three dogs and a rat. Will there be enough sausage to go around? Ed uses a fork to drop the sausages onto a plastic plate, then he breaks them into small pieces with his fingers. Steam rises into the frigid air. My mouth waters and I edge closer.

Ed wags a crooked finger at me. 'Just wait a little for it to cool.'

He wraps a piece of white bread around half a sausage and manages to take a bite with his gums.

Two stalactites of my drool plop to the ground.

'Mate!' says Jake. 'You should see someone about that drool problem.' I turn my head, confused. Is he serious? He barks out a husky laugh. 'Got ya!'

Once Ed has eaten his sausage sandwich, he gives each of us, including Betty, a bit of sausage. Betty clambers to the ground to eat hers, muttering something about Ed being a good bloke. Ed sips his coffee and watches us devour the food.

'What are you lot doing here, anyway? Hey?'

I nudge Panda forward and she tentatively lifts her paw onto his bony knee. Ed strokes her head then checks the tag on her collar. 'Peasemarsh Pound. So you're an escapee, hey? Clever girl. Well, Panda, if you need a home, you're welcome here. We're all escapees. Isn't that right, Jake?'

Jake gives a few croaky barks. 'I won't turn away a dog who needs a home.' He hops over to Panda and sits next to her.

It looks like they've bonded. All I need to do now is encourage Malcolm to provide the formal introductions.

21 ROSE

Rose dropped Ollie home then she drove to Phyllis's house. Rose wanted to establish what Mumford and Tony had argued about the night of the fire and broach the subject of Finn's trust fund. Did Phyllis have the right to draw down the capital, as Malcolm had proposed?

Rose found Phyllis's cat watching her though the sitting room window, her thick tail writhing one way and then the other. Rose had only just opened the garden gate when Phyllis appeared in her smart coat, which had a cat brooch on the lapel. On seeing Rose, the grandmother hurried up to her.

'You have news? Good news, I hope,' Phyllis said.

'I have some questions. Have you got a minute?'

'It'll have to be quick. My bus will be here in ten minutes.'

'I can walk with you to the bus stop, if you like?'

'All right, but don't dawdle.'

Phyllis shut her front door and then she and Rose hurried down the road.

'How is Finn?' Rose asked.

The pavement was narrow and Phyllis's huge handbag rhythmically smacked Rose's hip. It felt as if a brick was in there.

'He'd recover much faster if the coppers left him alone.'

'Has Finn told them anything?'

'He's gone silent again, blast their eyes. Hasn't said a dicky bird since they started hurling questions at the poor boy.' Phyllis glanced at Rose. 'Do you have anything new to tell me?'

Rose was disinclined to reveal the substance of her recent conversations with Mabey, Buttermere and Mumford until she could substantiate her suspicions. But she needed to know the answer to certain questions.

'Did Mervyn Mumford have a row with Tony the night of the party?'

'I did catch a glimpse of Tony and Mervyn in the study at one point, but they were whispering, so I didn't hear.'

'But there was tension between Tony and Mumford?'

'Of course there was! That weasel was pressuring my son to sell the farm. I wish I had eavesdropped, but I was distracted by the kids messing about outside.'

'Who was outside?'

'Jimmy, Sam, Alfie and Finn.'

'What were they doing?'

'Just messing around on farm machinery in the barn. They knew they weren't supposed to do that, so I called them back in.'

Rose rubbed her arm. Phyllis was lying.

'Did Finn play with matches or petrol?'

'That's exactly what DCI Leach accused Finn of. And I say to you what I said to him. Finn did not mess about with petrol or matches. Marie had made sure he knew not to touch either.'

Rose's pins and needles subsided.

'What about his friends Jimmy, Sam and Alfie? Did they ever play with fire?'

'They had nothing to do with it. They were ten years old, for goodness' sake.'

More pins and needles.

'Phyllis, please. I need the absolute truth, otherwise I can't find whoever killed Marie and Tony. Had one of the boys lit a fire in the past?'

'How would I know?'

Another lie. They had reached the bus stop. Phyllis clearly didn't want to implicate Finn or his friends.

'I have a question about Finn's trust fund.'

Phyllis's head whipped around, and her eyes narrowed. 'I already told you about it.'

'Are you allowed to touch the capital sum?'

'I can draw out small amounts to cover Finn's expenses. Nothing substantial, you understand.'

Now for the tricky question, Rose thought. 'How much of the fund has been spent?'

'That's none of your business.'

Okay, that didn't go down well, and Rose's next question would go down even worse.

'If Finn is found guilty of murder, he won't be permitted under British Law to benefit from his crimes, which is how the court will see the inheritance, and therefore he won't be able to touch the fund money. I believe it's called the forfeiture rule.' Rose had done her homework. 'What happens to the fund money if that happens?'

'It's your job to make sure that *doesn't* happen,' Phyllis said. She waved at the approaching bus.

'Phyllis, please answer my question.'

'Well, if Finn dies before his eighteenth birthday or is denied the money in the way you describe, I inherit it. But I don't want the money, Rose. I want Finn to have it. Which is why you have to prove him innocent.'

Phyllis got on the bus and Rose drove home in a quandary. Her client was definitely hiding something. She also had a motive to kill Tony and Marie, and then ensure that Finn was charged with their murder. Because Finn turned ten on the day his parents died, under English law he could be charged with murder. If it had happened a day earlier, he couldn't have been charged. Had Phyllis waited until he was ten years old before framing him?

The thought appalled her.

Rose couldn't believe that Phyllis would commit double murder and then frame her grandson. And why employ Rose to prove Finn innocent? Rose was more interested in the secret Phyllis was keeping about the night of the fire. She had to know what Finn and his friends were doing in the barn that night.

22 ROSE

At 8.50am on Monday, Rose pulled into Geldeford's fire station forecourt for her meeting with Tucker Hughes, the lead fire scene investigator on the Toyne Farm fire. The brand new fire station was also the headquarters for the county's Fire and Arson Investigation Unit. The building was impressive. It housed six fire engines, a kitchen, games and TV room, a training room, offices and gym, and could sleep twenty-four.

At the last minute, Rose had brought Monty along: she always felt more confident when he was at her side. The young woman who answered her knock directed her up the stairs. Hughes' office door was open. He and another man were discussing the details of a training session.

Hughes was not how Rose had imagined him. His phone voice had a maturity and efficiency that led her to expect an older man, but he was probably in his late twenties. She knocked and he looked up.

'Rose?'

'Yes. I can wait outside if you like.'

'No, no. Please come in.' Then to his colleague, 'Gary, can we do this later?'

'Sure.' Gary patted Monty on the head as left the office.

Hughes removed some files from a chair. 'Please take a seat.'

He was over six feet tall, with a runner's toned body. Rose was unable to take her eyes off him. She was so busy gawping that she very nearly missed the seat, only just managing to keep from falling to the floor. Her mind went blank. She had no idea what she wanted to ask him, beyond 'Are you married?'. She glanced at his ring finger: no wedding band.

Did she just do that? Miss I'm-happy-being-single. Worse, did he see her do that? Her hormones were on overdrive. *Stop this*, she told herself. *He's way out of your league.* She self-consciously tucked fluffy strands of wayward hair behind her ears, then clutched her hands tightly together in her lap.

'A private investigator? I've always wanted to meet one,' Hughes said, sitting at his desk. 'Do you mind me calling you Rose?'

'Rose is fine.' *You can call me anything you like*, she thought, then she gave herself a mental slap. *Get down to business!*

'Please call me Tucker. I googled you,' he said, smiling like a guilty schoolboy. Rose's heart did a backflip. *Please God, let it be good things.* 'The youngest on record to make detective in Geldeford. Solved two murder cases. At twenty-one, you set up your own PI business. Impressive stuff. But your photo doesn't do you justice.'

'Really?' Rose squeaked like a startled mouse. *Is he actually complimenting me?* She cleared her throat, aware that she was blushing, and tried to sound normal. 'I wasn't alone. I mean, my dog helped me catch the killers.' She stroked Monty's head. 'We work well together.'

Rose's mind wandered to romantic picnics by the river. Tucker holding her hand as they walked Monty. Their wedding. Their two kids.

Steady on Rose. Someone that good looking must have a girlfriend.

'How can I help you?' Tucker asked.

The question fazed her. Help her? Ah yes. That's why she was there. To ask questions. 'Five years ago you investigated the fire that killed Marie and Tony Toyne, is that correct?'

'That's right. I hear the cold case has been reopened. DS Varma spoke to me about it.'

'I'm investigating the same case on behalf of a client.'

'You know I have to be careful what I say. I can't discuss anything with you that isn't already in the public domain.'

'I read your fire scene report.'

'How did you…? Forget I asked.' He smiled.

'In your report you say that petrol residue was found all around the exterior of the house. The front and back doors were locked from the inside?'

'Yes. Somebody had key locked them, drawn the bolts across, then removed the keys. At least, that was the only explanation we could find.'

'Do you think it was to prevent fire fighters from getting in?'

'I think it's possible but more like they didn't want anyone getting out.'

'There were no keys left inside the house?'

'Not for the front and back doors, no.'

'Were the keys ever found?'

'Not to my knowledge.'

'Tony and Marie died in the upstairs bedroom. Finn's bedroom was next door to theirs. How did Finn escape?' Rose asked.

'That's the million-dollar question. There was nothing to indicate how he escaped, but my guess would be through the downstairs toilet window. A boy his size could have squeezed through it, but not an adult.'

'How did Finn and his dog manage to get downstairs when his mum and dad perished in their bedroom. I imagine the first thing they would try to do was hurry downstairs.'

'Ah,' said Tucker. 'Let me ask you, have you seen the autopsy reports?'

'Yes.' It was upsetting reading. 'Mercifully, Tony and Marie died of smoke inhalation before their bodies were burned.'

'Don't you think it odd that they didn't leave their bed?' Tucker asked.

'I do. Even if the smoke had reached their room, they should have been able to open a window or make it to their son's bedroom.'

'I have a theory,' said Tucker, 'and it's just a theory. This is just between us.' Rose nodded. 'Rohypnol is difficult to trace, especially when a body is burned to a crisp as theirs were.'

'You think Rohypnol could have been dropped into their drinks at the party?'

'It tends to work fast, so the party guests would have noticed their paralysis. But if it was put into their bedtime cocoa, for example, nobody would know.'

'How terrible. To know they couldn't save their boy or escape the blaze.'

'Except Finnegan survived, with his pup.'

Rose pondered this for a moment. 'Some believe Finn was outside the house before the fire began. They think he started the fire. What do you think?'

'I think I've speculated enough. I could be totally wrong about the Rohypnol and we'll never know, unless the arsonist confesses.'

'Your report says petrol was found on Finn's trainers.'

'And hands. The petrol cans in the barn were empty.'

'Where was he found, exactly?'

'In the barn, in a state of shock. He'd pissed himself.'

'Was anyone else present? A neighbour perhaps?'

'I don't believe so but you'd better ask the officer in charge of the investigation.'

Rose had asked all her questions but she didn't want to leave. *Think of something else to say!*

'What about the other boys at the party? Do you know if any of them have a history of lighting fires?'

'I don't, I'm sorry. I wish I could do more to help.' He smiled at her again.

She smiled back, mesmerised.

Tucker leaned across the desk. 'Rose, I know I'm being inappropriate here, and please tell me to piss off if you like, but do you fancy having dinner tonight?'

Without a moment's hesitation Rose said, 'I'd love to.' She flushed a deep red. *Oh my God! He just invited me out!*

'Shall I pick you up? At, say, seven?'

'Can we meet at...?' Where? It was so long since she had a dinner date that she couldn't think of anywhere to suggest. 'Have you been to the Drunken Duck in Nether Wallop?'

'No, but I'm happy to give it a try. I'll meet you there at seven.'

Rose floated out of the fire station. She put Monty in the car automatically and then when she was in behind the steering wheel and her door closed, she screamed with joy.

'I have a date!'

23 MONTY

Rose hasn't been the same since we left the fire station. For a start, she drove into town and went clothes shopping. This is weird! I've only known her to do this once! Sometimes she drops into second-hand and charity shops, but that's the total sum of her wardrobe shopping. Today, therefore, is a major event.

I sat in the back of the car like a good dog does and waited patiently for her return. It gave me time to think about Tucker Hughes, who seems to be the cause of Rose's sudden concern about how she looks. In my eyes, she always looks great, and more importantly, she smells perfect. Does her strange behaviour have anything to do with Valentine's Day? I wonder about this because Betty is also acting oddly. She can't stop talking about Sid and how handsome he is. In truth, my biggest concern is that Rose is meeting Hughes at the pub without me. What if he's not the nice man she thinks he is?

Does Valentine's Day have some kind of magic effect on the hoomans who are looking for love? And why do all the shop windows have red hearts all over them? I am very happy with my life. I love Rose, and Summer, and Betty, and they love me. What more could a dog want?

By mid-morning Rose is at her desk staring into space. Our investigation seems to have ground to a halt. I wish Ollie was here. He would know what to do. But Ollie's at school so I trot to Rose's desk where Kay's notebook sits next to her keyboard. I manage to lift my head high enough to nudge the notebook towards Rose as I wag my tail enthusiastically. She doesn't even notice! There's a knock on the door and Rose doesn't appear to hear it so I bark to draw her attention to it. Malcolm sticks his head inside

'Um, a PC Joe Salisbury's been trying to reach you,' Malcolm says. 'He asked me to ask you to call.'

'Joe? Why didn't he call my mobile?'

'He says he's tried everything – calls, texts, WhatsApp.'

Rose picks up her phone. 'Ah, he's left five text messages. Sorry Malcolm. I must have had my phone on silent. Thanks for passing on the message.'

'No problem. I was thinking, do you fancy a meal tonight? I could do my famous spaghetti bolognaise. To be honest, it's the only dish I cook, but it tastes good.'

'What a lovely idea but I'm already going out.'

'Are you? Oh.'

Malcolm leaves, looking dejected. If he were a dog, his tail would be between his legs. I wonder that Rose didn't notice.

She phones Big Man Joe and I eavesdrop. A baby is gurgling and a TV is on in the background. This must mean that Joe is at home and it's his day off work.

'You're a hard lady to find,' Joe says.

'Sorry, Joe, a bit distracted. I'm on a date tonight.'

'WHAT!'

Okay, that was loud enough for the whole neighbourhood to hear.

'Don't make a big deal of it, Joe. Please. I'm nervous enough as it is.'

'I thought you were off men. No dating, you said.'

'Well, this one's a bit special.'

'All right, spill the beans. Who is he?'

'I'm not telling, you'll probably do something embarrassing like turn up where he works to check him out.'

'Come on! I'm your mate. You have to tell me.'

'Joe, I'm kind of busy. What were you calling me about?'

'Oh all right, but you have to promise this is just between you and me.'

'I promise.'

'I mean it, Rose. I could get into huge trouble.'

'I promise. I won't tell a soul.'

'I overheard the DCI talking to Pearl. They think they'll have enough evidence to arrest Finn by tomorrow.'

Rose gasps.

I pant nervously. This must mean the Murder Squad knows something we don't.

'You have to tell me what they have on Finn. Pleeeeease, Joe.'

'No way, that would cost me my job.' His baby wails in the background, then his wife's soft voice soothes the child.

'Has Finn confessed?' Rose says.

'Nope. Rose, I can't say anymore. I'm only giving you a heads-up because I know how much this case means to you.'

'So I have twenty-four hours to prove Finn innocent?'

'Looks like it.'

'Thanks for this, Joe. I owe you.'

Rose ends the call and looks down at me, my jaw resting on Kay's notebook. 'Okay, Monty. We have to be super efficient. We're going to take a look at our suspects one by one and then we're going to talk to them in order of priority. Got it?'

I bark yes, my tail wagging furiously.

Rose drags a shiny whiteboard closer to her desk. Malcolm sometimes uses it to train his staff. She cleans the board and then takes the lid off a large and smelly pen. I lie on the floor and watch her write a list of names. When she's done, she points at the top one.

'Finn Toyne,' Rose begins. 'What is Leach's angle?' She pauses. 'Why would he do it?'

Anger, I think. I've seen his temper. Rose hasn't. Was he angry that night? Did he throw petrol around because his parents had told him not to? Was it some terrible mistake? A match struck and a blaze began before he realised what he had done? I'm sure he would never intentionally kill them.

Rose continues, 'He had nothing to gain from killing them.' She taps the smelly pen against the board. 'So why did Leach say that Finn had motive?' She stares at me as if expecting an answer. This is not a yes

128

or no situation. Unfortunately, I don't have the skills to communicate Finn's temper. Or do I?

I trot over to my desk – a.k.a. my bed – and take my tug-of-war rope in my mouth and slap it into the mat.

'Monty! Stop! What's the matter?'

I growl a bit as I slap the rope at the mat.

Rose says, 'You've never done that before. What's up, buddy?'

This isn't working so I drop the toy and trot back to where I was seated before. Rose stares at me with a confused look on her face, then she carries on.

'Finn had the means – petrol and keys to locks the doors. But he just wasn't capable of such a complex murder that required such planning.'

Rose stares into space for a moment. Then she phones someone. She asks to speak to Dr Doom, the psychiatrist. Rose puts her on loudspeaker.

'Hello, Rose! How are you?'

'Doing well, thanks, Doris. Um, did Phyllis O'Brien get in touch about Finn?'

'Yes. You're working for her, I hear? She gave me the go ahead to talk to you.'

'Great. Finn Toyne saw you for the eighteen months after he lost his parents?'

'That's right.'

'In your opinion, why was he unable to speak?'

'Trauma. The brain can shut down after a traumatic event and the body can be severely affected, too. He suffered from PTSD and carried a lot of survivor's guilt.'

'Do you think he refused to speak so that he didn't incriminate himself?'

'I don't believe so.'

'Was Finn capable of murder?'

I prick my ears. That is the question at the centre of this whole case.

'I don't believe he was. I know in this country that a ten-year-old is deemed capable of murder, but the murder of his mum and dad involved a degree of planning that I believe only an adult could do. And why would he kill them, Rose? He had a great life. Popular at school, doting parents, a beautiful home.'

'So if you were called as a witness at his trial, you would say this?'

'I would indeed. I absolutely believe that the arsonist was an adult.'

'Thank you, Doris, that's very helpful.'

'My pleasure. And is everything okay with you?'

'Yes, it's good to have such an important case to work on.'

'I'm delighted for you; and please, stay in touch.'

The call over, Rose smiles at me. 'I trust Doris.'

Doris Doom helped Rose move beyond her pee-tee-ess-dee. Therefore, I have to believe she knows what she's talking about. Finn may well have a temper, but I think I have misjudged him otherwise.

Rose points the pen at the second name on the whiteboard.

'Sasha Bassinger. Her boyfriend gave her an alibi that night. But she stood to gain the most from their deaths. I could try talking to the boyfriend but I can't imagine he would change his story unless some new evidence came to light that proves he lied. Didn't Malcolm say that Fred, his business partner, has a son who works for Sasha? Remind me to ask Malcolm about that.'

I bark yes, although I don't have opposable thumbs and therefore can't write notes. I hope I will remember. This is a big responsibility and I take it seriously. I repeat in my head, *ask Fred, ask Fred!*

'Next on the list, the vicar Reggie Mabey,' Rose announces. 'Why did he leave the party early and where did he go for that missing hour between leaving and arriving home?

Oooh! I know the answer to this question. But how do I tell Rose? He was with Karen Price, the lady from the choir. According to my friends from the pub, Shardie and Pinot, if Marie or Tony discovered the affair and threatened to tell his wife, Mabey would have motive to light the fire that killed them.

I sit up and bark keenly, telling Rose all of this but she's busy writing a list of actions on the whiteboard.

'That's got you very excited, Monty. I guess you don't like the vicar after he tried to hit Betty with a broom.'

I *hurrumph* and lie back down again.

'Next suspect is Mervyn Mumford.' Rose taps her pen at the name. 'He benefited financially from their deaths but he was very open about the sale of his farm. He's also a witness because he called emergency services and he found Finn outside the house. I think we leave him in the witness pile.'

I haven't met Mumford but I do know that Buttermere, the village gossip, pointed the finger at him, although it seems she did it out of spite.

I bark a yes in agreement.

Rose runs her finger down a list of three names. 'Finn's friends. Jimmy Fox. Sam Chang. Alfie Mumford. All at the party. Ten years old at the time. Phyllis saw them messing about in the barn that night but she wouldn't tell me what they were doing. I wonder if they were playing with matches, maybe the petrol can too, which could explain how Finn ended up with petrol residue on his shoes and palms.'

I bark a yes.

'The fire scene investigator didn't know if any of the boys had a history of starting fires. But house fires tend to make it into the local newspaper, so I'll make that an action.' Rose scribbles away on the board. 'I think we make talking to these boys a priority. And we must speak to Finn. He might know what new evidence the Murder Squad has. That is, if he's willing to talk at all.'

Rose gives me one of her loving smiles. 'If anyone can persuade Finn to talk to us, it's you.'

If a dog could blush, I would. I wag my tail across the floor.

'Sadie and Matilda Jones. Her parents said they were in bed asleep all night and they lived four miles away. Not easy for a ten-year-old to travel four miles in the middle of the night. I'm going to ignore them for now.'

Rose points to the last suspect. 'That leaves Phyllis,' Rose says. 'I can't believe she would do it.' She looks at me. I tilt my head to one side. 'I know, I know. I must keep an open mind.'

Rose sits at her desk and taps away at her computer.

'Interesting,' Rose says. 'A year before the farm fire, a house burned down in a nearby village. The owners admitted to placing drying washing too near a gas fire.' Rose looks up, grinning. 'The house belongs to Mr and Mrs Fox, Jimmy's parents. Were they covering for their son?'

Rose grabs her phone, car keys and notebook and I follow her out of the door. We head for the hospital.

24 MONTY

At the hospital we find Finn in his room watching a TV that's secured to the wall on a movable arm. He must be feeling better because he is not only sitting up, he also leans over the edge of the bed and gives me a pat. I wonder if he will speak to us. Phyllis said that he hasn't spoken a word since Leach started questioning him, not to Phyllis or the nurses. I jump up so my front paws are on the bed. Finn wraps his arms around me and breathes into the thick fur around my neck.

'Finn,' Rose says. 'Will you talk to me? This is important.'

Finn releases me from his grasp. His eyes flit to the door which Rose has closed. He parts his lips and says "yes" slowly.

'I know this must be difficult for you, but can you think back to the night of the fire on your tenth birthday?'

'Don't want to.'

His dark eyes grow watery. I smell his pain. I jump onto the bed and lie close to him so he can hold me close. He cuddles me like a teddy bear.

'I have suspects, Finn. I'm making headway. But I can't progress any further unless you tell me what you saw that night.'

'I'll try,' he says into my fur.

'You were found by the fire service outside your house. Can you tell me how you got there?'

Finn shook his head. Rose perches on the edge of his bed. 'If you're protecting someone, you need to start thinking about saving yourself. You are the only witness to how the fire started.'

'Can't remember.'

'Try, Finn. Who put you to bed?'

'Mum.'

'Okay, then what happened?'

I hear Finn's heartbeat racing. 'I heard Panda crying in the barn. Dad said she needed to get used to being an outdoors dog. He told me not to go to her because if I did she would always think that if she cried I would respond.' He stops speaking. His tears trickle beneath my fur and onto my skin.

'Then what?' Rose asks.

Finn sniffs. 'I crept downstairs and went to the barn.'

'Which door did you use to leave the house?'

'The front one.'

'Did you leave it open?'

Finn was quiet for a moment. 'I must've. It was the kind of door that locked behind you so I would have left it a little bit open.'

'And then?'

'I played with Panda in the barn. I heard a whoosh and smelt smoke. I picked up Panda. She was afraid too. Flames blew out the upstairs windows. I tried to open the door, but I couldn't.'

I watch Rose. She shows no sign of pins and needles in her body. Finn must be telling the truth.

'I'm sorry to have to ask this, but did you hear your parents call out?'

Finn squeezes his eyes shut. 'I don't think so.'

Rose ploughs on. 'Just a few more questions, Finn. Did you take the house keys with you?'

'No.'

'Did you lock the doors?' Rose asks.

'No!' he shouts. I look at Finn's hands. They are balled into fists. 'I didn't kill Mum and Dad,' he says.

I study Rose. She isn't showing signs of discomfort, so does this mean that Finn is still telling the truth?

'Somebody did, Finn. Did you see anyone else while you were in the barn?'

Finn turns his cheek so it rests on my back. 'Earlier, when I crept down the stairs, I think I heard footsteps, like someone was walking around the house. It scared me.'

'Do you have any idea who that person might be?'

'No.'

Rose wriggles her fingers. She stamps her feet. Pins and Needles. This is a lie.

'Did you see this person run away after the fire started?'

'Maybe.'

'What did you see?'

'I'm not sure. Between our farm and Mervyn's farm there's a bridleway. I saw someone there. Running.'

'On the bridleway?'

'I think so.'

'Male or female?'

'I can't remember.'

'You can tell me, Finn. They won't hurt you.'

Finn clamps his lips together and shakes his head.

'Finn, are you protecting someone?'

'No.' Even I can tell that he's lying. Fear smells like vinegar and it's coming off Finn in waves. Rose winces at her pins and needles.

'Does someone you know like to light fires?' Rose asks.

'No!'

Rose rubs her arm and moves her feet up and down, clearly experiencing discomfort.

'Your grandmother said that during the party she found you, Jimmy, Sam and Alfie in the barn. What were you doing there?'

'Messing about. Nothing.'

'Were you messing about with fire?'

'I didn't.'

'Who did?'

The door opens and a nurse walks in. 'Oh, you have visitors.' Then she sees me on the bed and her jaw drops. 'Dog!'

'A detective dog,' Rose says, reassuringly. 'Would it be possible to come back later? I'm investigating a case. Please, just five minutes?'

Wow! Rose said that with such confidence. I'm so proud of her!

'Oh I see,' the nurse says. 'All right.' The nurse closes the door behind her. Rose repeats the question.

'Who was messing about with fire that night? Was it Jimmy?'

Finn shakes his head.

'Alfie?'

He won't look at Rose and he stays silent.

'Sam?'

No response.

'How did you get petrol on your hands and shoes?'

'Can we stop? I'm tired.'

'Just two more questions. Did Mervyn Mumford get angry with your dad because he wouldn't sell the farm?'

'Don't know.'

'Did they have angry words?'

'Sometimes.' Finn turns away and lies on his side. 'I don't want to do this.'

Rose and I leave the hospital. I sense Rose's disappointment.

'Finn knows who started the fire,' Rose says aloud. 'But he won't say. What do you think, Monty? Did Jimmy and Finn mess about with petrol and matches, and it got out of hand? Was it a terrible accident?'

I don't know what to think so I stay quiet.

Rose continues, 'And what about the person Finn thought he heard outside the house and then saw on the bridleway? Could that be Jimmy? Would a ten-year-old be capable of finding his own way home in the dark? Hmmm.' Rose pauses. 'I really don't think they could. Even so, we must speak to all the boys. We'll start with Jimmy Fox.'

25 MONTY

R ose and I have just jumped into the car when Malcolm phones.
'Bad news. I went to see Ed today, to see how he felt about
possibly adopting Panda. The poor man's caravan has been trashed.'

My ears prick up.

'How terrible,' Rose says. 'Is he okay?'

'He's devastated. The van is all he's got. Can you come over here and
talk to him? He's refusing to call the police. I think he might listen to you.'

'Why me? I don't really know him.'

'Well, I'm getting nowhere. Every time I suggest reporting it to the
police, he threatens me with a frying pan.'

'All right. I'm on my way.'

Rose turns in her seat and looks at me. 'Change of plan. We'll leave
the car at home, then we'll walk to Ed's caravan.'

Rose sets off for home. I pace back and forth like a caged animal at a
zoo. I want to comfort Ed. Is Jake okay? And why would anyone wreck
an old man's home?

Rose pulls up in our driveway. Summer and Panda peek around the
corner. Perhaps they sense something is wrong. Rose spots them and
calls them over. 'We might as well all go.'

We set off across Winterfold Heath. Sun periodically breaks through the grey clouds and the air is rich with squirrel smells, although none of us are in the mood to play chase with a squirrel. As we get close to Ed's home, I bark a warning to Jake that I have Rose with me. I wait for his reply. Seconds pass and I grow agitated. Why hasn't he responded? Then I hear his rough voice.

'It's a sad day,' is all he says.

Ferns around the caravan are trampled and Ed's metal mug lies in the mud. The caravan is old and rusty but he keeps it neat and tidy, only now, his pots and pans, his washing that hangs on a line, and the seat cushions from inside the caravan are scattered across the ground. His coffee pot lies in the ashes of his fire and the legs of the small wooden stool he sits on have been broken. There's something written in red on the caravan's exterior.

We all stop in our tracks. Rose gasps. I move carefully through the mess, sniffing the ground. The camp smells of strangers. Jake's bulk appears in the doorway. He hangs his head, the sign of a defeated dog.

'Ed? Malcolm?' Rose calls.

Ed appears in the doorway behind Jake.

'Get out of here!' he yells, brandishing a carving knife.

He is unsteady on his legs, his thinning hair all awry.

'Ed, it's me, Rose from Duckdown Cottage. This is Monty, you know Monty. Malcolm asked me to come over.'

'Rose? Oh yes and there's Monty.' He lowers the knife. 'Thought them bastards had come back.'

Jake hops out of the caravan and takes a tumble when he lands badly. He comes over to me. 'I need your help to find who did this. They gotta pay.'

'Of course I'll help you. They need to go to jail,' I say.

'Jail's too good for them,' Jakes says.

'Monty! Leave the poor Staffie alone,' Rose says.

Ed takes the step down from the van slowly, then throws his arms wide, his eyes traveling across the carnage. 'Why?' Ed asks.

Malcolm comes out of the van and jumps down. 'Hey, Rose.'

'Can't offer you a coffee,' Ed says. 'They put a hole in me pot.'

The old man looks close to tears. Malcolm points to the word written in red paint on the side of the caravan.

"What kind of person writes "scum" on someone's home?' Malcolm asks, shaking his head.

'Kids, probably.' Ed gestures to the little wooden stool. 'They broke my favourite stool. Trashed my caravan. They pissed on my bed.' Ed lowers his head into his hands. His sobs are heart-breaking. Jake slinks over and rests his head on Ed's boot. 'Not your fault, Jake.'

Panda, Summer and I whimper in sympathy.

'Ed, we should report this to the police.'

'Cops! I don't want them coming near me. They're as bad as the bastards that did this. They've tried to evict me. Came here and told me I had to leave.'

'This isn't right,' Rose says, 'people can't go around destroying other people's property. They can't intimidate and threaten like this.' Rose stares at the word painted on the caravan. 'I have a friend who's a PC. He's a good man. He'll take your complaint seriously.' I'm pretty sure she's talking about Big Man Joe.

Ed sighs. 'Do what you like. There's nothing left except Jake, my loyal buddy. The council and all them nasty villagers have got what they want. I'll move on. There's nothing left for me here.'

Rose wanders away and I overhear her speaking to Joe on her phone. It sounds like he's started his shift.

Malcolm places a hand on Ed's shoulder. 'I've had a look around. We can clean off the red paint. A spring clean, a new mattress and bedding and new cushions and it'll be home again.'

'You're a kind man, but the only money I had was in a tea caddie and them bastards took it. A hundred and ten pounds it was. My life savings.'

'Ed, we'll find a way to get the things you need.'

'PC Salisbury and PC Barika Zaid are on their way,' Rose announces, putting her phone away and kneeling next to Ed. 'Did you see who did this?'

Ed wipes his running nose on his coat sleeve. 'Nah. I wasn't here, was I? I got a job, see? Gardening work. Dog came with me. Wish I hadn't taken 'im now. Jake would have defended the place, wouldn't you, my old friend?'

'Too bloody right, I would have,' Jake growls. 'If I find who did this, I'll sink my teeth into 'em.'

Nose to the ground, I start the slow and meticulous process of inhaling scents. Summer and Panda do the same.

'Ed, you can't stay here tonight,' Rose says. 'Come and stay with me. And of course bring Jake.'

'I don't need no charity,' Ed says, raising his saggy chin. 'The mattress is ruined, but I can sleep on the floor.'

I hastily return to Ed's side and rest my chin on his bony knees. I want him to know that he's most welcome at Duckdown Cottage.

'It's not charity, Ed, it's neighbourliness. I'd really like you to be my guest for as long as it takes to get your van cleared up so you can live in it again.'

'Very kind of you, but I'll be all right.'

Rose chews her lip. 'There is something you can do for me, Ed. If you can help me with this, you can stay at my house. How does that sound?'

'Sounds possible. What is it?'

'When you lived in Nether Wallop you had an allotment. Your shed was burned down. Do you remember?'

'Of course I do. That shed was my pride and joy.'

'Who set fire to the shed?'

'Kids.'

'Can you remember their names?'

'Let me see. Sam something or other. Jimmy Fox. I remember him. He was big for his age and gave me lip, the cheeky bugger. And one more...he was tall. That's it. Alfie Mumford, the farmer's son.'

'Was Finn there?'

'Finn, you say? Phyllis's grandson?'

Rose nods.

'No. He'd never do anything like that.'

'Did you see who lit the fire?'

'Nah, I saw them run away, is all.'

'Thanks, Ed, that's very helpful,' Rose says. 'Now I owe you, so why don't you allow me to pay my debt and have you stay at my house tonight?'

'All right. That's a deal,' Ed says.

All three of us dogs have hopped into the caravan and we've sniffed the interior, especially the duvet which reeks of human pee.

'Do you recognise the hooman scents?' I ask Panda and Summer.

'One of them is familiar,' Panda says. 'From a long time ago. Someone at the party on that frightening night.'

'So you'd recognise their scent again if you met them?' I ask.

'I think I could,' Panda says.

26 ROSE

Rose felt like the dog version of the Pied Piper of Hamelin as she walked across Winterfold Heath followed by four dogs. She had left Ed and Malcolm with the two police officers and was heading home.

At the back of her mind was her date with Tucker. She wanted to conduct a few more interviews and then get home to settle Ed comfortably. Then, she hoped, she could still make her date.

Why was it that, just when she had the chance to get to know someone really special, not only did she have a house-guest, she also had to solve a difficult case, all on the same day? Her wheels were spinning but she wasn't confident she was achieving much.

When they reached Duckdown Cottage, she found a bulging envelope with her name on it under her back door. Opening it, she found a handwritten note from Phyllis:

Rose,

I enclose copies of my bank statements for the last five years. You'll see I have drawn on the capital in Finn's trust fund three times. Once to pay for Finn's bloody hopeless psychiatrist. Once for a school trip to France, and once to cover his electric guitar lessons which was the only thing he seemed to enjoy after his parents' passing.

Phyllis

Rose sat at the kitchen table and scanned the bank statements. It was exactly as Phyllis had described and Rose felt terrible that she had suspected Phyllis of stealing from Finn.

Monty sniffed the documents in her hands.

'Well, Monty, this confirms that Phyllis didn't steal from Finn. She's now off our suspects list.'

Monty wagged his tail enthusiastically.

Next, Rose fed all the dogs, told Monty to look after Jake, and then headed into Geldeford.

Trent Insurance was housed in a three-storey, boxy grey building surrounded by ornate, lush gardens. The original Victorian house had been bulldozed to make way for this corporate building, but thankfully, much of the original grounds and established trees had been kept, including a stone-walled sunken garden complete with stone bird bath, and a rose garden with a well in the middle.

A sullen receptionist took Rose's name and phoned Jimmy's mum, Violet Fox, explaining it was about a police investigation. Rose chewed her lower lip: she'd pushed the truth a little, hoping it would be enough to scare Violet into meeting her. After all, it *was* a police investigation – just not *her* police investigation.

Violet was an overweight woman in her forties with long corn-blonde hair held back by an Alice band. She wore a mackintosh with daisies on it. The hairband and the mac had a childish look about them, as if Violet liked to believe she was younger than she was. She wheezed as she hurried to greet Rose.

'Can we talk outside? It's my ciggie break.' Violet wiggled a cigarette held between two nicotine-stained fingers. In her other hand was a purple Zippo lighter.

The day was cold but dry. Violet led Rose through the garden to a bench beneath a Japanese Maple. The leaves in Autumn would have been a magnificent red, but in February the branches were bare. Last night's rain had left droplets on the bench's wooden slats. Rose used her palm to brush the water away before she sat.

Violet lit her cigarette and inhaled deeply before blowing smoke at the sky. 'This about the fire five years ago?'

'Yes.'

'I already talked to a detective. A well-dressed Indian bloke. Very nice man.'

That was DS Varma, who was, indeed, a very nice man, and a great detective. Rose guessed that Varma's focus was on Finn. 'The case has been reopened now that Finn has shown signs he can speak.'

Violet snorted. 'How very convenient.'

'What is?'

'Well, I mean, it's obvious, isn't it? Finn burns down the farmhouse, then suddenly he can't talk, which means they can't get him to confess. That boy always was a wily little shit. But he's smart.' Violet tapped a finger against her temple. 'Too bloody smart for you coppers.'

'I used to be a police officer, Mrs Fox. Now I'm a PI and I'm doing my own investigation.'

'Why you doing that?'

'A client has commissioned me to do it.'

'Who? Oh I know. I bet it's Phyllis. Damn her.'

Violet clearly didn't like Finn or Phyllis and yet her son had been best friends with Finn.

'Why would you be upset if Phyllis appointed a PI?'

'She's a bossy cow, that's why. Just like her daughter. Marie thought she knew better than everyone. Stuck up, she was.'

Phyllis certainly was opinionated. However, this was the first time Rose had heard anyone criticise Marie Toyne.

'Why didn't you like Marie?'

'She thought she was better than us. Went to some fancy art college and studied fashion design. She looked down her nose at me, I swear she did. It's not my fault we can't afford fancy clothes.'

'I understand that Finn and Jimmy were good friends.'

'Yes, although I tried to stop it.'

Rose moved on.

'Mrs Fox, I understand you lost your house to fire six years ago. How did the fire start?'

'It was my fault. I put a clothes horse with washing on it too near a gas fire. We lost most of the house, but it happened while we were out, so nobody got hurt.'

'Did the insurance company investigate?'

'Of course they did.'

'Did they discover any foul play?'

Violet's eyes disappeared into a pudgy face as she frowned at Rose. 'What are you going on about?'

'Could someone have lit the fire deliberately?'

'No. I told you, it was an accident.'

'On the night of Finn's tenth birthday, your son was in the barn with Finn, Alfie and Sam. Would they play with matches?'

'Don't be stupid. They were ten years old.'

Rose felt a wave of pins and needles travel up her legs.

'Has Jimmy lit fires?'

'My Jimmy's a good boy. He'd never do that.' The wave turned into an arrow of pain that shot up her legs. Violet was lying.

'When Jimmy was nine he, Sam and Alfie burned down Ed Penrose's allotment shed,' Rose said.

'That was an accident. That old bastard made out it was deliberate, which it wasn't! Jimmy was having a smoke behind the shed with his mates. Jimmy dropped it into dead grass. It was a dry summer and the fire spread. They panicked and ran away.' So far Rose hadn't had any sensation that told her Violet was lying. 'Then bloody Alfie went and told his dad that Jimmy did it on purpose. That boy's a liar.'

'They were smoking at ten years old?' Rose couldn't help being shocked.

'Didn't you try a ciggie when you were young? They were just experimenting.'

'No.'

Violet took a portable ash tray from her pocket, stubbed out her cigarette in it, closed the lid and pocketed the tin. She then heaved herself up. 'Stay away from my son.'

Rose watched Violet Fox walk away.

Had Jimmy been playing with matches and petrol in the Toyne's barn on the night of the fire?

27 ROSE

Sam Chang's mum, Daphne, had agreed to see Rose at four. They lived in a flat in the hilly suburb of Castleford. When Rose knocked, Sam, who was still in his school uniform, opened the door.

'You're the PI?' Sam asked.

His features were delicate and made him look younger than his fifteen years.

'Yes, nice to meet you. I'm Rose.'

'Come in. Mum told me you were coming.'

'Sorry I'm a few minutes late.'

Rose followed Sam into the sitting room, furnished with a sofa and two armchairs. The room's balcony provided a view of the city's castle. The city lights, sparkling in the early winter darkness, were pretty spectacular, which made up for the flat's otherwise small rooms.

Daphne appeared from a bedroom, wearing a blouse and skirt, her black hair neatly tucked behind her ears. Up until that point, the name Daphne Chang hadn't rung a bell. Now Rose recognised her.

'Do you work at the Ace Tennis Club? I think I've seen you there.'

'Yes. Sorry, have we met?'

'No, I was at the club the other day and I noticed you in the office.'

'Please don't mention to anyone you saw me there. It was a job interview. The receptionist's job at the club pays double what I'm getting now.'

'My lips are sealed. How did it go?'

'Okay, I think. The club manager seemed to like me, so fingers crossed. Take a seat.' She gestured at the two-seater sofa. Daphne took one armchair and Sam, the other. 'You said you wanted to talk about Marie and Tony's deaths?'

'Yes. As I mentioned, I'm a private investigator. Have the police spoken to you about the case?'

'No, although a detective Kamlesh Varma has left a message.'

None of the suspects she'd met had mentioned DI Pearl. It seemed like Varma was doing all the work while Pearl, as usual, was taking the glory.

'That's good. I used to work with Kamlesh. Mrs Chang, I understand you dropped Sam off at the birthday party and then picked him up at the end, but you didn't attend. Why was that?'

'I was working.'

'What time did you pick him up?'

'I can't remember exactly. Maybe nine o'clock.'

Rose turned to Sam, stiff-backed in his chair, his hands grasped together.

'What I'd like to do, Sam, is ask you about the party. At what point did you, Finn, Alfie and Jimmy go to the barn?'

'It was after the cake was cut and we'd stuffed our faces with food. The grown-ups were getting loud, drinking wine and beer. We wanted to run around and explore.'

'What did you do in the barn?'

Sam flicked a nervous look at his mum. 'Not much. Snooped about. Played with Finn's puppy.'

'Did you explore the shelves? There were containers of fertiliser, week killer, petrol, that kind of thing?'

Sam clenched his hands together until his knuckles went white. 'I can't remember.'

Rose's pins and needles warned her he lied. 'Please try. If you don't, the wrong person might be accused of causing the fire.'

Sam rolled his lips together for a second or two. 'I can't talk about it.'

'Why not?' Rose asked.

'I promised. We all promised.'

Rose felt a flutter in her chest, a feeling she got when she was nearing the truth. 'Who made this promise?'

'Me, Alfie, Finn and Jimmy. It was all Jimmy's fault.'

'What was Jimmy's fault?'

'I can't say.'

His mother spoke up. 'If you know something about that fire you must tell the nice lady.'

Rose waited. Seconds ticked by loudly as the hands of the carriage clock on a mantelpiece marked time.

Sam spoke, but he wouldn't make eye contact. 'Jimmy took the lid off the petrol can. Boasted he could burn the whole barn down in minutes. It scared me. Finn told him to put it down. When Jimmy wouldn't, Finn gave me his puppy to hold then he grabbed the petrol can. It sloshed on his trainers. They were a birthday present, so he was very upset. He told Jimmy he was stupid to play with fire and he'd get someone killed one day.'

Sam was telling the truth. At last, Rose knew why Finn had petrol residue on his shoes and hands.

Daphne asked her son, 'Why didn't you tell me?'

'When we heard the house had burned down and Finn's parents were dead, Alfie made us all promise to keep quiet about Jimmy's fire habit,' Sam said.

'Alfie?' Rose asked in surprise.

'Yes.'

'Did you or any of your friends stay behind after the party?'

'I don't think so. Mum collected me. Alfie and his dad walked home across the fields. Jimmy's mum picked him up.'

'Did you actually see them leave?'

'I saw Jimmy go. I didn't see Alfie and his dad leave. His dad was drinking a lot and didn't look like he wanted to go anywhere. He was very loud.'

'Did anyone that night argue? Get angry?'

'I don't remember. Oh, hold on,' Sam said. 'Finn's mum went for a walk with Alfie's dad at one point. It looked like they were planning something secret.'

This was the first time Rose had heard about this. She knew Mumford and Tony had talked in the study, but nobody had mentioned that Mumford and Marie had gone for a walk together.

'What made you think they were being secretive?'

'They were whispering and kept looking behind them, furtive-like. They wandered out of the yard.'

'Did you overhear any of their conversation?'

Sam shook his head. 'I heard Tony calling Marie inside. He went after them. He was angry. He said Marie and Mervyn were up to something.'

What were Marie and Mervyn conspiring about? Could this altercation have led to Mervyn killing Tony and Marie?

'Did Finn ever mention that his parents were going through a rough patch?'

'He said they argued all the time about selling the farm.'

'I understood they didn't want to sell it, is that right?'

'I don't know,' Sam said.

'I can tell you about that,' said Daphne. 'Marie and I were great friends. She was my saviour when my husband walked out on us. Marie was always there when I needed a shoulder to cry on. And I did the same for her. Many a time she came here and she bawled her eyes out. She was so unhappy, you see.'

'Unhappy?' Rose said.

'Yes. Marie had always wanted to be a fashion designer. Her designs were stunning. She was the star of her art college. Then she met Tony and fell in love. He had inherited the fruit farm by then – it had been in his family for generations. Tony asked Marie to marry him, and she had to choose between a designing job in London or life on a farm with Tony. She chose Tony, but I know there were times when she deeply regretted her choice. Farm life is hard. Marie had no time for her art and it affected her deeply. Marie loved Tony and Finn, but she longed for more. She was a city girl. She loved beautiful clothes. By the time of the party, their marriage was on the rocks. She wanted Tony to sell the farm to Bassinger Homes. Then they could start a new life, the life Marie longed for.'

Everything Daphne was telling Rose was true – she hadn't had a single tingle in her arms and legs. Rose swallowed what felt like an angular humbug stuck in her throat.

'So you're saying that Marie wanted to accept the offer from Sasha Bassinger but Tony refused to take it.'

'That's right. Tony was being selfish. It was a good offer, and he knew how much Marie hated the farm. With the money from the sale, they could have bought a house and invested in Marie's designer business. Tony wouldn't have needed to work after that, if he didn't want to.'

'So what was she talking to Mervyn about on the night of the party?'

'Marie and Mervyn were going to work together to convince Tony to sell.'

Rose stared down at her notes, her heart pounding. 'You didn't mention this in your police statement. Why was that?'

'Marie was dead. I didn't want people thinking badly of her.'

'Are you absolutely sure that Marie and Mumford had a plan to convince Tony to sell?'

'Yes, she was so happy the night of the party. She whispered to me that she would soon be off the wretched farm and Mervyn was going to help her.'

'Would you be willing to make a police statement to this effect?'

A vein on Daphne's right temple pulsed under her skin. 'Will I get into trouble?'

'No. And I can come with you if you wish. It was an omission, Daphne, not an outright lie.'

'You think it's important?'

'I do.'

'All right then.'

They agreed Rose would arrange for Daphne to meet a detective. On the way home, Rose left a message for DS Varma, who would be more understanding of Daphne Chang's omission from her original statement. This could be enough to stop Leach from charging Finn with murder.

28 ROSE

Rose put fresh sheets on the spare bed and laid a bath towel on the duvet for Ed. Downstairs in the kitchen there was a *click click click* of dog claws on the floor: Jake was pacing, anxious to see his owner again. She checked her watch. It was 5.19pm.

I can still make it, she told herself. She was due to meet Tucker Hughes at the Drunken Duck at 7pm. But would Ed be all right in the house without her?

'Of course he will,' she mumbled.

Rose skipped into her bedroom and laid out her new clothes on the bed.

She had a new pair of black jeans and a pink-champagne, sequined, ruched top which she had bought especially for the occasion. It was more glamorous than Rose usually liked to wear, but this was a special date and she wanted to look her best. As a back-up, she had also purchased a pink spotted cotton blouse, a simpler affair which was more her style. It had been an age since she'd been clothes shopping and she'd secretly enjoyed it, although she wasn't sure how she would pay off her credit card at the end of the month. Her bank account was almost empty. Still, there was no point worrying about that now.

A car came to a stop in her drive. That would be Malcolm and Ed. By the time she was down the stairs, Jake and the other dogs were out the front, greeting them with raucous barking. Rose hurried out to welcome them. Ed carried an old rucksack over one shoulder. Malcolm offered to take it. Ed snatched it away from him.

'I'm old, not decrepit, thank you, Malcolm.'

Malcolm, Ed and the dogs followed Rose into the kitchen.

'Tea?' she offered.

'Ta, three sugars,' said Ed, sitting in the nearest chair.

He wore his trench coat and cloth cap, which he seemed in no hurry to remove.

'Do you want me to stay tonight,' Malcolm asked Rose. She stared at him blankly. 'You're going out tonight,' Malcolm clarified.

'Oh I see. You're most welcome, but I guess that's up to Ed,' Rose said. 'Ed, I'm due to meet a ... friend at seven just for a couple of hours. I was planning on making you dinner before I go. Will you be all right on your own or do you fancy company?'

'Stop your fussing girl. I'll be fine. And I won't be alone, will I?' he gestured to the four dogs seated close to him.

'Okay, then,' Malcolm said. 'I'll be off.' He smiled at Rose. 'By the way, your police friends were great. They are sending a forensics person round in the morning to dust for fingerprints.'

'That's good news. Perhaps they will have the vandals' fingerprints in their database.'

Rose put the kettle on.

'Oh, I forgot to tell you,' Malcolm said. 'Fred spoke to his son about Sasha and the Toyne fire.'

'What did he find out?'

'Not much. His son likes working at Bassinger Homes and says Sasha is a good boss. Unfortunately, he joined the company after the fire so he doesn't know anything about the deals struck or any animosity between the parties involved. Sorry about that. I was hoping it might be more useful.'

'It is useful, Malcolm. A number of people have expressed their dislike of her. It's good to know that an employee likes her. Thanks for asking.' Rose poured the boiled water over the teabag in the mug. 'I found out something interesting today. A friend of Marie's claims that Marie hated farm life and wanted Tony to sell to Bassinger Homes. Tony refused, so Marie and Mervyn Mumford made a pact to make him do it. We don't know what that pact was, but what if they thought they could burn down the house and force the sale because it was under-insured?'

Monty gave her a fixed stare, his ears pricked, as if he were hanging on her every word.

'If that was their crazy plan, it went terribly wrong,' Malcolm says. 'Well, I'd better be going.'

Malcolm's boots crunched the gravel as he headed for his car. When Rose had made Ed's tea she discovered Jake curled up on the old man's lap. At last, the Staffie was happy.

'You make a lovely cuppa,' Ed said, drinking the sweet tea.

'How does chicken, barley and vegetable casserole sound, with bread and butter? It won't take long to defrost.'

'Sounds nice,' Ed said, looking around the kitchen. 'Good to see you haven't changed the kitchen much. Brings back fond memories.'

Rose popped the frozen casserole in the microwave to defrost. Then she sat at the table and drank a glass of water. 'You know the house well?' she asked.

Ed had constructed a wire-mesh fence for her a while back. Unfortunately, Monty discovered that he could dig underneath it or squeeze through the Hawthorn hedge at the back if he wanted to go off exploring, as he often did. Ed had never mentioned that he had fond memories of the place before Rose lived there.

'Oh yes,' Ed said, giving her a wide, gummy smile. Rose wondered if Ed had remembered to bring his false teeth with him. The casserole might be difficult to eat without them. 'Kay and I were good friends,' Ed said.

Rose's surprise must have been written on her face because Ed chuckled. 'I bet there's a lot about your aunt you don't know. Did you know I asked Kay to marry me?'

Rose's eyes went wide. 'No. Tell me about it.'

'It was a long time ago, mind, when I was an estate agent and lived in Nether Wallop. Kay was quite a bit younger than me, but I wasn't bad looking back then.'

'How did you meet?'

'At the village hall. She did a talk about policing. She was a great speaker and passionate about her job. We chatted afterwards and I asked her on a date, then and there.' Ed smiled ruefully. 'I couldn't believe it when she said yes.'

Rose only had memories of Kay living alone at Duckdown Cottage. From the age of six, Rose spent two weeks every summer with her aunt. It was a welcome respite from the chaotic and noisy bed and breakfast her parents ran in Cornwall, where she always felt like an unwanted appendage. Kay taught Rose about plants and insects, how to grow vegetables and bake bread, and they'd go for long, lazy walks on Winterfold Heath with Kay's Dachshund, Legless. Oh, happy days! Kay's relationship with Ed must have been over by the time Rose became a regular visitor.

'How long did you go out with each other?' Rose asked.

'Nine months. I loved her very much and I asked her to be my wife.' Ed's smile faded. 'She wanted time to think about it. I spent an agonizing week waiting for her answer. In the end, she said no. She didn't have time for marriage. Her career meant everything, and she needed to give it one hundred percent.' Ed shook his head. 'She broke my heart.'

'Oh, Ed, I'm so sorry. In those days, women in the police were not taken seriously. Kay made it to the rank of Detective Inspector, which was exceptional back then. She worked long days and I suspect she knew it would be unfair to you.'

'I know, but I would have been happy to support her in her career. Anyway, what does it matter now? Kay and I stayed friends but neither of us married.' Ed sighed. 'I miss her, even now.'

Rose reached across the table and squeezed Ed's arthritic hand. He stared down at the table, clearly lost in memories. 'I was with her when she died, you know. At least I could do that for her.' He looked up. 'Kay was a fine woman who knew what she wanted and I see much of her in you. I can see you love being a detective. But a word of advice. If you find the love of your life, don't let them slip through your fingers.' Ed pulled his hand away and drank the remainder of his tea in silence.

Rose thought about the man she was meeting tonight. Could he be the one for her?

'Would you mind if I had a look around?' Ed asked.

'Of course not. Shall I show you to your room?'

'Is it upstairs? 'Cause my knees ain't so good these days.'

'Yes.'

'Then I'll make my way up there later. So I don't have to keep going up and down. All right, Jake, up you get. Let's find the TV.'

Jake opened his eyes and then jumped to the floor, landing on the side where his back leg was missing. It didn't appear to hurt him. The dog had a shake. Ed used the edge of the table to help him stand, then he turned to the hall and tripped, falling with a *thunk* on the floor.

'Ed!' Rose knelt down. 'Are you hurt?'

Ed lay there for a moment, seemingly stunned. He tried to sit up.

'Let me help you.'

Jake was barking in Ed's face, which wasn't helping. Rose took Ed under his armpits and helped the old man to sit up.

'No harm done,' Ed said. 'Just a few bruises. I'll be all right.'

'Stay where you are a moment so you can catch your breath,' Rose said, worried about how she was going to lift Ed to his feet. He was lean, but he was still quite a weight. Monty pushed his head under one of Ed's arms. 'Come to help me, Monty?'

'He's a good dog,' said Ed. 'I wasn't sure about him when we first met. But he's turned into a very good-natured fellow.'

Rose took Ed's weight on the right side and Ed used Monty's shoulders as a prop to help him push up on his left side. Together they managed to get Ed onto a dining chair.

'Anything broken?' she asked. Ed was the kind of guy who would downplay his injuries. 'Concussion?'

'Stop your fussing, Rose. You have a friend to meet. Why don't you go and get yourself ready?'

'It's not important,' Rose lied. 'I'll cancel tonight, then you and I can spend a cosy night in.'

She was disappointed. But after that fall, she couldn't leave Ed alone in the house. She just hoped that Tucker would be understanding.

29 MONTY

I stare at Ed's false teeth in a water glass by his bed. I can't wrap my head around the idea that Ed is able to take his teeth out of his mouth and then put them in again, whenever he likes. My teeth are firmly attached to my jaw and I'd be lost without them. I tilt my head as I study them. His teeth are small, especially his canines, which are hardly worth having.

I am not allowed upstairs but Ed's snoring is shaking the house walls. He fell down earlier in the evening and I have come upstairs to check he hasn't got something stuck in his throat which might explain his thunderous noises. I snuck into his room – which used to be Kay's bedroom – and found Ed on his back, mouth open. There is nothing unusual in his mouth, though.

Rose's bedroom door is shut. I expect that's because of the noise Ed is making. Rose was sad at having to cancel her date with Tucker. At least he was gracious about it and suggested tomorrow night instead.

I head down the stairs and then poke my nose into the hole in the skirting board.

'Betty?'

Her whiskers tickle the tip of my nose. I pull my head back and Betty wriggles through the hole, but her middle section gets stuck. 'Blimey! I swear this hole is shrinking. Must be dry rot that's doing it.'

I hear her back paws scratching the floorboards and, with one huge effort, she pops out and slides across the floor, spinning like a top.

'What's up?' Betty says, 'And who is the dinosaur roaring upstairs?'

'Follow me.'

I wake Panda, Jake and Summer with a nudge of my nose. They blink at me sleepily, then follow me outside where we can talk without waking the hoomans. I quickly clue in Betty about Ed, his caravan, and the insult painted on the wall.

'Bloody hoomans,' says Betty. 'They can be so cruel. What did poor Ed do to hurt anyone? Nothing! I say we find the bastards who did this.' She sits up with her front paws on her hips. 'Who's with me?'

'Me,' I say.

'I'm in,' Jake growls. 'I'm going to tear them limb from limb.'

'Jake, my friend, if you bite a hooman, you know what will happen.'

'I want justice and justice is worth dying for,' Jake says, puffing out his chest.

'All we need to do is find where the vandals live. Rose will make sure the police arrest them.'

'That's not enough,' Jake mutters. 'They are vermin.'

'We can find the vandals through their scent,' I say. 'We all smelt them, right?' They nod. 'Two hoomans. One of them smelt of limes and the sharp smell of the goo hoomans use in their hair, and sunburnt skin.'

Summer said. 'That hooman also smelt like curry.'

'Yes,' says Panda.

'The other scent was harder to work out,' I say. 'A sweet fragrance. And nail polish. Rose has some in her bathroom cabinet.'

'And tennis balls,' says Panda. 'When I was held at the pound, they would exercise me in a yard by throwing a tennis ball for me to collect.'

'Right!' says Betty, clapping her front paws together, 'how do we find these toerags?'

'Tonight, we go back to the caravan, follow the scents and see where they lead. If we're lucky we'll find out where they live.'

'What if they used a car?' Summer asks.

'Then we have a problem. But if they are kids, as we think they are, they probably walked there.'

'I will stay here,' Summer says. 'I'll just slow you down. I hope you find them.'

It doesn't take long for three dogs and one rat-who-thinks-she's-a-jockey to reach the caravan on Winterfold Heath. It's eerily still tonight. Not a leaf stirs. The caravan is cordoned off by police tape strung up between four trees. In silence, we slip under the tape and congregate at the caravan steps. The van door is ajar. The door is dented and won't close properly.

'I think we should split up,' I suggest. 'Betty, you know what Ed smells like. I need you to get to know the other two smells in the van.'

'Easy-peasy.' She scurries up a tyre and into the caravan that way.

'Panda, you're nimble. You check the bed and other higher surfaces. Maybe they left something behind by mistake.'

Panda noses the broken door open and disappears inside.

'Jake, you and I will search for scent trails out here. You do the area inside the crime scene tape and I'll do the area outside it. Okay with you?'

'Fine with me.'

I smell nothing of the vandals until I'm nose to the ground and halfway between the third and fourth trees that support the tape. The scent of tennis balls and a sweet fragrance hits me like I've run into a wall. I pull my nose away from the ground and notice the heather has been squashed in the shape of a footprint. I circle around the footprint. A little to the right, another footprint. I catch the whiff of burnt skin and a weird smelling sweat like curry. I explore a wider circumference and it becomes clear that the vandals followed this path through the forest as their escape route.

'Over here,' I bark.

Panda and Jake arrive almost immediately, and they sniff the footprints. Betty doesn't appear, so I jump into the caravan to hurry her along. Milk has been poured over the carpet and is turning sour. The stench of hooman pee on the bedding is even stronger than before.

'Betty?' I bark.

There's a squeak from the side of the bed nearest the wall. Betty's bottom points skywards, her head hidden by the duvet. I jump on the bed and see something shiny and circular in Betty's mouth. It must have fallen down the side of the bed. Betty gives another tug and frees a smooth gold bangle. She drops it on the duvet.

'Take a whiff of that,' Betty says.

I inhale its scent: tennis balls, nail polish and a fragrance that reminds me of sweetpeas.

'Great work, Betty. Can you loop it around my collar? That way, I can show it to Rose. It's evidence.'

'Easy-peasy,' says Betty, taking the bangle between her jaws and climbing up my leg. I then feel the hard metal slide under my collar. It presses against the skin of my back but it's not uncomfortable. 'Done.'

'Hang on tight, Betty,' I say. 'I've found the path the vandals took.' We join Jake and Panda outside. 'They went that way.' I point with my nose in the direction we should go.

'Well, what are we waiting for?' Jake growls impatiently and sets off. One, two, three, hop. One, two, three, hop.

The terrain is easy to cross: a sandy path, heather, bracken. Their scent takes us to Cissbury Lane. The hoomans then walked along the side of the lane and into Little Wallop.

'It was bound to be one of the villagers,' growls Jake. 'They made Ed's life a misery. Tormenting him. Complaining to the council and park rangers.'

Little Wallop is, as the name implies, little. No shops, no church, not even a bus stop. We keep going, passing some very big houses and large gates. There are a couple of sixties-style bungalows and the scent stops outside number two. We all halt. The village is sleeping. Not house number two. I hear music and see light coming from the back. We stealthily follow a paved path to the back garden.

In a glass conservatory, the lights are on. Music pulses. A teenage male and a female are dancing with beer bottles in their hands. The girl is laughing. A window is open. I hunker down low and reach the window. I lift my nose and sniff the warm air coming from the conservatory. I smell tennis balls, nail polish and a sweet fragrance. The girl's fingernails are painted black. The boy smells of burnt skin, lime hair gel and sweat; it smells less like curry than the trail we followed, but it's still present.

The girl takes the boy in an embrace and kisses him. The gold bangles on her wrist jangle. 'When's your dad back?' she asks.

'Not for ages,' he says with a cheeky grin, as he begins to undo the buttons on her white blouse.

'Not here,' she says. 'Upstairs.' She leads him away. The lights are switched off and new lights go on upstairs.

Jake's shoulders are hunched with tension and he's emitting a low and threatening growl.

I lead everyone back to the street. If Jake attacks the hoomans, he will be put down and nobody will pay any attention to the bangle dangling from my collar.

'It's time to get Rose here,' I say in a quiet yowl.

'Will she follow you?' Panda asks.

'All I can do is try.'

'Stay here and watch them. But don't show yourselves or attack them. Promise, Jake?'

'I'll do my best,' he growls.

I sprint all the way home.

30 MONTY

The handle to Rose's bedroom is like a horizontal stick. I close my jaw around the handle and tilt my head one way, forcing the end of it downwards. The door opens a fraction. With the top of my head I gently push the door further open and walk in, hoping Rose won't be too concerned about the slobber now coating the handle.

Rose is curled up in bed with the duvet tucked under her chin. On her bedside table, her mobile phone is linked to the wall by a cable, which she calls "recharging". The watch she wears, that was once Kay's, lies next to it. I push my nose so close to hers they are almost touching. I make a *mrrrrrr* sound, a whine that isn't as shocking as a full bark. She doesn't stir. I move a notch closer and give her a single, light-weight bark.

Rose's eyes spring open and she sits up like a jack-in-the-box. 'What? What?'

She fumbles blindly for the bedside lamp switch, and after a few misses she finds it. She squints at me through barely opened eyelids.

'Monty?' Her voice is raspy. 'Intruder?'

We've had an intruder before. That intruder nearly killed Finn and me.

I bark twice – a no – and then leave the bedroom, hoping that she will follow me. I hear the rustle of her dressing gown being pulled on, then she appears on the landing in her slippers. Her attire isn't exactly right for a run through the heath to Little Wallop and this is where my plan is a bit hazy. Unless Rose is prepared to follow me into the freezing-cold night, I don't know how to indicate that we have found the caravan vandals. Our yes and no communication works well in most situations but this is more complicated.

Rose switches on the stair light, then follows me down, where she finds me and Summer staring up at her from the bottom of the stairs.

Will Jake's and Panda's absence be enough to get her moving where I need her to go?

'What on earth is going on?' she asks.

I lead her to the kitchen and tug at my lead, dangling from a hook. Rose scratches her messy hair.

'This isn't about a walk, is it?' She checks the wall clock. 'Eleven thirty-three. Hmmm.' Her gaze wanders around the kitchen. 'Where are Panda and Jake?'

She calls their names out of the back door and when they don't appear, she looks at me with a worried frown.

'Did they go out?'

I reply with one loud bark – yes.

Her heart rate speeds up. 'The caravan! Did Jake and Panda go to Ed's caravan?'

That is not where I want Rose to go but it is on the way to Little Wallop. I scratch my ear while I think about how to answer the question. I finally bark – yes.

Moving close to her, I lower my head, hoping she will notice the gold bangle hanging from my collar.

'What's that?'

I feel Rose's hand touch my neck. 'I won't touch it. Could be evidence.'

She pulls on her yellow rubber washing-up gloves and undoes my collar, frees the bangle, then does up my collar again..

'Where did you get this?' I look up. Rose stares at the bangle. I nudge her hand. Then I pull at my lead on the wall hook.

'Do you want to show me where you got it from?'

One bark from me. And one bark from Summer. I glance at my mother. *Thanks, mum,* I think.

Rose grimaces out of the window. I'm not surprised she's reluctant to go outside. It's almost freezing out there. 'I'll get dressed,' Rose says.

Not long after, Rose is dressed in her puffy coat and gloves, with a red bobble hat on her head and her red Wellington Boots on her feet. She places the bangle in a transparent zip-lock bag and puts it in her coat pocket, then she takes a torch from the cupboard under the sink. She tells Summer to say here and look after Ed, then she and I leave. She shuts the back door behind her.

Rose walks fast for a hooman and we reach Ed's caravan on Winterfold Heath in no time at all. I duck under the crime scene tape but Rose tugs on my lead and I stop.

'It's a crime scene, Monty. I can't cross the line.'

I put my weight into dragging Rose a little closer to the tape, her boots sliding across the sandy soil.

'Is this where you found the bangle?'

I bark once and she drops the lead. Rose ducks under the tape then follows me into the caravan, her torch light bouncing around objects in the cramped interior. I rest my front paws on the duvet.

'Did you find the bangle on Ed's bed?'

One bark.

'What is a woman's bangle doing in here?' Rose says to herself. Then she looks at me. 'The vandal was a woman?'

One bark from me.

'Good boy, Monty! I'll get this to Joe in the morning.' She pats my head. 'But where are Jake and Panda? I thought I'd find them here.'

I jump outside again. Rose follows.

'Slow down, Monty!'

Rose jogs to catch up with me and grabs the lead. We set off at a fast pace along the path to Little Wallop. We startle a couple of rabbits who zip into ground cover. Our breath forms little clouds of warm air and her torch bobs over heather and into the tall pine trees. By the time we reach number two, Cissbury Lane, Rose's nose and cheeks are flushed with the cold.

Two pairs of eyes watch us from behind a pot plant. First Jake and then Panda come out of hiding. They greet Rose silently by snuffling her gloved hands.

'Is this the vandal's house?' Rose whispers.

I give Rose the quietest bark I can muster. The bedroom light is still on upstairs and from the sound of the two voices, the boy and girl are still awake.

'I can't knock on someone's door at midnight,' she whispers. 'I'll come back tomorrow.'

I run to the front door, dragging Rose behind me.

'Monty!' she whispers. 'Stop!'

She looks up at the bedroom window, hears a woman's laughter and a man's voice. She chews her lip, then lifts her hand so that her finger hovers in front of the door bed.

Go on Rose, ring the bell, I urge her in my head.

The male laughs loudly, a nasty sneering laugh. 'Look at him squirm!'

Rose must have heard it too. She rings the doorbell.

The girl squeals, 'Shit! Your dad!'

'Can't be,' the boy says. 'He's got a key. Get dressed.'

The boy opens the bedroom window and leans out. He tugs down a sweatshirt as if he has only just put it on. 'What do you want?' he yells.

Rose squints, her vision blinded by the bright light from the bedroom. 'I'm PI Rose Sidebottom. I'm sorry to disturb you but—'

'Piss off. It's fricking midnight.'

Car headlights lights up the lane. The boy sees it too, swears, slams the window shut and yells at the girl to put her jeans on. Jake and Panda crouch behind the pot plant, out of sight. The car slows and turns into number two's driveway, the glare of the headlights spotlighting Rose and me on the doorstep. From inside the house comes the sound of footsteps on the stairs, then the boy throws the door open. Simultaneously, the driver of the BMW gets out.

'What the hell is going on?' the man says.

'Mervyn Mumford?' Rose says, aghast.

Mumford comes around his parked car and stares at Rose and I, bathed in the light from the hallway. 'I know you. You're the PI from the tennis club.'

'Yes.' Rose turns her head to look at the boy framed in the doorway.

He looks more like a man to me, but I've always found guessing a hooman's age difficult. 'And this must be Alfie, your son.'

Alfie Mumford was one of the three boys who were at the party the night Finn's parents died. He must be fifteen hooman years old.

I haven't met either the father or the son before, so I sniff the father's jeans. He's been at a pub: the smells of beer, beef burger and burning wood from a log fire cling to the cotton and dominate my senses. Beneath those superficial aromas, I try to detect his innate scent. His skin smells strange, an aroma I've not come across before. I manage to identify the whiff of recently ploughed fields and a yeasty smell. I'm fairly certain that he isn't the person who vandalised Ed's van.

I then shift close enough to Alfie to sniff him – he has the exact same scent that we found at Ed's van. How could he be so cruel to Ed? Peering over Alfie's shoulder is a girl with the sweet fragrance mixed with tennis balls and nail polish. These two hoomans are the vandals.

'Yes, this is Alfie,' says Mumford. 'Look, I don't mean to be rude. But what are you doing here so late?'

'Can I come in?' Rose asks.

Beneath her puffy coat she is sweating. She's nervous.

'No, you can't,' Mumford snaps. 'What do you want?'

Panda whimpers from behind the flowerpot. Mumford's aggression is scaring her.

'I think it would be better if we talk inside,' Rose says with authority. 'You don't want the neighbours involved, I'm sure.'

He pulls in his chin and hesitates.

'All right, but this is grossly inconvenient.' Mumford barges past us and into the hall where he mutters to Alfie, 'Keep your trap shut.'

Alfie and the girl step aside. The girl glowers at Rose. We step into the toasty warm hallway. Mumford tells Alfie to shut the door and then frowns at me.

'Not the bloody dog!' Mumford says. 'He'll put mud on my cream carpet.'

We're standing on a giant doormat.

'We can talk here,' Rose says. 'I'm Rose Sidebottom, I'm a private investigator.' Rose looks at the girl who slouches against the wall. She has shoulder-length blue hair and a jewel on one side of her nostril. I've never seen a hooman with blue hair before and I can't help staring.

'Can I have your name?' Rose asks.

'Mind your own business,' she sneers.

Rose's grip on my lead tightens. 'You must be, what? Fifteen? Do you want to tell me why you had your blouse off in Alfie's bedroom?'

The girl glares. 'Piss off.'

'Alfie?' Mumford says. 'What have you been–?'

'We're not doing anything, Dad,' Alfie snaps.

'I've told you before, if you want to go to university you have to stay focused on schoolwork.'

'Oh Dad, give it a rest.'

'No, I won't give it a rest. You have the chance to be someone. Don't muck it up, wasting your time on girls.'

'I'm right here,' says the girl, sulkily. 'Don't talk about me like I'm invisible.'

Rose focuses on the sulky girl. 'If you don't wish to be invisible, tell me your name.'

The girl holds up a middle finger.

'Oh, for crying out loud, she's Tammy Mendelson,' says Mumford. 'Look, I'm tired. I want to go to bed. What's so important that you have to see us tonight?'

Rose takes the transparent bag from her pocket. She holds it up so that the girl can see it clearly. 'Does this bangle belong to you?'

Her eyes bulge. I smell vinegar: she's afraid.

'No.'

It's a lie. I know it. Rose knows it because she winces and shifts her feet from side to side.

'This bangle is going to a forensics lab in the morning. I believe it's yours. Lying to me just makes you look more guilty.'

'Dad! Tell her to leave!' Alfie pleads, a bead of sweat trickling down his temple.

'It's mine. I lost it,' says Tammy, 'So what?'

'It was found in the caravan belonging to Ed Penrose on Winterfold Heath. His home was vandalised earlier today and the word *scum* painted on the side of the van. The caravan is now a crime scene and I'm helping the police with their enquiries. I believe that Alfie and Tammy are the perpetrators,' she says to Mr Mumford.

I watch the father carefully. He locks eyes with Alfie and gives him a dagger stare. He knows that Alfie is guilty. Then he smiles at Rose, a fake smile. 'If Tammy's bangle was found at that tramp's van, it's because he stole it. Isn't that right, Tammy?'

'Yes, that's right,' says Tammy.

'I'd like you to leave now,' Mumford says, attempting to reach out and open the door, but too many of us are crowding the hallway.

Rose pockets the bangle. 'Mr Mumford, by protecting Alfie and Tammy, you are an accessory to the criminal act. I'd think very carefully about what that means. You will hear from a police constable in the morning. One more thing. About the night of Finn Toyne's tenth birthday party: can you confirm that Marie wanted to sell the farm, whereas Tony didn't?'

'I'm not confirming anything. Now please leave.'

Alfie squeezes past us to open the door. 'Go away.'

Rose and I step out of the house, the front door slams behind us and Rose calls Jake and Panda to her.

We walk home as a pack.

'Mumford isn't the nice man I thought he was,' Rose says. 'His son is even worse. As for the girlfriend, I didn't like her at all.' She looks down at me. 'You're such a clever dog. I don't know what I'd do without you.'

Don't worry, I think, *I'll always be there for you.*

'You're all very clever dogs,' Rose says, 'and when we get home you'll all get some treats.'

31 ROSE

At 9am on Tuesday morning, Rose arrived at Geldeford Police HQ. In her handbag was Tammy Mendelson's bangle. She had rung Joe Salisbury earlier, so he was expecting her. He met her in reception and led her to a ground floor meeting room.

'What have you got?' Joe asked.

Rose gave the transparent bag containing the bangle to him. 'Monty found it in the caravan. On Ed's bed. I think you'll find it belongs to Tammy Mendelson. She's Alfie Mumford's girlfriend. They both go to Geldeford High. I can't prove it but I believe Alfie and Tammy vandalised Ed's caravan.'

'Did you see Monty find the bangle, or did he bring it to you?'

Rose grimaced. Joe was only doing his job, but she knew that she couldn't say for certain where he found it. She was tempted to tell a little white lie and say that she saw her dog find it. But Rose couldn't do it. She explained how Monty had woken her in the night and dragged her to Ed's caravan. He had then made a big show of pointing at the bed.

'He's a clever dog, Joe,' Rose said. 'You know he is. He was very specific about the bed.'

'I know, Rose, but all this is hearsay. I'll have a chat with Tammy and Alfie about it but unless they confess, there's not much I can do.'

Rose was about to argue that the bangle should go to forensics, when Joe asked, 'Isn't Alfie one of Finnegan Toyne's mates? He was at the fatal birthday party, wasn't he?'

'Yes. So was his dad. Which reminds me, can I speak to DS Varma? I have some information relating to that case.'

Varma hadn't returned her call and Rose was keen for Daphne Chang to make a new statement as soon as possible. The Murder Squad didn't know that Marie and Mervyn Mumford had cooperated to force Tony to sell the farm. This was a whole new line of enquiry that might exonerate Finn.

Joe shook his head. 'You're too late.'

Her stomach plunged. 'How do you mean?'

'Finn has been charged with the murder of his parents. Varma, Leach and Pearl are with him now.'

'No,' she moaned.

Rose splayed her palms on the table's cool surface, trying to think how to stop the process. 'So many people had motive to light the fire. How can the DCI be so certain?'

'A witness came forward. He saw Finn messing around with a petrol can the night of the party.'

'Who's the witness?' Rose asked.

'You know I can't tell you that.'

It could only be Sam, Alfie or Jimmy. The boys were in the barn unsupervised for a while, until Phyllis ordered them into the house. Rose ruled out Sam, given his honesty with her yesterday. The new witness had to be either Jimmy Fox or Alfie Mumford.

'That witness could be lying, Joe. I know that Marie Toyne wanted to sell the farm. She was conspiring with Mervyn Mumford to put pressure on Tony to agree to it. That's why I want to see Varma. Daphne Chang wants to make a new statement.'

'It's a bit too late. Finn confessed.'

The ground shifted beneath her. 'What? No, he wouldn't.' Rose gripped the edges of the seat.

'He confessed, Rose. His lawyer and grandmother were with him.'

Rose slumped in her chair. 'I don't understand. Finn asked me to prove him innocent. Why would he confess?' She shook her head. 'I've failed him. And Phyllis.'

Joe gave her a sympathetic smile. 'Rose, Leach had the whole Murder Squad working this case. They had the manpower and forensic support. You didn't. You did all you could.'

Rose left the police station and sat in her car, trying to take in what had just happened. Not only had she failed to help Ed, Finn and Phyllis, but she had also failed to crack her one and only official case. If she had succeeded, business would have poured in. As it stood, she was no further forward than she had been last week. She was clientless and her bank account was almost empty. What was she going to do now? Would she have to shut down The Nosy Detectives and get a regular job?

A police car left the station, and she watched it drive away. Finn had been charged with double homicide but he was a minor and therefore he would be treated differently from an adult. Rose had not been involved in a case like this before so she was unsure what would happen to Finn now, especially since he was medically unable to leave the hospital.

It would be a while before the case was heard in court, so she still had time to find proof that someone else committed the crime.

Rose turned the ignition and headed for the hospital.

Rose found Phyllis seated in the hospital café, quietly weeping over her untouched mug of tea. Phyllis looked older; her face drawn. Rose sat opposite her and the old woman didn't even look up.

'I'm so sorry,' Rose said.

Phyllis had a cotton handkerchief balled in one palm. She opened it out and blew her nose. 'My darling boy.'

'Is it true that Finn's confessed?' It wasn't that Rose didn't believe Joe, but she needed to hear it again from Phyllis, just in case there had been some terrible mistake.

'Yes,' Phyllis wailed. 'Lord knows why. He's innocent.'

Heads turned and people stared.

Rose leaned across the table and spoke quietly. 'Can you tell me what he confessed to exactly?'

The precise wording was important. For instance, *I was messing about. I never meant to burn the house down* was completely different from *I lit the fire because I wanted my parents dead.*

'I…I can't believe it.'

'Believe what?' Rose coaxed.

'Finn said he hated his parents. It's just not true.'

'That's it? A ten-year-old boy hates his parents? Kids that age say all sorts of things they don't mean.'

Phyllis shook her head. 'He explained how he did it.'

'Which is?'

'He said that he snuck out of the farmhouse when his mum and dad were asleep. He checked his puppy was in the box in the barn. Then he took a can of petrol from the shelf, went back into the house, found matches next to the gas stove. He knew the back door was locked and the key was in the door. He took that key, and the key for the front door.' Phyllis clenched her eyes tightly shut. 'I can't bear to think about it.'

'Take your time,' Rose said.

Phyllis wiped her eyes with the paper napkin next to her tea mug.

Phyllis continued in a broken voice, 'He claimed he poured petrol over the sofa, curtains and stair bannisters. What utter rubbish! He just wouldn't do it.'

'What else did he say?'

'He threw a match, he said, then locked the front door from the outside.

'What did he say he did with the keys?'

'He refused to say.' Phyllis sniffed. 'They'll send him to a secure children's home. I've lost him forever.'

'You haven't lost him yet. He hasn't been found guilty in court. Do you believe him?' Rose asked.

'No, I do not,' Phyllis sounded angry. 'I don't know why he's saying all this stuff. I've asked for an MRI. There's something wrong with his brain. Has to be.'

'Is he lying to protect someone?' Rose asked.

Phyllis looked alert for the first time since Rose had joined her in the hospital café. 'That could be it. But who?'

'Who would Finn risk going to prison for?'

'Me, I suppose, but I didn't kill them.'

Rose hadn't totally dismissed her theory that the trust money was a motive for murder but Phyllis clearly adored her daughter and grandson. 'Who else?'

'Nobody.' She was silent for a while. Rose waited patiently. 'Well, I suppose Finn might have lied to protect his friends, but he's no longer close to them. They fell away when he couldn't speak.'

Rose scratched her head. 'Did Finn have a visitor yesterday, someone who might have put pressure on him to admit to a murder he didn't commit?'

'I wasn't here the whole time. I didn't see anyone. You could ask the nurses on duty.'

'I will. Where is Finn now?'

'Here. Handcuffed to the bed.'

'Phyllis, you must delay his departure from hospital for as long as possible. Get some more medical tests done. Whatever it takes. And I'll try to find enough evidence to prove Finn can't have lit the fire.'

'How on earth will you do that?'

'I have an idea. But first I need the keys to your house. And some instructions.'

32 MONTY

Ed is on a deck chair, enjoying the winter sun as if he were on a summer holiday in Spain. He took a long bath this morning and shaved away his raggedy beard. Even to my eyes, he looks younger. Panda, Summer, Jake and I are sprawled in the grass near him, also enjoying the sunny nook outside the tool shed. I hear the distinctive sound of Rose's car engine approaching and I race to greet her.

Rose runs to the back door and ducks into the house. I follow. She snatches my lead from the hook and clips it to my collar. She's like a Beagle following a scent – nothing will distract her. I sniff her jeans; she's been to the cop shop and the hospital, but why the urgency to go for a walk? Not that I'm complaining. I'm always up for a walk. Rose leads me to where Ed sits in the deckchair, his eyes closed.

'Ed. I need your help,' Rose says, waking Ed from his snooze with a jolt.

'Oh, it's you,' Ed says, raising his hand to shelter his eyes from the low sun. 'Help, you say? What's happened?'

'Finn has confessed to a murder I don't believe he committed. I have to find new evidence to prove Finn didn't light the fire. The farmhouse keys were never found and Finn saw someone running along the bridleway near the house when the fire had already started. My only hope is finding the keys and hoping they will lead us to the true killer.'

'You want to find a needle in a haystack, hey?'

'It's a huge task, I'll admit,' Rose says. 'Can you remember the boundaries of Toyne Fruits as it used to be? It's now a sprawling gated community and I have no idea where the farm used to sit.'

He struggles to sit up in the deckchair.

'I could work it out.' He sucks his lips into his mouth and rolls them over his toothless gums. 'If I remember rightly, a public bridleway marked the northern perimeter of the farm. It separated Toyne's farm from Mumford's. If the bridleway is still there, I can probably work out which properties now sit on what used to be farmland.'

'That's great, Ed. I have to go to Phyllis's house to collect a few things, then I'm picking up Ollie – the lad who assists me – then I'll be back. Can you be ready to leave in, say, an hour?'

'If I can get out of this awkward contraption, yes.'

Rose pulls Ed out of the deckchair. Ed is a little unstable. Rose hangs onto him until he stops swaying.

'I'll be back as soon as I can.' She turns to leave, then looks back. 'Kay kept old maps in her study. See what you can find. There may be one that shows the farm as it used to be.'

'Will do.'

I walk with Rose to the car with less enthusiasm than I felt earlier when I thought we were walking on the heath. A trip to Phyllis's house involves facing Tiffany the cat.

Rose drives to Nether Wallop and then we pause outside Phyllis's front gate. I sniff the air for Tiffany's corn chip scent which is strong. She's not far away. Rose takes from her handbag a key on a keyring that's shaped like a cat's head with sharp triangular ears. It is covered in Phyllis's scent. My tail droops. Does this mean that Phyllis isn't inside the house? This isn't going to be pleasant!

'Okay Monty. Tiffany may not take kindly to us turning up.'

Rose looks down at me and I look up at her and I swallow hard. My stomach makes gurgling sounds, much like when I've eaten a food scrap that's gone off and it gives me the runs. Is Rose about to do what I think she's about to do? Before I can bark a warning, she opens the creaking gate and calls out Tiffany's name.

The cats I know don't react to their name unless you are about to feed them and I'm pretty sure that Rose isn't about to do that. I sense Tiffany's presence and the fur down my spine sticks up like a hedgehog's prickles. She's watching us. I sniff the air, swivelling my head side to side, homing in on her exact location. I look up. There is a hanging basket of pink winter petunias and behind them is a mass of grey fur.

'Here, kitty!' Rose calls out. 'Phyllis gave me a key.' Rose jangles the key in the air. 'I have her permission to enter your home.' Then Rose mutters, 'I must be insane. I'm talking to a cat!'

Oh boy! This is getting worse by the second. There's a screeching *meeeeeow* and Tiffany leaps out of the hanging basket. She lands on the porch and arches her back, hissing.

Rose and I step back.

'You will not enter here!' Tiffany yowls.

'Nice kitty,' Rose says.

I step forward to protect Rose, although I keep a close eye on Tiffany's claws, which are extended and ready to swipe. I say, 'Phyllis has given Rose permission to enter.'

Tiffany swirls her tail around like a whip and snaps my cheek with it. 'Liar! My mistress would never allow strangers in her house.'

'Rose is trying to save Finn,' I bark. 'He's confessed to murder. Rose wants to prove he's innocent.'

Tiffany's paw extends so fast I only just rear back in time. Her claws narrowly miss my nose. 'Liar!'

Rose pulls me back by the lead. 'I don't think barking is helping, Monty.'

If I don't convince Tiffany we are friend and not foe, we are not going to get past her. I don't want to disobey Rose but, oddly, Tiffany is more likely to listen to me. Dogs are known for their truthfulness.

'It's true, I swear. Why else would we risk coming here? Rose is trying to save Finn from being sent to a children's home for criminals.'

Tiffany's arched spine straightens. 'One wrong move and I'll rip you to shreds.'

She steps out of the way and her claws retract.

Rose breathes a sigh of relief. 'I guess that means we can proceed.'

Rose shuffles around the cat, with me close at heel, and unlocks the front door. Tiffany darts past us, then sits on the bottom stair, tail writhing like a snake, her eyes fixed on Rose.

'Right,' Rose says. 'I need to collect three things. A spade that Tony used to use. A hairbrush Marie used to use. And Finn's boxing gloves. Let's start with the boxing gloves.'

Tiffany zips upstairs. We follow. She darts into Finn's room. Again, we follow. We find Tiffany behind the bedroom door and staring upwards. Hanging from a hook on the door is Finn's dressing gown and a pair of red boxing gloves. Am I imagining it, or is Tiffany helping us?

'Thank you, Tiffany,' Rose says.

She unhooks the boxing gloves. Yep, they definitely belong to Finn – they smell of his sweat and the metallic tang which comes from his guitar strings.

'Right. Now we need Marie's hairbrush.' Rose scratches her head.

Tiffany slinks behind the door and runs down the landing and into Phyllis's bedroom. Both Rose and I hesitate. This is the old lady's sanctuary, and it feels like we are invading it. Tiffany meows to us to come in, so I take the initiative and walk in first. The cat sits on an antique, dark wood chest of drawers with oblong brass handles. Her paw touches a drawer. Rose opens it. Inside it are a hand-held mirror, a couple of hairbrushes, a glass bowl filled with hair curlers and long plastic pins, and a porcelain jar with cotton wool balls inside. Tiffany rests a front paw on one of the hairbrushes.

'A Mason Pearson brush,' Rose says, observing Tiffany suspiciously.

I don't blame Rose for being careful. One swipe from that paw and Tiffany's claws will draw blood. Some long black hairs are caught in the bristles of the brush. Rose picks it up. 'This has to be Marie's,' Rose says, studying it.

I point my nose at the brush and inhale the scent. It's definitely not Phyllis's aroma. Instead, I detect watercolour paint, chocolate cake and the faint scent of silk.

Rose puts the brush in a resealable bag and drops it in her handbag. 'I guess the spade is in the shed.'

Tiffany darts down the stairs and out of the cat flap in the rear door. The lock has a key which Rose turns and we spot the cat licking her paws in the sun at the shed entrance. The path to the shed has disappeared beneath the tall grass and weeds which have taken over the garden. The shed is at the far corner and smells of treated wood. Rose pulls the shed door open. There's a lawnmower with a heavy roller that requires pushing, a gardening fork, one spade, several trowels and plenty of terracotta flowerpots. I sniff the spade – ripe strawberries, damp soil and a shaving foam with a strangely citrus smell.

'That's all I need,' Rose says, grabbing the shovel.

'Thank you,' I bark at Tiffany.

Rose is eager to get going. I'm surprised when Tiffany walks with us as we enter the house and Rose locks the back door.

'There's something you should know,' says Tiffany. 'Marie wanted to sell the farm and Tony didn't. They rowed about it a lot. I fear she was at her wit's end and thought she could burn down the house and force Tony to sell.'

I wag my tail. Tiffany really does want to help us.

'Rose has that theory too. But how does destroying the farmhouse force them to sell to Bassinger Homes?'

Tiffany walks with us to the front door.

'The house was under-insured,' Tiffany says. 'It meant that to rebuild the house would cost way more than the insurance company would pay. She and Mervyn wanted to force Tony's hand.'

'Do you think Finn helped his mum to light the fire?' I ask.

'Finn had nothing to do with it.'

'Hurry up, Monty!' Rose calls out. 'And stop barking at the cat!'

I risk asking another question. 'You believe Finn is protecting his mother's reputation?'

'Why else would he stay silent all this time?' Tiffany says. 'Although I never did understand why Marie used petrol. She didn't like Tony keeping cans of it in the barn. She complained it was too risky, especially with a kid about. A simple match dropped on their sofa cushions would have been enough to start a fire and would have given them time to get out.'

I wonder if Marie had someone helping her. Someone who was happy to use petrol.

We step onto the porch. Tiffany jumps outside too, before Rose shuts and deadlocks the front door. 'Whatever you may think of me, I love that boy,' Tiffany says. 'You have to save him, Monty.'

Rose has to drag me up the path to the car because all I can do is stare at Tiffany. Perhaps I have been wrong about her. Everything she has done is to protect the hoomans she loves.

33 ROSE

In his Crossland X, Malcolm followed Rose's car to Meadowbank Close. Rose hadn't wanted to ask him for yet another favour but Ollie phoned the vet hospital before Rose, who was driving, could stop him.

Rose glanced at his car in her rear-view mirror wondering what she had done to deserve such a good friend. Seated next to Malcolm was Ed, with Jake on his lap. Malcolm laughed at something Ed said. Just seeing him laugh made her smile too.

'Can't wait to use them metal detectors,' Ollie said, pushing his glasses up the bridge of his nose. 'Never used one before.'

Monty poked his nose out of one of the back windows, his ears flapping, the fur on his back vibrating. Panda, head out of the other open window, was taking bites of air, her thick coat shimmering in the winter sun. Rose hoped that Monty, Panda and Jake would act as sniffer dogs.

Ollie went on, 'Malcolm knows so many people. Managed to get the metal detectors dirt cheap from a guy who has goats. Turns out Malcolm is their vet. The farmer runs the local metal detecting club. You know, maybe I should become a vet instead of a detective. I like animals.'

Rose snuck a look at the seventeen-year-old next to her. He had come a long way in the last year. When she first met him, he had no qualifications and he was involved in a bad gang. Now he was taking eight GCSEs and kept much better company.

'You can do anything you set your mind to, Ollie. Do your GCSEs and then decide what you want to be. You have the makings of a great detective, but I can also see you as a vet. You could ask Malcolm for some work experience, if you like.' Although Rose had to admit she would miss Ollie's company terribly.

'Nah, I like doing stuff with you.'

'What about the classes you're missing today?' Rose had hesitated about asking Ollie to join her, but she needed as much help as possible, and Ollie would never forgive her if he missed out on searching for an important bit of evidence.

'All good,' Ollie said. 'Told them I wasn't well.'

Rose slowed the car through Nether Wallop and past St Bartholomew's church. Rose hadn't even had the chance to speak with the vicar's secret girlfriend. Finding the missing house keys was her best option right now.

'So what's the plan?' Ollie asked. 'That posh housing estate is huge. Where do we start?'

'The person who lit the fire would want to get rid of the keys as soon as possible, in case they were stopped by the police. They could have done this on the Toyne's land, along the bridleway where they were seen running, or on Mervyn Mumford's land. I think it's least likely to be on Mumford land, because if the killer ran that way, they were heading away from Nether Wallop and Little Wallop, where all the suspects lived at the time.'

'Unless the killer is Mervyn or Alfie,' Ollie said.

'True. Still, I think it's more likely to be hidden on the Toyne's farmland or the bridleway.'

'Okay, so what's first?'

'We see what we can find on what used to be Toyne's farmland.'

Rose turned into Meadowbank Close's private drive. As usual, the uniformed security guard bustled out of his hut next to the boom gates and made a note of her number plate on his clipboard. Malcolm pulled up behind them.

'I'll need to do some sweet-talking. Here goes,' Rose said, stepping out of the car.

'Hello, Aaron.'

'Hello, Rose, nice to see you again. Any luck solving the case?'

'Well, the case is why I'm here. I need your help, actually.'

Aaron Brown stood a little taller and tried to pull in his midriff that was bulging over his belt. 'Help solving the case?'

'Exactly.'

'Well, I've always fancied myself as a detective. What can I do?'

Rose could feel Malcolm, Ed, Ollie and the dogs watching her. She cleared her throat.

'I believe a critical piece of evidence is buried right here in Meadowbank Close and I need your help to find it.'

'What evidence?'

'Can I trust you, Aaron? This must stay between you and me.'

'You can trust me. I'm a security guard after all.'

'Okay. We have to find a set of house keys. I think the killer buried them or threw them away on land that used to belong to Toyne Fruits, which, as you know, is now part of Meadowbank Close.'

'Where in the close?' Aaron asked.

'It will be on or near the land that used to be Toyne Fruit Farm. We need your help approaching the house owners who now live on that land to get their permission to use metal detectors.'

Aaron sucked at his teeth. 'I'll get fired if I do that. I'm supposed to keep the riffraff out, not help you dig up their gardens.'

Rose wouldn't give up. Without Aaron, the only area they could search was along the bridlepath, which was public land. Ed had found an old map in Kay's study that showed the farm's boundaries, which he'd transferred onto a map of Meadowbank Close. A total of ten houses fell within that boundary.

'Aaron, this is a murder investigation. If you help me solve this, your name will be all over the news. You'll be famous.'

Aaron's eyes lit up. 'All right. What do I say to the house owners?'

'Tell them that the Nosy Detectives are investigating a double homicide. We believe a set of keys may have been buried on their land five years ago and we want their permission to use metal detectors. Anything we find that doesn't pertain to the case is theirs to keep.'

Aaron scratched his belly through his shirt. 'If the keys were buried before this place became a building site, won't the keys have been built over?'

'Maybe. But we have a fifty-fifty chance of finding them.' It was probably way lower than that, but she had to make Aaron believe that putting his neck on the line was worth it. 'This could be your moment of fame, Aaron.'

Aaron looked up the lane at the houses he was paid a pittance to protect, then back at Rose. 'I'll do it. I'm fed up with this shitty job anyway. But I can't leave the gate unattended. I have to call Barry and ask him to come in.'

Rose didn't have time to wait for Barry, even if Barry was willing to come in on his day off. 'We can't wait for Barry. We have a deadline to solve the case. Can you leave the boom gates open?'

'I can't do that.'

'Okay, I have an idea. Do you happen to keep a spare work shirt with you?'

'Yes, why?'

'Can you hang on a moment?'

'Sure.'

Rose jogged over to Malcolm's car and explained the problem. 'Ed, how do you fancy playing security guard for a few hours? All you have to do is jot down the vehicle number plates and open the boom gates.'

'To be honest, I'm relieved you asked me that. I'm not sure me legs are up to traipsing around with metal detectors. As long as I can sit down, I'm happy.'

Ed changed into the white shirt, donned the guard's black jacket and clutched a clipboard. He then sat in the hut, looking every bit a security guard. Rose made sure each dog had sniffed Tony's shovel, Marie's hairbrush and Finn's boxing gloves. If the keys had been buried without any covering, the scents of Finn, Tony and Marie would have faded long ago. But if they found the keys wrapped in plastic or another material, the dogs could tell them if they were the right ones.

Aaron got into his white Suzuki and led them to the first house on Ed's map. Rose accompanied Aaron as he explained the situation to the elderly couple. They readily agreed, as long as they didn't dig up their spring bulbs. Malcolm and Ollie started at that house with a metal detector each. Jake remained in Malcolm's car – Rose couldn't risk the dogs upsetting the residents. The dogs were to be used once they had found something promising for them to sniff.

Rose followed Aaron to the next house but no-one answered the doorbell. Disappointed they moved onto house number three. A young mother with a toddler was reluctant to oblige but when Rose assured her that anything they found in the ground, other than the keys, would be handed to her, she acquiesced. Monty and Panda stayed in her car, on standby. Monty whimpered, clearly not happy.

The morning passed quickly. Between them, they had used a metal detector at seven out of the ten houses that used to be on Toyne Fruits' land. Nobody was home at two of the houses and when Aaron phoned them, they didn't pick up. The last remaining house was the biggest and belonged to Sasha Bassinger. Rose was dreading knocking on her door. Nevertheless, she and Aaron did so. Sasha opened the door in a gym top and lycra pants.

'Oh it's you,' she said to Rose. To Aaron she said, 'And what do you want? I'm doing Zumba on Zoom.'

Aaron told her why they were there.

Sasha laughed. 'Are you nuts! Go away. Both of you!'

Sasha began to close the door.

'Mrs Bassinger,' Malcolm shouted from the road. He waved at her from his vehicle.

'Oh, Malcolm.' Sasha grinned. 'What are you doing here?' She beckoned him over.

Malcolm looked nervously at Ollie and then joined Rose and Aaron on the doorstep. 'Do come in,' Sasha cooed to Malcolm. 'My darling cats will be so happy to see you.'

Was Rose imagining it, or did Sasha flutter her eyelashes at him?

'Mrs Bassinger, I…I'd love to another time, but this search for the keys is vitally important. Can you please allow us to use our metal detectors?'

'Oh Malcolm, you know I would if I could, but my partner would be upset if I allowed you in. He's a very private man.'

'We won't enter your house, Mrs Bassinger,' Malcolm said, 'just your garden, if you don't mind.'

'I have to say no.' The gushing smile was fading.

Malcolm dragged his fingers through his thick black hair. 'You're a long-standing client and I'd be very happy to waive any vet bills for the next six months if you would give us access to your property for, say, twenty minutes?'

Sasha licked her lips. 'What a lovely offer and I accept. Your friends can use their metal detectors but you, Malcolm, must sit with me and have a cup of coffee.' She took his hand and led him inside, closing the door behind her.

Rose and Aaron walked to her car to pick up the metal detectors. 'He's a brave lad,' Aaron said. 'That woman eats men for breakfast.'

Rose felt a stab of jealousy. She didn't like the idea of Sasha Bassinger flirting with Malcolm.

He's not my boyfriend, she told herself.

And then a little voice in her head said, *Maybe he should be?*

34 MONTY

From where I sit in Rose's car with Panda, I hear an occasional beep from the metal detectors and hooman chatter. I wish I was out there with them. Aaron, Ollie and Rose have so far found nails, scraps of corrugated iron, a key to a window lock, and even a gold wedding band, but not the keys we are looking for.

Bored, I poke my head out of the open window and see Rose handing Sasha the wedding ring they found. Sasha's expression is sour, and she looks more annoyed than thankful. Malcolm almost runs out of the door, looking flustered, and heads for his car. Sasha waves goodbye to him with a cheeky smile.

'Are you all right, mate?' Ollie asks, leaning against the Crossland's bonnet.

He doesn't look all right to me.

'She's terrifying,' Malcolm says. 'I spent the whole time trying to put some distance between us but she kept fondling my hair and telling me I was a strapping man.'

Ollie laughs. 'Strapping! Blimey. She's got the hots for you.'

'And don't I know it!'

Rose, Aaron, Ollie and Malcolm huddle together in conversation.

'It looks like it's the bridleway next.' Rose lays out a map on the car bonnet. 'The bridleway extends three miles. This half-mile section here used to border Toyne Fruits. On the other side of it was Mumford's farm. It makes sense that if an intruder lit the fire, they would run along this path until they reached Nether Wallop, here.' Rose points at the map. 'I suggest we start from where the bridleway begins at Nether Wallop.'

'What if we find nothing there, either?' Ollie asks.

'Well, by then it will be lunchtime. We'll go to the pub and come up with a new plan.' Rose is using her upbeat voice but worry emanates from her skin like heat.

Ollie's face lights up at the thought of food.

Me too!

This time, us dogs lead the search. We are now in the section of bridleway that runs between what was Toyne land on one side and Mumford land on the other. If the keys were thrown into bushes years ago, our noses can find them without having to use the metal detectors. Panda, Jake and I have our noses to the ground, vacuuming up smells as we go. Our job is made harder by the strong aroma of horse. The bridleway is lined with hedgerows, bramble bushes and trees but the path itself is sloshy with loose mud that has been churned up by hooves. Rose uses her metal detector on the right-hand side of the path and Malcolm uses his on the left. Ollie and Aaron come up the rear and use their metal detectors on the actual path.

I look behind me at Jake. He is moving slower – he's getting tired. Panda is still buzzing with energy. She sniffs in urgent, short bouts, then lifts her head, runs forward and then back skittishly. So far, the metal detectors have beeped at lots of useless pieces of metal, including a rusted bicycle and a shopping trolley, but no keys. Rose slows her pace and I sense her confidence in her plan is waning.

'Maybe I should get back to work?' Aaron says, sounding deflated.

'You might as well hang on a few more minutes,' Rose says. 'You could miss the moment we find them.'

Aaron shrugs and shuffles along behind us. Even Ollie is quiet.

'We could show the dogs the scent items again,' Malcolm suggests. 'They need constant reminding.'

Malcolm has the spade with him. Ollie carries the hairbrush in his pocket and the boxing gloves are draped over his shoulder.

Ollie calls me, Panda and Jake over and we sniff each item again. Then we set off once more.

My paws slosh through puddles and mud squelches between my toes. My nose stays just above the ground.

'Too many smells,' Panda whimpers.

I bark back. 'Just try to focus on the three things we sniffed.'

Jake sticks his head into a bramble bush and comes up with a McDonald's burger box, which still smells of the burger it once contained.

'Leave it, Jake,' Rose says. 'You'll get a special meal when you reach home.'

Jake reluctantly drops it.

Ahead, two horseback riders are approaching, and we all step out of the way. Their hooves splash through puddles and kick up small stones. One of the horses tramples an area of tall grass and low-lying ferns to one side of the path. The horse's tail swooshes, and the rider thanks us. Just then, I smell Tony's scent. As soon as the horses are out of the way, I dash across to the place where the ferns are snapped and compressed.

'Do you smell it?' I bark at the other dogs excitedly.

We all have our noses to the ground. Tails wag.

'Yes,' Jake says. 'I smell Tony and Marie. Them keys are here somewhere.'

Panda dashes about in circles. 'Yes, me too!'

'I think they've found something,' Rose says, running her metal detector over the area.

The machine gives a long, high-pitched beep.

I start to dig where the smell is strongest. Panda joins me. She is fast, like a squirrel. Jake does his best to help us, but it's hard for him to dig with only one back leg to balance on.

The hoomans crowd around and watch.

Soon we have cleared the ferns and grass. The hole in the dark soil is growing wider. Our paws dig in a rapid blur. The hole is as deep as two dog bowls piled on top of each other. Every so often I stick my snout in the hole and inhale. Tony's and Marie's scent grows stronger. There's another scent that I find distracting.

'Something smells bad,' Jake comments.

'Petrol,' I say.

My paw snags on a plastic bag with something inside it.

'Wait!' Rose says, taking me by the collar and pulling me back. 'Malcolm, can you pull Jake and Panda away?' Both dogs resist but in the end they comply and sit at the edge of the hole, panting from their exertion.

'Monty! Stay!'

I don't want to stay. I want to keep digging. But I stand patiently, tongue lolling, and watch her pull on latex gloves. She kneels down. 'Well, it's not a key, but it must smell important. Ollie, can you video this on your phone. If this is evidence, we need to record the discovery.'

'It could just be rags,' Aaron says, scratching his belly.

'Maybe, but the dogs went ballistic, which means it probably smells of either Tony, Marie or Finn.'

Ollie films Rose as she gently scrapes damp soil away from the object in the hole, revealing cloth inside a clear plastic bag. The smell of petrol is coming through a hole in the bag. Rose tugs at the bag and it comes free from the dirt. She lays it on some grass.

The transparent bag is tied at one end in a tight knot. She turns the bag around and we all see that it is a pair of badly burned jeans. I can't hold back any longer and lunge at the jeans, nostrils pulsing. It's difficult to bypass the intense petrol stink but I keep inhaling. There's a faint smell of aftershave and Marmite, which Rose puts on her toast in the mornings, oh and a strange skin smell.

I lift my head. 'The killer wore these jeans,' I bark.

Jake barks too. 'Petrol!'

Panda squeals, as if she's been kicked. She darts away and hides behind Malcolm's legs.

'The poor dog's terrified,' Malcolm says, stroking Panda's head.

'Aaron, can you run your metal detector over the bag but please don't touch it.'

'Sure.' He lifts his metal detector and holds it above the bag. The detector emits an ear-piercing screech. 'Definitely metal in there somewhere.'

Rose sits back on her haunches. 'This might be nothing or everything. We need to be absolutely certain these jeans are linked to the double homicide before we hand them over to the police.'

Rose runs her hand along the length of the bag. 'There's something hard in here. I'll have to widen the hole.' She tears at the plastic and slides her gloved fingers over the jeans and into a pocket. She tries another pocket. This time, she pulls out four small, flat, identical keys. 'Oh my God!'

'Are they what I think they are?' Malcolm asks.

'It's possible, yes. The front and back doors had mortice locks and the key was the same for both – a slim, small Chubb key.

'That's a Chubb key,' Malcolm says. 'Perhaps the others were spares?'

We all stare at the keys. The smell of mint, Marmite and burnt skin is blowing my senses. I bark, 'The killer took these keys!'

Rose looks at me and then back at the keys and burnt jeans. 'Please keep filming while I phone the police,' Rose says.

Ollie nods.

Rose calls Leach's mobile phone. It goes to voicemail.

'I think we've found the missing keys to the Toyne farmhouse. They were buried under ferns on one side of the public bridleway that runs behind what used to be the Toynes' farm. There's also a burnt pair of adult jeans. Please call me ASAP.'

Rose stares at her phone as if trying to decide what to do next.

'I'll call the nick.' Rose dials and is told that Leach, Pearl and Varma are unavailable. She leaves a message, explaining what they have found. Exasperated, she calls Varma's mobile phone. He answers.

'Rose, can I call you back?' Varma sounds flustered. Varma *never* sounds flustered. Something is wrong.

'What's happened?' Rose asks.

'Finn tried to take his own life.'

35 ROSE

Rose ran through the hospital's main entrance, up the fire stairs and burst through the ward's double doors. She found chaos. Outside Finn's room, a nurse, a doctor, Phyllis and Leach were arguing, voices raised, faces flushed. Standing nearby was Pearl, who leaned against the wall, his arms folded. She couldn't see DI Varma.

The attempted suicide of a minor charged with murder was a big issue for the police officer in charge and that officer was DCI Leach. It was also a big issue for the hospital.

Rose's heart pounded. All she cared about was Finn. She ran down the corridor, determined to get some answers. Leach saw her coming and said something to Pearl who stepped into the middle of the corridor to block her path.

'Go home, Rose. This is none of your business,' Pearl said.

'Is Finn alive?'

'Yes.'

'Can I see him?'

'No, now go home.'

Phyllis screamed at Leach. 'Stay away from him!' She turned to the doctor. 'Tell him! Tell him to leave Finn alone. He's in a fragile state.'

'Detective,' the doctor said, 'I must insist that the patient is given twenty-four hours to recover. He can't be moved or see anybody but his grandmother.'

'Phyllis!' shouted Rose. 'I came as fast as I could. What happened?'

Phyllis smacked Pearl on the back. 'Get out of the way, you oaf!'

Pearl glared at the old woman but when Leach nodded at him, he allowed Rose to pass.

'He tried to hang himself, poor love,' Phyllis said. 'Thank goodness the rail came out of the wall.'

'How long was he without oxygen?' Rose asked.

'We're unsure,' said the doctor, 'We need to monitor him for signs of brain damage.'

It was like being hit by a truck. Finn had been through so much already, and now this?

'You drove him to this,' Phyllis accused the DCI, stabbing her finger at his barrel chest. 'I'm going to the press! I'll have you sacked!' Then she rounded on the nurse. 'And what the hell were you doing? You were supposed to look after him!'

Monty was waiting in the car, guarding the plastic bag containing the jeans and four keys. Rose hadn't wanted to remove the evidence from the bridleway, but she couldn't leave it there to be trampled by horses. Nor could she expect Malcolm, Ollie or Aaron to stand there for goodness knew how long and guard it. She had placed the evidence in her car, asked Malcolm to see to it that everyone who needed to get home got home, thanked everyone, and had driven to the hospital just as fast as she could.

Everyone at the hospital was tense. Now was not the time to tell Leach that she had evidence that might prove Finn's innocence. Of course, until the forensic team had looked at the bag's contents, nobody knew who had handled the keys and jeans. One thing Rose was certain of was that the jeans were adult size.

However, she wanted to pass on the new evidence as soon as possible. The only detective who might be willing to listen to her was DS Varma.

'Where is Kamlesh?' Rose asked.

'At the nick,' Pearl snapped. 'It's time to leave, Rose.'

Rose left. She would drive to the nick and hand everything to Varma for forensic testing.

Monty had managed to steam up the car windows with his heavy panting, but the evidence bag was still there in the footwell of her car.

'Good dog!'

Rose set off for Geldeford Police HQ. When she got there, she automatically drove around the back to the police officers' private car park where she used to park. Realising her mistake, she carried on down the street and luckily found a one-hour parking spot. That should be enough time to hand the evidence to Varma.

Rose pulled on latex gloves, placed the evidence in a shopping bag, told Monty that she wouldn't be long, and set off. An unmarked police car she recognised drove past and she caught a glimpse of Pearl in the driver's seat. He entered the police car park. This didn't change Rose's plan. She would present the evidence to DI Varma. But she would wait five minutes. She really didn't want to bump into Pearl.

Rose shivered in the cold and when five minutes was up, she followed the path to the front of the building. She stopped in her tracks. There stood Pearl, a lit cigarette in his hand. He was laughing with his smoking companion – Tucker Hughes.

What was Tucker Hughes doing with Dave Pearl? Rose had forgotten that she was seeing him that night. To be honest, going on a date was the last thing she felt like doing after the shocking news of Finn's attempted suicide.

Something about their body language suggested they were friends. Rose ducked behind a parked vehicle. Tucker hadn't mentioned that he was mates with people from the Murder Squad, where he knew that she used to work. Her stomach squirmed. She had a bad feeling about this. She crept closer, using the parked vehicles to hide her presence.

'You're such a charmer!' Pearl said.

'It was too easy,' Tucker said, smirking. 'She's gagging for it.'

'Watch her, mate. She's a troublemaker. Just find out what she thinks she knows that we don't. Now that the boy tried to top himself, the commander is all over this case like a rash.'

'Don't worry, mate. She'll be putty in my hands.'

Pearl snickered. 'You dirty dog!'

Rose swallowed the bile creeping up her throat. Tucker didn't fancy her. It was a trick and Pearl must have put him up to it. It didn't take an Einstein to know she would want to talk to the case's fire scene investigator. How could she have been so stupid? Why would a good-looking man like Tucker Hughes want to date a plain-Jane like her? She wrestled with her hurt and fury, and fury won.

She came out of her hiding place and, walking tall, made a beeline for them. Tucker saw her first. He stared at her like a fox caught in a hen-house. He nudged Pearl, who smirked.

'Tucker, I should have known you were friends with Dave. You're both lying, vain bastards!'

'You can't talk to me like that,' Pearl blurted.

'Shut up, Dave. Does Tucker know that this is all about your dented ego? Does he know that when I started work here, you asked me on a date, and I said no!'

'You're talking shit,' Pearl said.

'You did everything you could to sabotage my career, but do you know what I've realised? I'll always be a better detective than you because I care. I don't do it to show off to my mates. I do it because I want justice for the victims and closure for their loved ones.'

She turned her back on the both of them and strode away, head held high. There was no snide come-back from either man, and when she reached the car, adrenaline powering through her veins, she felt a little glow of pride that she had finally stood up to Pearl.

It was only when she sat behind the steering wheel that she realised she hadn't given Varma the evidence. She didn't dare go into the police station after her outburst. She tried phoning Varma one more time, with the intent of asking him to meet her in the street. No answer.

As her heart rate slowed and the adrenaline melted away, she felt wrung out.

'I've had enough. I'm going home. What difference does one day make?'

Before she drove home, she dialled Phyllis.

'Phyllis, can you talk? It's important.'

'Finn's having an MRI. I'm so worried.'

'I want you to know that I think I found the farmhouse keys today. Chubb keys for a mortice lock.'

'Yes, yes, it was a mortice lock. Where did you find them?'

'The bridleway that used to border the farm. And there's a pair of jeans buried with it. They're badly burned.'

'You think they're the killer's?'

'Possibly.'

'Have you told the police?'

'I have the evidence with me. I'll hand it over tomorrow morning. I thought you might like some good news for a change. But keep it to yourself, okay?'

36 MONTY

I am in the garden with the other dogs trying to work out who the jeans belong to. The mood is glum – we are all worried about Finn. Ed is napping on the sofa in the lounge room, the TV on low, and Rose hasn't come home yet.

'Finn must be so unhappy,' Panda says with a huge sigh. 'All those things I said about him. I called him mean. I am a very bad dog.'

'You're not a bad dog, Panda,' Summer says, who is lying on the lawn next to me. 'Try not to judge yourself so harshly. The best way to help Finn is to make sure the real killer is caught.'

I turn my muzzle towards Summer. My mother is very wise. 'You're right. Moping around like this isn't doing any good. The problem is I can't make up my mind who the killer is. Any ideas?'

'I'll bet two dog biscuits it's that Alfie boy,' Jake says. 'He's got a nasty streak in him.'

'Panda? What do you think?' I ask.

She scratches an ear ferociously. 'I don't know. What about Reverend Mabey? I heard Marie arguing with him in the barn that night.'

I'd forgotten about the vicar.

'What do *you* think, Monty?' Summer asks.

'Tiffany thinks Marie and Mervyn Mumford planned to burn down the farmhouse so that Tony would have to sell it. Perhaps the fire got out of control?'

'Tiffany! You believe a cat?' Jake asks.

'I think she was trying to help.'

Jake grunts. 'Has she bewitched you?'

'No, Jake. She loves Finn and she doesn't want him taking the blame.'

'Well, now I've heard everything,' Jake rests his jowls on a paw.

'Sam Chang's mum told Rose the same thing,' I say. 'Both Marie and Mervyn desperately wanted Bassinger to buy the farm. The question is how far were they prepared to go to make this happen? Would they set fire to the place to force Tony's hand?'

'Tell me again about the jeans you found,' Summer says.

'The problem was the petrol,' I say. 'It's such an overpowering smell. I thought I detected aftershave, Marmite and a strange skin smell.'

'You think it was aftershave and not a female's perfume?' Summer asks.

I look at Jake. 'What do you think?'

'No idea, mate. I can't tell the difference,' Jake says.

Panda scratches an ear. 'The pig farmer who left me at the pound used to go out with his wife to a restaurant every now and again. He normally smelt of pigs and manure, but when he went to the restaurant that changed to a citrus and bergamot smell that tickled my nose. The fragrance on the jeans smelt a bit like that, so I think it was a male scent.'

'And what do you think the peculiar skin smell is?' Summer asks.

'That's a hard one,' I say. 'A bit like hooman skin that turns red with too much sun.'

'Have you met anyone who smells like that?' Summer asks.

In the last few days I have sniffed so many suspects, I am quite muddled. I stand up. 'I need my bed to jog my memory.'

I trot into the kitchen and bury my nose in my dog bed. Every person I have sniffed carries a unique scent which rubs off on me. When I lie down on my bed, some of that smell transfers to the bed cover. I start sniffing at one corner and detect Phyllis, Tiffany and Finn. Next Malcolm, Panda, Jake and Ed. I move past Big Man Joe, Leach and Pearl and pause as I inhale the smell of Sasha Bassinger and Frances Buttermere. I wasn't with Rose when she interviewed Violet Fox about

Jimmy, or when she met Sam Chang and his mum, Daphne, but some of their scents have rubbed off on Rose and they, in turn, rubbed off on me when Rose hugged me at home. None of these hoomans smell of Marmite, aftershave and strange skin.

My nose has reached the middle of my dog bed. Tammy's fragrance is nothing like the one on the buried jeans, but Alfie's scent makes me pause. If I ignore his other smells – limes, hair gel and curry – there is an underlying aroma of sunburn. I pull my head back. I already know that he trashed Ed's caravan, and it is his piss on Ed's bed. But could Alfie, at ten years old, have lit the fire that killed Finn's parents?

I have to be sure.

I sniff the exact spot on the fabric again until I have the complex mix of aromas locked inside my mind and then shift my nose across the bed. I find Mervyn Mumford's scent, which stinks of pub food and wood smoke from a log fire. I push my nose deep into the bed. A yeasty smell, not dissimilar to the smell on the jeans. And then another smell that I can't work out, a bit like the one when Rose gets her hair caught inside the hairdryer.

The sound of Rose's car arriving home has me darting out the back door and down the side passage to greet her. I bark at her, desperate to know if Finn is going to survive. Panda and Jake join in the barking.

'Quiet, all of you.'

In her hand is the plastic bag with the jeans and keys and we all follow her into the house, where Summer waits patiently. Rose gives her a pat.

Ed calls out from the lounge room and Rose leaves the plastic bag on the kitchen table. Rose looks weary. She sits in an armchair and tells Ed about Finn's condition and how he tried to hang himself and how the boy might have brain damage. I hang my head. Panda whines.

'What did them coppers say about the evidence you found?'

'Ah,' Rose says. 'I didn't quite get around to handing it in. I was a bit distracted. You see, I was going on a date tonight with the fire scene investigator. I thought he liked me. Turns out he was doing it because DI Pearl wanted him to pump me for information about the case.'

'What a nasty thing to do,' Ed said. 'You're better off without men like that.'

'You're right. I just feel so stupid.'

I lick the back of her hand. I want Rose to know she's a very clever hooman.

'His loss, Rose,' Ed says. 'You're a lovely woman. Pretty, clever, kind. You deserve someone special.'

'Oh Ed, you are sweet. But I don't think I'm destined for love. And besides, I'm happy with my doggie companions. Fancy a cuppa?'

'That would be lovely.'

I follow Rose into the kitchen.

From the hole in the skirting board Betty squeaks, 'Rotten scoundrel! I'll find him, I'll bite his ankles.'

Rose makes two cups of tea and takes them into the lounge room.

While she's gone, Betty squeezes out of her hole and announces, 'Rose is always unlucky in love. It's time we did something to fix it.'

'Maybe when this case is over,' I say.

'What could be more urgent than match-making?' Betty asks, coyly.

I hear a big vehicle entering the drive. We seldom have visitors, so I am instantly on high alert.

'Jake!' I bark, and he runs into the kitchen.

'What's up?' Jake asks.

'Guard the evidence. Don't let anyone touch it,' I say.

Jake positions himself between the back door and the table. Panda crawls under the table and lies there, shivering with fear.

Rose comes into the kitchen. 'I wonder who that is.'

The back door swings wide open and there stand Mervyn and Alfie Mumford.

37 ROSE

Monty's barking was loud and frantic. He only barked like that when he sensed a threat. The warm tea in her stomach churned.

'Get your dog away from me!' Mumford shouted from her kitchen doorway.

'Monty!' she called, but he ignored her.

Monty's eyes were locked on Alfie and his teeth were bared. His tail was curled over his back and his stance was wide. It was a defensive posture she'd seen before, and her dog's fear made Rose very nervous. Was he defending Ed from Alfie? What were the Mumfords doing here?

Alfie backed out of the door, clearly frightened, but his father stood his ground.

Rose reached for Monty's collar and drew him back a few steps. But she wasn't going to dismiss her dog's instinctive reaction to the new arrivals. Time and time again Monty had proved to be spot-on about people, and he clearly found Alfie a threat.

Now her dog was under control, Alfie's arrogance returned. He patted his hair into position and swaggered into her kitchen. 'You should muzzle that thing!'

'He's guarding my home. Why are you here, Mr Mumford?'

'I want you to leave me and my son alone. We are law abiding citizens. You must stop this vendetta against my son. He's a good boy.'

Monty growled. Clearly, he didn't agree.

Rose guessed that Joe Salisbury had paid them a visit about the vandalism of Ed's home. Joe could be quite intimidating in his police uniform, even if he was a total sweetie at heart.

'Really?' Rose said. 'Alfie's a good boy to piss on an old man's bed, is he? He's a good boy to destroy the few possessions Ed has?' Rose looked at Alfie. 'I'm watching you, Alfie. Try anything like that again and I'll make sure you are charged.'

'Yeah, right!' Alfie sneered. 'Nobody believed you this time, and they won't next time.'

Mumford smacked Alfie across the back of his head.

'Shut up!' Mumford put on a fake smile. 'Rose, please be reasonable. All this rubbish about Alfie vandalising the tramp's home has to stop. I was called in to the headmaster's office today. Somehow he had got wind of it. I can't allow you to jeopardize my son's future.'

'I'm not the one jeopardising his future, Mr Mumford. If you turn a blind eye to what he and Tammy did to Ed's caravan, you're effectively telling him it's okay to break the law. What might he do next?'

'Oh for heaven's sake. What utter crap.'

Alfie had edged closer to the table. 'Dad. Look!'

Monty was straining to get away from Rose's grip. She could feel growls vibrating through his body.

'So it's true,' Mumford said. 'You found the keys to Toyne Farm, and something else by the looks of it.'

How could they know that? Rose thought.

Only DS Varma and Phyllis knew what she had found on the bridleway. Rose sighed. Of course. Lord knows why Phyllis would tell Mumford, but the news had reached him. Why hadn't Phyllis kept the discovery to herself as Rose had asked?

Rose released Monty's collar and positioned herself between Alfie and the table. Monty stood beside her.

'If new evidence has come to light,' Rose said, 'that's a matter for the police.'

Mumford tried to take a closer look. Jake let rip with a ferocious growl.

'This house is full of dangerous dogs.' Mumford stepped back. 'I'm going to the police. I'll have them destroyed.'

'It's time you got off my property.'

Ed appeared at the doorway, no doubt woken from his nap by the barking and raised voices. 'You,' he said pointing at Alfie! 'You're always tormenting me!'

'Shut up, old man!' snapped Mumford.

'I will not!' Ed said. 'This boy trashed my home. He's shouted obscenities at me. I'd recognise him anywhere.'

Mumford said, 'Alfie, let's go.'

'But Dad!'

'Now, Alfie.'

Rose helped Ed to a chair and shut the back door. Tyres skidded on gravel as Mumford and his son sped away. Jake sat at Ed's feet, panting.

'Good boy, Jake,' Ed said, stroking his dog.

'Thank you for protecting me.' Rose hugged Monty until her heartrate settled. 'Ed, I have to go back to the nick.' She scooped up the evidence bag. 'Too many people know about it. Lock the door behind me, will you, and keep the dogs inside?'

Monty followed her to the door. 'All right, Monty, you can come with me. Ed has more than enough protection.'

38 MONTY

The tension in the house tonight is as taut as a rubber band.

Since Rose handed in the jeans and keys to DI Varma and returned home, everyone in the cottage is on edge.

'Boys like Alfie go through life causing nothing but pain to others,' Ed says, slurping loudly as he eats his minestrone soup. 'They trample on the small people and get away with it. Well, I'm not having it. I'm going to the cop shop tomorrow and demanding they arrest that boy.'

Rose toys with her soup. 'I'll come with you, if you like.' Her voice is flat.

Ed studies her face. 'You worried about Finn?'

'Yes,' Rose says. 'I spoke to Phyllis. She says the MRI doesn't indicate brain damage, which is good news.' Rose puts the spoon down on the table. 'I guess I'm annoyed at her for telling people about what we found on the bridleway. She boasted to the vicar that I'd solved the case, when I haven't, and you know how village gossip spreads. Those keys and jeans could belong to someone totally unrelated to the Toyne fire. Unless the forensics team confirms the keys are indeed the farmhouse keys and they can identify from DNA and fingerprints the person who took them, we may be no further ahead than we were yesterday.'

Rose picks up some bread and butter, dunks it in her soup and chews unenthusiastically.

'A good night's sleep will do you a power of good,' Ed says. 'When you've finished your soup, you go up to bed. I'll clear up here.'

'Thanks, Ed.' Rose gets up. 'I'm not that hungry.'

She pours the remainder of the minestrone soup down the sink. I am disappointed that she hasn't poured it into the dog bowls, but I guess she's distracted tonight.

Rose uses the long black key in the back door to lock it. She must be scared because I hardly ever see Rose do this. 'The front door can't open – it's warped with damp and age – but I'm locking the back door tonight.'

'Right you are,' Ed says.

Panda is under the table and even though she is totally still, her eyes dart around the kitchen and her ears are pricked. Summer lies on her dog bed. By now she is normally asleep, but tonight her eyes are open and alert. I follow Rose to the stairs and watch her climb them. I want to stay close to her. I lift a paw onto the first stair. Rose looks over her shoulder and tells me to stay. I lie down at the foot of the stairs and listen to Rose brushing her teeth and the creak of her bed as she gets into it.

In the kitchen, Ed does the washing up. I smell brandy, then Ed takes a glass of it upstairs. Jake joins me at the foot of the stairs and collapses next to me with a loud sigh.

The house goes dark as the landing light is switched off.

Through the hall window I watch clouds blow across the half-moon. The wind howls through the trees and whistles under the tiny gap beneath the front door. Jake starts snoring but I can't sleep. Panda's claws are tap-tapping across the linoleum floor – she can't sleep either. I get up and head for the kitchen and push my snout into the hole in the skirting board in the hope that Betty is home.

Panda watches me.

Betty wriggles out of the hole and sits in front of me, her whiskers twitching.

'There's something in the air,' Betty says. 'Something bad. Even the birds sense it.'

'Can you keep me awake, Betty? I must guard the house.'

'I'll keep you company, my friend. It's our job to keep Rose safe. We make a good team, don't we?'

'Yes, we do. Tell me, how are you getting on with Sid?'

'He's a dirty rat!' Betty hisses, loud enough to freak out Panda, who yelps and dives under the table. 'Turns out Sid has a long-term girlfriend. She went away to visit family and now she's back. I caught them together, canoodling on a hymn book. He's got pups too, the lying toerag!'

'I'm so sorry, Betty. I really am.'

Betty shrugs her tiny shoulders. 'Oh well, what can I do except move on. Maybe I'm getting too old to find a boyfriend. I noticed the other day I have some white fur around my jaw.'

'It's a sign of maturity and wisdom. Nothing to be worried about.'

She peers up at me with her bulbous eyes. 'You think I'm wise? Really?'

'I do.'

'Aww shucks!'

Crunch!

Betty and I both hear it and turn our head towards the front of the house.

Crunch!

The sound of hooman feet on the gravel drive.

'Could be a fox, or a stray dog,' Betty suggests.

Crunch, crunch!

The sound is getting nearer. I sneak down the hall. I nudge Jake in the neck and he wakes instantly. He takes one look at my pricked ears and the raised fur down my spine and he knows we have a problem.

Jake follows Betty and me to the sitting room. We can see the driveway through a large window. Rose's car is parked close to the side passage. The front boundary of the cottage is lined with a hedge, but there is no gate to bar entry. Betty clambers up onto my head and peers through the window too. The crunching has stopped. Then I see the silhouette of a hooman moving like a ghost cross the lawn. They are heading straight for us. They hold something shaped like a bottle in their hand.

I sound the alarm, barking as loudly as I can. Betty is jolted off my head and lands on my back, then scurries to the floor. Jake gives a deep croaky bark. From the kitchen, Panda squeals, then dashes to our side, and barks frantically. A light goes on upstairs – its brightness permeates the space down the stairs and reaches into the sitting room. The intruder runs straight at the house as if they are going to run right through the living room window.

'Run!' I bark.

We turn as one and charge out of the lounge room and race down the hallway. The sitting room window shatters. A wave of heat, like a giant flaming hand, propels all three of us into the kitchen. I tumble and roll. There's an almighty boom, so loud my ears ring and my head spins. I get up on wobbly legs. Then I feel the heat on my back and the true meaning of terror hits me.

Fire!

Tall orange flames. The stink of petrol.

If there is one thing that all animals instinctively fear, it is fire. Our very natures tell us to run. I race over to Summer who is already up and heading for the back door. But it is locked.

Upstairs, Rose screams. I run to the stairs and bark and bark. The sitting room curtains peel and curl, turning black and gold, then the flaming fabric falls to the floor. The sofa is alight and black fumes swirl above it. I retch. The fumes from the foam cushions are like poison and I cough. Rose is yelling at Ed to get up. I race up the stairs and find her in Ed's room. She throws the bed clothes off him. Ed blinks, bewildered, then starts to cough as the smoke rises up the stairs.

'Hurry!' Rose urges. 'Fire!' Rose puts an arm around him and steers him to the landing.

I bark frantically, urging them to be quicker.

As they descend the stairs in their bare feet, Ed slips and almost drags Rose down with him, but she grabs the banister rail just in time and they hasten to the bottom of the stairs. The sitting room is ablaze, the stench of petrol fumes and black smoke makes my eyes stream. My lungs burn. I honk like a dog with kennel cough.

Rose and Ed stagger into the kitchen. Panda circles us, her cries desperate. Rose trips over her, falling to her knees. Ed manages to save himself by grabbing the edge of the table. He bends double, retching. 'Can't…breathe.'

I nudge Rose and whimper, 'Get up!'

She coughs so hard that I fear she will cough up her lungs. I take her pyjama top in my teeth and pull her towards the back door.

Rose holds my collar and stands unsteadily, then staggers to the back door. She turns the key and pulls the door open. A rush of cold, clean air fills the room. The fire behind us roars like a jet engine, as if the new air is fanning the flames. In the garden, the ducks are quacking and squawking in panic. A fox screams a warning to others. Rose and Ed stumble out of the house, beyond the patio and onto the grass, where Ed collapses into the frost-covered lawn. Jake, Panda and I follow, coughing and retching. I feel as if my heart will explode. Betty squeaks in terror as she dives under the willow. A boom shakes the ground. Birds fly into the sky. The roof has a hole in it and flames lick the black sky. I suddenly notice that Summer isn't with us.

Where is she? 'Summer! Mum!'

I bark at the other dogs. They haven't seen her.

'This way!' Rose commands, waving us away from the house.

I stare into the kitchen. My skin already feels scorched; the heat is unbelievable. Through the open door I see the hall carpet and banisters are alight. I cannot see into the kitchen because of the swirling smoke, but my mother must be in there.

I look behind me for a second. Rose is on the phone.

'Fire,' she says to the operator. She gives her address.

I inhale some cool breaths and run back into the kitchen.

'Monty!' Rose calls, 'Come here!'

I should obey Rose. But now I know that she is safe, I have to find Summer.

'No!' screams Rose.

I can't see anything. My eyes are streaming and the smoke is black. I head for Summer's bed but miss my mark and bang into the table leg. I keep going. I hear a gagging sound. Summer lies on her side, her back legs draped over the bed, her upper body on the lino. Her eyes are half closed and she's choking.

I bark. 'Mum! Get up!'

Summer moves her head a fraction. She's too weak to move. I close my jaw around the loose skin at her neck, my gums covering most of my teeth as Retrievers can do, and I drag her across the kitchen floor, the cooler cleaner air guiding me in the right direction. She isn't heavy, but my energy is low. I can't catch enough breath and if I cough I will lose my grip on her.

'Monty!' Rose yells, dashing to my side.

She grips Summer's collar and together we drag her out of the house and onto the pavers where I collapse, gasping. Then my whole body convulses and I vomit ash and bile. Rose picks up Summer in her arms and carries her down the garden to where Ed lies under the oak tree with the other dogs. I can't move.

Then I feel Jake bump me with his snout.

'Get up!' he growls. 'Save yourself!'

On weak legs, I raise myself up and walk away from our burning home. I collapse next to Summer, who coughs and coughs but her eyes are open. Rose sits in her pyjamas next to Ed.

'My house,' Rose says, forlorn. 'Everything I have is in there.'

Ed looks at her. 'But everything you love is right here.'

In the glow from the inferno, I see Rose smile. 'That's true.'

Betty sniffs my face. 'You were very brave, Mr Monty. Are you okay?'

I'm still gagging up phlegm and ash. I can't answer.

'That was a petrol bomb,' Betty says. 'I know this because some evil hooman threw one into the Euro Tunnel when I lived there. It was meant to stop the train. No hooman was hurt but it killed a lot of rats in a truly terrible way.'

'Who attacked us?' Jake asks, his throat rougher than ever.

'I think I know.'

But I have to be sure. I drag myself up and plod forward like an old dog and head for the front garden. Jake comes with me.

I sniff the grass and then the gravel where the intruder walked. I know his scent and I follow it, across the road and into Winterfold Heath, with Jake at my side.

This time, he is not going to get away with it.

39 MONTY

The hooman has a torch and the beam bounces as he runs across Winterfold Heath. He has a head start on us, but we keep him in our sights. He misses his footing and falls to his knees, which gives us a chance to draw closer.

Jake and I can see very well in the dark. The hooman, even with a torch, finds it hard to see. He slows right down, trips over tree roots and stumbles over uneven ground. The filthy smoke from the fire still irritates my lungs and I choke. Despite the howling wind, the hooman hears me. He turns and points his torch in our direction. We both hunker down in the heather and stay very still while the beam of light sweeps over us. The hooman sets off again and takes a lesser-known path through the tall pine trees. The branches whisper in the wind.

'Who is it?' Jake asks, his voice reedy with exhaustion.

'We will see.'

A high-pitched howl pierces the night, sharp enough to shatter glass. It is Panda's voice. I imagine her, head back, jaw wide open, her eyes locked on the moon.

Help us! A hooman set fire to Duckdown Cottage. He smells of smoke and petrol and he's running across Winterfold Heath. Stop him!

Her howl is quickly joined by Summer's breathy baying and she repeats the same message. My lungs are burning as we pursue the culprit, but I am invigorated by the howl-a-thon. Soon dogs in Farley Green, then Nether Wallop and Little Wallop join in the howling, repeating the same story. Their message is picked up by other dogs and it travels for miles and miles. Then the wind carries the wail of a fire engine siren. Will they save our home?

The hooman is slowing down. I hear his heavy breathing. We are approaching Ed's caravan. Does he mean to hide there? His torch bounces off the straight, slim tree trunks. Jake is tiring. He trips and rolls over, growling.

'Hurt me leg,' Jake says. 'Keep going! I'll follow you.'

I set off. The hooman has sped up and the forest is full of shadows. The howl-a-thon has receded into the distance. My paw snags on a clump of heather, but it doesn't hold me back. I burst through a bush and onto the road that leads to Little Wallop. The dark figure's torch illuminates a car that's parked on the soft verge.

Oh no!

If he gets in the car I won't be able to keep up. I accelerate, my lungs complaining, my muscles aching. He slows to a lumbering walk. He clicks the remote to unlock the car. I draw on all my remaining energy and sprint.

He must hear me because he spins around and points the torch in my eyes. I head straight for the blinding light and leap.

My front paws and chest collide with the man, and he falls backwards. He lands on dead leaves and mud, with me on top of him, gnashing and snarling. I stare into his blue eyes, which are wide with terror. He hits me on my head with the torch. I scream in pain and shock, but my head is hard. I sink my teeth into the arm holding the torch: I want him to drop it.

As my teeth slice through his rain jacket and they graze his flesh I taste yeast and finally I know what it is. Rapeseed. Strongest of all is the strange taste of burnt and healed skin. The texture of his flesh is ribbed and rough. I know who tried to kill us tonight and it isn't Alfie. It's his father, Mervyn Mumford.

He screams and releases his grip on the torch, which rolls into the road. He tries hitting me with his fist, then he grabs my collar and uses it to push me away. He's stronger than I imagined. Must be all that tennis he plays. I dig my teeth deeper into his arm and he screams in pain, releasing my collar.

Behind me there is rustling and Jake's ragged breathing.

Jake latches his jaw around Mumford's other arm. The man whimpers and complains but he strops struggling.

'I'll skin you dogs!' he bellows.

From down the road, a German Shephard appears. 'Want some help?'

'Stand over his face,' I say.

The German Shepherd looks down at the man's face and snarls, his huge canines dripping with saliva.

'Dear God! Somebody help me!' Mumford cries.

A Jack Russel darts out of the heath and leaps onto the man's stomach, his sharp teeth bared, his yips angry.

I hear a police siren, then a glimpse of blue flashing lights. The car headlights flood the road and the vehicle skids to a halt. Doors open.

'Monty! Are you okay?' Rose asks.

The police officer with her says, 'Looks like Monty and his gang have everything under control. And this must be the man who set fire to your house?'

'Yes and I suspect you'll find he's behind the fire that killed Marie and Tony Toyne,' Rose says.

I know the officer's voice: it's Big Man Joe. He kneels down and holds out handcuffs. He looks at me. 'You can let him go now.'

I withdraw my teeth and back away. The other dogs do the same, although Jake hangs onto the man's arm for a little longer before he drops it. Big Man Joe handcuffs the killer.

'Mervyn Mumford, I'm arresting you for the attempted murder of Rose Sidebottom and Ed Pascoe and I'm taking you in for questioning in relation to the murder of Marie and Tony Toyne.'

Joe explains what Mumford's rights are. All I care about is that Rose is safe and Finn is innocent. I lie in the damp leaves to rest my aching limbs. I thank Jake, the German Shepherd and the Jack Russel.

'I guess we were wrong about Alfie,' growls Jake.

'Not totally wrong,' I say. 'He trashed Ed's caravan. But I suspect that Mumford killed Marie and Tony, not Alfie. We will know soon enough. The jeans and keys we dug up hold the answer.'

40 MONTY

It's the evening of Valentine's Day and Rose is at her office. In one corner is a camp bed, made up with sheets and pillows and a thick duvet, loaned to her by Phyllis, who is busy tucking the sheet under the mattress.

'Are you sure you want to stay here?' Phyllis asks. 'It's freezing and what happens if you need the loo in the night?'

Rose, Summer, and I are homeless. Phyllis has given Ed a place to stay until he can get his caravan into a habitable state. Jake is with Ed – I pity him having to contend with Tiffany but Jake's a tough dog and I've no doubt that he will cope.

Betty has moved into the garden shed until a new house is built. The fire obliterated almost everything downstairs at Duckdown Cottage, which upset Rose greatly because precious photos of her and Kay were lost forever. Luckily, Rose's clothes and other items in her bedroom were undamaged, although they reek of smoke. The staircase is unsafe and the upper level is propped up with metal poles. The downstairs area is little more than charred brick and ash cordoned off by crime scene tape. Somehow, the fridge and its contents remained intact – it's always important to look on the bright side.

'Malcolm has given me a key to the vet hospital bathrooms,' Rose says.

Phyllis picks up her enormous handbag. 'Right you are then, I best get going. Ed needs his dinner.'

'Thank you for the sandwiches,' Rose says.

Phyllis has left some ham and cheese sandwiches and a slice of chocolate cake on Rose's desk. Who would have thought she could be so kind to Rose when only a few weeks ago she regarded Rose with such suspicion? Come to think of it, I misjudged Tiffany, too. She's not as scary as she first appears, and I realise now that her aggression was about protecting Phyllis and saving Finn. One thing I have learned during this case is that you can't judge a book by its cover, or a cat by its hissing.

Even Rose, who is a brilliant detective, misjudged some of the suspects on her list, including Mervyn Mumford. She fell for his charm. And just because a hooman does some bad things in their life, it doesn't mean they are a killer. Take the vicar, for instance, or Jimmy, who really did set fire to his home as a kid and who did mess about with a petrol can on the night the farmhouse burned down. But neither the vicar nor Jimmy had anything to do with Marie's and Tony's deaths. And Marie's friend, Daphne Chang, had Rose believing that Marie lit the fire deliberately to force Tony to take Bassinger's offer. But Mrs Chang misinterpreted the conversation that she overheard between Marie and Mumford that terrible night. When Marie had said "tonight is the night", she only meant that after the party she would insist on Tony selling the farm. Nothing more sinister than that.

Phyllis pauses at the office door and looks back at Rose. 'I'm sorry about your cottage. It's my fault you lost your home. I should never have confided in Reverend Mabey. You'd have thought I could trust a vicar, but it seems our vicar is of the untrustworthy variety. I still can hardly believe he was stupid enough to tell Frances Buttermere. He might as well have put up a ruddy great poster once he'd confided in that gossipmonger. Buttermere went and told Mervyn Mumford, the evil swine.'

This was how Mumford knew Rose had evidence that could land him in jail. When he and Alfie barged into our home on the pretext that Rose was maligning Alfie, Mumford's fears were confirmed when he saw his own jeans on our kitchen table. The very same pair of jeans he had buried on the bridleway five years ago, along with the keys he took from the farmhouse. However, Mumford didn't know that Rose then handed in the evidence to DS Varma, so his attempt to destroy it with a firebomb was fruitless.

'It's not your fault he firebombed my house,' Rose says. 'He's responsible for his own actions and he'll spend the rest of his days behind bars, not just for what he did to us, but for what he did to Tony and Marie, and the trauma he's put Finn through.'

Phyllis smiles. She actually smiles! Will wonders never cease?

'Good night, then,' she says, and departs to catch the bus home.

What almost threw me was the strange skin smell on the buried jeans. I had never come across the smell of burnt and scarred skin before. When I met Mervyn Mumford for the first time outside his house on the night I dragged Rose there, his clothes reeked of pub smells, including the aroma of burnt wood from a log fire. I therefore didn't put the smell of fire and skin together until he came to Duckdown Cottage. I should have realised that the yeasty smell he carried, which I thought was Marmite, was in fact the rapeseed he used to grow on his farm. Rapeseed has a strong yeasty smell and after thirty years of growing it, the smell was part of Mumford's innate scent.

I wondered why Panda didn't recognise Mumford as the arsonist the night Rose accused Alfie and Tammy of vandalising Ed's caravan, but remembered that she was cowering behind a pot plant, terrified of Mumford's anger, so she wasn't close enough to detect his unique smell.

Alfie smelt of sunburnt skin which confused me, too. I overheard Big Man Joe tell Rose that when they searched Mumford's house they discovered a sunbed which Alfie used so he could keep an all-year tan. Why do some hoomans want to change their skin colour?

Rose shuts her laptop.

Summer, who has recovered from the smoke inhalation, jumps onto Rose's camp bed and closes her eyes for a snooze.

'Well, Monty, Happy Valentine's Day,' Rose says.

I hear the hint of loneliness in her voice. I lean against her leg. I wish I could tell her how much I love her. Perhaps Betty was right. Rose deserves a nice hooman in her life.

Someone knocks and Malcolm sticks his head in. He's not wearing his white vet's coat, so I guess that means he's finished work. He glances at the camp bed and the sandwiches and cake wrapped in cling wrap.

'Please don't sleep here tonight. It's freezing. Come to my flat. You can have my bed.' He blushes. He hastily adds, 'I'll sleep on the floor.' He lives in the one-bed flat above the vet practice.

'I'm fine. Really. Are you off anywhere nice tonight?'

'Me? No. Why would I? I mean, I don't do Valentine's Day.' He looks down and scuffs the sole of one shoe across the concrete floor. 'I mean, I would celebrate it…if, you know, oh it doesn't matter.'

If Malcolm is attempting to invite Rose to his flat for a romantic evening, then he's doing a really bad job of it. His heart is beating fast and he's wearing aftershave: I think this is the first time I've smelt it on him. He's also made an attempt to tame his wild, black hair. I decide to give him some help. I put my front paws on Rose's desk and grab the package of cheese and ham sandwiches in my jaws, drag them over the edge and onto the floor, then I rip at the cling wrap.

'Stop that!' Rose cries and dives at the sandwiches.

I pick up the messy bundle and run around the room. A slice of buttered bread falls out, followed by some cheese slices. Malcolm corners me and takes away what remains of the sandwiches.

'I can't believe he did that!' Rose says. 'Bad dog!'

Malcolm has a twinkle in his eye.

While Rose peers at her messed-up sandwiches to see what, if anything, can be salvaged, he gives me a wink. Malcolm and I are on the same wavelength. The sandwiches are covered in slobber, exactly as I had planned. This means Malcolm can now step in and save the day.

'That settles it,' Malcolm says. 'I'll cook dinner at my place and you can stay the night.'

'You've already been so generous; I really can't impose on you.'

He takes a couple of steps closer. 'Please join me, Rose. I'd…' *Come on Malcolm, you can do it*, I think. 'I'd …like your company.'

'Really?' Rose says.

'Really.'

I bark once, a loud yes!

'Okay, then I'll buy us dinner. Do you like curry?' Rose asks.

'My favourite,' Malcolm says.

'I won't take your bed, Malcolm, but if you are able to help me get this camp bed up your stairs, I can sleep in your sitting room.'

Malcolm smiles broadly. 'We might have to get Summer off it first,' he jokes.

It turns out that the bed is easy to fold, and Malcolm carries it up to his flat in a few easy strides. B, his puppy, greets us and is very proud to show Summer and I around. Soon we are settled in Malcolm's cosy flat, and Rose has phoned the local curry house and ordered home delivery. He offers Rose beer or wine, and she opts for beer.

They both say at once, 'You've got to have beer with curry.' Then they laugh.

I settle at Rose's feet. It's so good to hear Rose laugh again.

'How is Finn doing?' Malcolm asks.

Rose and Malcolm are seated at opposite ends of his three-seater sofa.

'No long-term damage from his attempt to hang himself and the charges against him have been dropped. He's back home with his grandmother and he has Panda with him. He says he wants to keep her.'

'That's great news. Do you know why Finn confessed to the murders?'

'Once Mumford was under arrest, Finn admitted that Mumford had threatened to kill Phyllis if he didn't admit to murdering his parents.'

'So Mumford coerced the boy?'

'Yes, Phyllis is all Finn has left in the world, so the poor boy took the blame.'

'Mumford really is a hideous human being. I can't believe I was so wrong about him.'

'You and me both,' Rose says. 'I've misjudged a few people during this case. The fire scene investigator gave me a bum steer when he suggested that the killer might have used Rohypnol on the parents to ensure they couldn't escape the fire. I was also wrong to doubt Phyllis.'

I rest my head in Rose's lap and look up at her. I want her to know that none of that matters because we got there in the end.

'And Mumford did it for money?' Malcolm asks.

'Yes. If Tony had persisted in refusing to sell his farm, then Bassinger Homes would have withdrawn their offer to buy Mumford's. Mumford lied to me when he said that his sale would have gone ahead regardless.'

Malcolm shakes his head. 'It's incredible what people will do for money.' He sips his beer. 'Those burns on his legs, they must have been agony. Did he accidentally spill petrol on himself?'

'It was only a few dribbles, but it was enough to set his jeans on fire.'

'His burns would have needed treatment. I'm surprised the police didn't contact hospitals at the time and ask about burns victims.'

'I'm told they did. But Mumford went to a hospital in another county and the investigating officers didn't extend their enquiries that far. And his burns weren't bad enough to keep him in hospital.'

'How was it that the police didn't notice his injuries?' Malcolm asked.

'Once he'd torn off the burned jeans and buried them with the keys, he went home, did his best to tend to his burns and then he called emergency services. He managed to hide his burns while a police officer asked him what he knew and then, when the officer had gone, Mumford drove to a hospital. He must have been in agony.'

'Serves him right,' said Malcolm. 'And I guess he kept the scars hidden under trousers, so he didn't have to explain the burns?'

'Must have. Apparently, he always played tennis in white trousers rather than the shorts most of the other members wore.'

DS Varma told Rose about this. He also thanked her for finding the keys and jeans. Not surprisingly, Leach and Pearl haven't acknowledged our contribution to solving the case.

'What about Alfie and Tammy? Are they going to be charged with vandalism?'

'Alfie is. There's not enough evidence to link Tammy to the damage. The bangle could have been lost on the heath, as she claimed. However, pissing on someone's bed leaves DNA behind. Alfie will probably end up having to do community service and I hope he'll see the error of his ways.'

I look up at Rose doubtfully. She always sees the best in everyone.

'Well, you and Monty solved the case. Congratulations!' They clink bottles. 'The Nosy Detectives are off to a great start.'

I bark a loud and joyous, yes!

Rose's phone rings. From the frown I'd say that she doesn't recognise the caller's number. 'Could be the home delivery person. Maybe they can't find us.' Rose answers. Listens. Pulls her notebook from her pocket and makes some notes. 'Okay, I'll see you tomorrow.' The call ends.

'Everything okay?' Malcolm asks.

'That depends.'

'On what?'

'That was Sasha Bassinger. She just offered me a rent-free house until Duckdown Cottage can be rebuilt.'

'What! That's very nice of her.'

Sasha hasn't struck me as the kind of hooman who does something out of the goodness of her heart, but I should give her the benefit of the doubt.

'There are strings attached.'

Aha! Just as I thought.

'Which are?' Malcolm asks.

'Her husband died eleven years ago.'

'I thought she lived with her husband.'

'He's her boyfriend,' Rose says, shutting her notebook.

'So what does she want you to do?'

'Sasha says her husband faked his own death. She's been receiving threatening notes recently and she's convinced they are from him.'

'Does the gold wedding band we found on her property belong to the husband?'

'She tells me it does.' Rose looks down at me. 'What do you think, Monty? Does it sound like the kind of mystery we should solve?'

A dead man who isn't – that sounds exactly like the kind of case we should solve.

I bark a resounding *yes!*

ACKNOWLEDGEMENTS

The inspiration for this book, and the two preceding novels, is my beloved Golden Retriever, Pickles, who passed away at the age of twelve. He was at my side for every book I wrote, and I miss him terribly. For a month, I couldn't write at all.

I hadn't realised that Pickles was also my motivation. If I didn't sit down at my desk by the usual time, he'd come up to me and give me a reproachful stare, then insist I follow him. He'd then settle on his dog bed in front of my desk. When he considered it was time to take a break, he'd nudge my leg and we'd walk up the road for coffee or go to the park, and then return to my office to write some more. I found completing this novel helped me to manage my grief. It made me smile and I hope it has brought a smile to your face, too.

I want to thank my brother, Nick Young, and my husband, Michael Larkin, for their encouragement and support for my writing career. I grew up in England and our house was always full of dogs, mostly adopted from rescue centres. At one time we had three Dachshunds whose quirky personalities inspired the characters of Shiraz and Shardie.

I also want to thank David Gaylor and Carolyn Tate who gave me such fantastic feedback on the first draft; my literary agent, Phil Patterson; my publisher, Lindy Cameron; and my editor, Narrelle Harris. You have helped me make *The Nosy Detective* the best it can possibly be. I should add that any deviation from real legal practices, policing, or property development was done by me to add drama and excitement to the story.

Most of all, thank you to everyone who has read this book, and to every reviewer and book blogger. I love reading your comments and I thank you from the bottom of my heart.

Finally, can I ask you a small favour?

Please give your dog a hug from me.

AUTHOR BIO

Louisa studied Literature at the University of London and went on to learn Canine Linguistics from her Golden Retriever, Pickles, which is how she discovered what dogs really get up to when we're not around. Truth be told, the beloved and much-missed Pickles came up with the idea for the Monty Dog Detective Mysteries, and Louisa just transcribed it. She was faster on the keyboard and less easily distracted by food and passing squirrels.

There are now three humorous mysteries starring Monty the Dog Detective and his hooman pal, Rose Sidebottom.

Louisa's golden retrievers Lilly and Tigger continue to be the inspiration for this feel-good series.

Louisa also writes crime-thrillers as L.A. Larkin and teaches crime writing at the Australian Writers' Centre.

To find out more about Monty the sniffer super-sleuth:

https://lalarkin.com/cozy-mysteries/

BOOKS BY LOUISA BENNET

THE MONTY DOG DETECTIVE SERIES
Monty & Me
The Bone Ranger
The Nosy Detectives
Short story 'When the Chips are Down' in *Who Sleuthed It?*

WRITING AS L.A. LARKIN
Next Girl Missing – Sally Fairburn book 1
Her Deadly Truth – Sally Fairburn book 2
The Safe Place
Widow's Island
Prey
Devour
Thirst
The Genesis Flaw

AVAILABLE AT CLAN DESTINE PRESS

www.ingramcontent.com/pod-product-compliance
Lightning Source LLC
Chambersburg PA
CBHW020610030726
47497CB00007B/2178